"Maybe you didn't think our marriage was real, but I did," Jack said.

Annie froze. "You just took off, leaving that stupid note. 'When you come to your senses, you can join me.' You're supposed to be so good with women, Jack. Did you really think *that* was going to make me fly off to the ends of the earth to be with you?"

"You're not like other women. You're *Annie*." Annie, his friend, who had stood beside him in a gaudy little wedding chapel and promised to be with him forever....

"I wasn't expecting to leave the country practically the minute I got married! I wasn't expecting to get married at all! Then you got that call. Everything happened too fast."

"Look, Annie, we've got to get some things settled...."

"You want a divorce...."

"Divorce? I'm not here to ask you for a divorce. I'm here to claim the wedding night we never had."

Dear Reader,

Happy New Year! Silhouette Intimate Moments is starting the year off with a bang—not to mention six great books. Why not begin with the latest of THE PROTECTORS, Beverly Barton's miniseries about men no woman can resist? In *Murdock's Last Stand,* a well-muscled mercenary meets his match in a woman who suddenly has him thinking of forever.

Alicia Scott returns with *Marrying Mike... Again,* an intense reunion story featuring a couple who are both police officers with old hurts to heal before their happy ending. Try Terese Ramin's *A Drive-By Wedding* when you're in the mood for suspense, an undercover agent hero, an irresistible child and a carjacked heroine who ends up glad to go along for the ride. Already known for her compelling storytelling abilities, Eileen Wilks lives up to her reputation with *Midnight Promises,* a marriage-of-convenience story unlike any other you've ever read. Virginia Kantra brings you the next of the irresistible MacNeills in *The Comeback of Con MacNeill,* and Kate Stevenson returns after a long time away, with *Witness... and Wife?*

All six books live up to Intimate Moments' reputation for excitement and passion mixed together in just the right proportions, so I hope you enjoy them all.

Yours,

Leslie Wainger

Leslie J. Wainger
Executive Senior Editor

Please address questions and book requests to:
Silhouette Reader Service
U.S.: 3010 Walden Ave., P.O. Box 1325, Buffalo, NY 14269
Canadian: P.O. Box 609, Fort Erie, Ont. L2A 5X3

MIDNIGHT PROMISES
EILEEN WILKS

Silhouette®

INTIMATE™MOMENTS®

Published by Silhouette Books

America's Publisher of Contemporary Romance

This book is for Bill and Martin, who serve the best
Key lime pie in the world.

Thanks for sharing Denver with me—
live long and prosper!

SILHOUETTE BOOKS

ISBN 0-373-07982-6

MIDNIGHT PROMISES

Copyright © 2000 by Eileen Wilks

All rights reserved. Except for use in any review, the reproduction
or utilization of this work in whole or in part in any form by any
electronic, mechanical or other means, now known or hereafter
invented, including xerography, photocopying and recording, or in
any information storage or retrieval system, is forbidden without
the written permission of the editorial office, Silhouette Books,
300 East 42nd Street, New York, NY 10017 U.S.A.

All characters in this book have no existence outside the imagination of
the author and have no relation whatsoever to anyone bearing the same
name or names. They are not even distantly inspired by any individual
known or unknown to the author, and all incidents are pure invention.

This edition published by arrangement with Harlequin Books S.A.

® and TM are trademarks of Harlequin Books S.A., used under license.
Trademarks indicated with ® are registered in the United States Patent
and Trademark Office, the Canadian Trade Marks Office and in other
countries.

Visit us at www.romance.net

Printed in U.S.A.

Books by Eileen Wilks

Silhouette Intimate Moments

The Virgin and the Outlaw #857
Midnight Cinderella #921
Midnight Promises #982

Silhouette Desire

The Loner and the Lady #1008
The Wrong Wife #1065
Cowboys Do It Best #1109
Just a Little Bit Pregnant #1134
Just a Little Bit Married? #1188
Proposition: Marriage #1239

EILEEN WILKS

is a fifth-generation Texan. Her great-great-grandmother came to Texas in a covered wagon shortly after the end of the Civil War—excuse us, the War Between the States. But she's not a full-blooded Texan. Right after another war, her Texan father fell for a Yankee woman. This obviously mismatched pair proceeded to travel to nine cities in three countries in the first twenty years of their marriage, raising two kids and innumerable dogs and cats along the way. For the next twenty years they stayed put, back home in Texas again—and still together.

Eileen figures her professional career matches her nomadic upbringing, since she's tried everything from drafting to a brief stint as a ranch hand—raising two children and any number of cats and dogs along the way. Not until she started writing did she "stay put," because that's when she knew she'd come home. Readers can write to her at P.O. Box 4612, Midland, TX 79704-4612.

IT'S OUR 20th ANNIVERSARY!
We'll be celebrating all year, starting with these fabulous titles, on sale in January 2000.

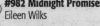

Chapter 1

"Did you hear the news, dear? Jack Merriman is in town."

Annie didn't actually sway. Her head went light and dizzy and the attic's dusty air got stuck in her lungs, keeping her from drawing a breath, but her body didn't move. That was fortunate, since only half of her was in the attic. The other half was in Mrs. Perez's garage, with her size-five work boots planted on the highest rung of the stepladder.

"Jack is back?" she managed to say as soon as her lungs started working again. "Are you sure?"

Annie couldn't see Mrs. Perez, who had been determined to stay in the garage while Annie worked so she could steady the stepladder with all ninety-five pounds of her aging body. It was an unnecessary caution. The ladder was sturdy, and Annie had a head for heights.

At least, normally she had a head for heights.

"Oh, yes," the older woman said. "I heard it directly

from Ida Hoffman when I went to the grocery store this morning.''

Ida had been the Merrimans' housekeeper for thirty years. ''It must be true, then.''

''He showed up yesterday afternoon without a word of warning. Ida said she nearly fell over when she opened the door and there he stood, grinning at her.''

''That sounds like Jack. Unpredictable.'' Annie was pleased with herself. She didn't sound angry or upset or afraid, though she felt all of that and more. How typical of Jack to show up without a word to her! ''I'll bet Ida was surprised.''

''That's an understatement. She was thrilled, of course. She always did have a soft spot for that rascal.''

So what else was new? Women always liked Jack—all women, all ages.

''Ida was so excited about having Jack home. She's looking forward to cooking for him. With that big old house standing empty ever since Sybil Merriman's death, she hasn't had much to do.''

Annie agreed without really listening, her attention trapped between the past and the present. She frowned at the dust motes sifting lazily down the band of sunshine admitted by the attic window. Jack was a lot like those dust motes—always in motion. Even when everything was smooth and peaceful, he couldn't be still, couldn't stay in one place. One little puff of wind and he was gone.

He'd proved that, hadn't he? A little over two months ago, when he left her.

She wasn't here to contemplate past follies, she reminded herself, and trained the beam from her high-powered torch on the wiring she'd just finished redoing. It looked fine. The damned beam was trembling, though. So was Annie's hand. She scowled and shut the torch off. ''All done here,'' she said, and started down the ladder.

"I appreciate you coming out to fix this so promptly."
Annie's former teacher held the ladder for her until Annie
had her feet once more on the ground. "Give me a moment
to find my checkbook, and I'll pay you for your time.
Though I still don't understand why you're doing handyman work instead of teaching."

"Mrs. P—"

"Never mind." She patted Annie's shoulder. "I promised not to nag, and I won't."

While Mrs. Perez went in search of her checkbook, Annie made out her bill on the kitchen table. She was determined not to let herself start brooding over past mistakes
or her current lack of direction. She'd done too much of
that already. After years of working determinedly toward
one goal, taking step after difficult step along the path she'd
set for herself—a path she had chosen in part because of
the woman whose wiring she had just fixed—it had been
more than upsetting to learn she'd been wrong about her
life's work. It had shaken her world.

Which was how she'd ended up making the second big
mistake of her life.

Annie shook her head. She was *not* going to think about
Jack. She wasn't going to speculate about why he was here,
or what he intended to do. With Jack, she assured herself
as she tore off the bill, speculation was pointless.

Mrs. Perez's voice came to her from the back of the
house. "Why do you suppose Jack Merriman is in town?"

Of course, it was hard to put him out of her mind when
people insisted on talking about him. "Who knows? Jack's
reasons don't always make sense to normal people."

"He didn't return for his aunt's funeral."

"He was in Borneo, for heaven's sake. I'm sure he
would have been here if he could have made it in time."
She bit her lip, annoyed at the way she'd automatically

defended Jack—and that she'd given away her knowledge of his whereabouts.

"Here it is!" Mrs. Perez returned, waving her checkbook triumphantly. "Ida was hoping Jack might have decided to move home for good. He owns that house now, after all."

"I imagine he'll sell it. Jack doesn't need a house here, not when his job takes him all over the world." Which was just how he liked his life to be—in motion. Annie held out the bill. "Here you go, Mrs. P. You let me know if there's anything else I can do for you."

Mrs. Perez glanced at the bill, then fixed Annie with the steely look that had always made Annie confess to anything in high school. "This can't be right."

"Is it too high? Let me run the figures again."

"Nonsense. You know very well you haven't charged me enough."

Annie also knew that Mrs. Perez's husband had been in the hospital twice this year. She tried to look innocent. "Ah—senior citizens' discount?"

Mrs. Perez charmed Annie by rolling her eyes. "Shall I tell all my age-disadvantaged friends that you will do their work for less than half the going rate, then?"

That might be a problem, given the current state of her bank account. "Age-disadvantaged?"

The old eyes twinkled. "Never mind. You're a rascal, Annie, but a bighearted one." She bent and wrote out the check. "Now, when you see that other rascal, you be sure and tell him I expect him to come visit me." She cocked her head to one side, looking like a wrinkled sparrow. "You know, back when you and Jack were in high school I used to wonder if you two would make a match of it."

Annie concentrated on tucking the check away neatly in a bank deposit pouch. "I can't imagine why."

"Oh, I don't know. You were such good friends and you had so much in common, in spite of your differences...I suppose I thought you might be a good balance for each other. You're so level-headed. Jack could use a touch of your caution.''

"Except that it usually worked the other way around," Annie said dryly. "Just ask my brothers. Jack always could talk me into…'' She flushed. That came too close to home. The last escapade Jack had talked her into had been a good deal more serious than the high school high jinks she and Jack and her brother Charlie had sometimes pulled.

Mrs. Perez looked at her over her glasses. "Perhaps you could use a touch of his impulsiveness, too."

Definitely not. She'd proved how poorly acting on impulse worked for her. She started for the door. "Don't let Ben hear you say that."

Mrs. Perez followed, opening the door for her. "Ben means well, but brothers aren't always realistic about their little sisters. And you've always possessed a surfeit of brothers.''

She grinned, liking the phrase. Since she had three older brothers, it fit all too well. "You do have a way with words, Mrs. P. How would you say that in Spanish?"

"Una plaga testosterone," the older woman replied promptly.

A testosterone plague? Annie laughed and took her leave. She was still grinning as she climbed into her Bronco. The first thing she did was check her to-do list and cross off Mrs. P.'s job.

Jack was back.

There was no point in writing that down. She wasn't going to forget, and nothing Jack Merriman was likely to do would fit neatly on any list.

Though it was only September, the air had a bite to it. She shrugged into her jacket so she could leave her window down. Annie liked to feel connected to the world around her—to the quiet bustle of her hometown, and to the wild and rugged peaks surrounding it. The air streaming in her window was spiced with pine and juniper, sharpened by a hint of ozone. Breathing in the familiar mingling of scents comforted her.

Whatever mistakes she might have made, coming home to Highpoint wasn't one of them. The big city hadn't been right. Not for her.

It was late afternoon. Thunderheads building to the north had darkened the sky, making the air dreamy with dusk. Annie took note of the storm that was headed their way and smiled. She had a fondness for storms.

As she turned onto Main, her cell phone rang. She crossed her fingers as she thumbed the connect button, hoping it was someone calling about work.

It wasn't.

"What the hell is Jack Merriman doing back in town?" her oldest brother's voice growled in her ear. "And why didn't you tell me about it?"

"Gosh, Ben, I wish you'd quit beating around the bush," she said dryly. "Just come out and say what's on your mind."

That low, rumbling noise was his chuckle. "So, how was your day, Annie? Nice weather we're having. What do you think of those Bulls? And why didn't you tell me Jack was coming home?"

"Because I didn't know. I just heard about it from Mrs. Perez."

There was a moment of silence. "I guess you think I'm overreacting. But after all the trouble Jack dragged you and Charlie into, can you blame me for being edgy?"

"That depends on whether you called Charlie to lay down the law, too."

"I don't lay down the law. A little advice from your big brother—"

"Which tends to sound a whole lot like orders. I think

I've mentioned this habit you have of thinking I'm still fifteen and in need of a curfew.'' Annie had been ten when their parents were killed. Ben had been twenty-two. He'd quietly put his own life on hold in order to keep the family together, a sacrifice she was only beginning to understand. But he drove her crazy sometimes.

Which was why she hadn't told him about Jack. Her conscience twinged. She changed the subject. ''I'm going to swing by the grocery store on my way home. Is there anything you need? You *do* remember that it's your turn to cook tonight, don't you?''

Ben made his usual grumbling protest, and the familiar debate over who was cooking, who was cleaning up and who had the night off soothed her. It was almost like old times. Her second-oldest brother, Duncan, was in the Special Forces, so she rarely saw him. But her next-oldest brother, Charlie, was a long-haul truck driver, and when he was in town he lived with her and Ben in the old house where they'd all grown up.

''All right,'' Ben conceded finally. ''I'll fix chili if you'll pick up some jalapeño peppers. Get a half dozen.''

''Two.'' Even without the fresh peppers, Ben's chili could dissolve a spoon if you didn't eat fast.

''All right, all right. Look, I'm sorry I jumped all over you earlier, half pint. I guess I did act as though you were still in school and trying to hide whatever you and Jack were up to.''

A sick lump formed in the pit of her stomach. ''I'm used to it,'' she said lightly. ''Listen, I'd better go before this call eats up my entire earnings for the day.''

As soon as her brother said goodbye she disconnected, swallowing hard, but the sour taste of guilt didn't go away. She'd lied to her brother. Of course, that was nothing new—she'd been lying to him, by omission if not out loud, for months now. But she'd also lied to Mrs. Perez. Shoot, she'd been trying to lie to herself.

Annie had a pretty good idea why Jack was in town. Much as she might try to deny it, she thought she knew what he wanted.

A divorce.

Day was sliding into dusk as the bruised-looking storm-clouds rolled in. On the McClains' front porch, a man paced. He had an easy way of moving in spite of a slight limp, and the kind of smooth, rangy body that draws women's eyes. His hair was short and mink brown, as dark as the clouds overhead.

As dark as the scowl on his face.

Pacing made Jack's knee ache. He'd been on one plane or another for fourteen hours yesterday, followed by the drive here from Denver, and his stupid knee had stiffened up. He didn't consider sitting down to wait for Annie to get home, though. After only one day in this blasted town, his feet were already itching to leave.

Highpoint wasn't the only reason for his restlessness. He'd left a lot unresolved back in Borneo, and the need to find out who was responsible for that mess burned in him. He'd have to make a trip to Denver soon to see what he could do to track down the thief.

But he didn't intend to leave without Annie. Not this time.

Fortunately he had plenty of room for pacing. The McClains' front porch ran the entire length of the house. It was the sort of porch people used to sit on during long summer evenings, a place where a young boy might steal a kiss from his first girlfriend. Not that Jack had stolen any kisses here. Annie McClain had been the little sister he'd never had, a freckle-faced tagalong who had turned into a good friend.

Somewhere along the line, she had changed. Or he had.

There was a wooden porch swing at one end of the porch. It was painted a bright, incongruous turquoise. Annie's doing, Jack thought, pausing. The hard line of his mouth softened. Annie loved bright colors. Not in any big, splashy way, of course. Annie didn't do anything in a big, splashy way. Her love for vivid color had to sneak in under those cautious fences she'd built around her life, popping up as a turquoise porch swing or a pair of screaming red sneakers.

A marmalade-colored cat the size of a bear cub lazed on that porch swing. In the half hour Jack had been waiting, the sum total of the animal's movement had consisted of an occasional twitch at the tip of its tail. The cat watched him pace with a certain lazy interest, much as an adult might keep an indulgent eye on a child's energetic antics.

"So," Jack said, sticking his hands in his back pockets, "you seem to belong here, big fellow. What time does Annie usually get home?"

"About now."

The voice came from behind him. Jack turned around slowly. "Annie."

She stood at the foot of the steps that led onto the porch, her arms wrapped tightly around two brown grocery bags as if their weight could keep her earthbound in the gusting wind. Now that she was here, standing in front of him, he didn't know what to say. He just wanted to look at his old friend without words, without letting the needs of the present and hurts of the past crowd in.

Her hair was slightly longer than it had been the last time he'd seen her—long enough for her to pull into a ponytail that the wind was whipping around. It was the same soft, reddish brown as always, though. He liked it pulled back that way, liked the way it left her face bare to the world. Annie had a pretty face, with a soft curve to her cheeks and forehead, a stubborn chin and eyes as green as the Irish hills she'd never seen. At the moment, those eyes were bright with suspicion.

He stepped closer, looking down at her. She was such a little thing. He tended to forget that. Physically there wasn't that much of Annie, yet she vibrated with so much energy it was easy to forget her actual size, as if she'd been given more life than such a slight body could contain without it spilling over onto those around her. "You're looking good," he said softly.

"Oh, sure. I always look my best in work clothes, with no makeup and my hair all over the place."

He shook his head. "The proper response to a compliment is 'thank you.'"

Suspicion vanished in a flash of humor. She chuckled. "Imagine you worrying about the proper response to anything."

His eyebrows went up. "Believe it or not, I do have a few ideas about what's proper. For one thing, I think a married woman ought to wear a wedding ring. Where's yours?"

She bit her lip. "Have you told anyone about—about Vegas?"

"No. Once I realized you preferred to keep our marriage a deep, dark secret, I covered for you. Haven't I always?"

"It usually worked the other way around," she said dryly. "Look, we have to talk. I know that. But could we do it inside, out of the wind?"

Jack stepped aside, letting her come up on the porch. He didn't offer to take her bags, though it was obviously awkward for her to juggle them long enough to get her key out and get the door opened. He didn't offer because he was too damned angry. Still. Again. Jack was used to temper hitting fast, like a flash flood, then draining away completely. The sullen core of anger that had refused to leave him the past couple of months was new to him.

He didn't like it. He followed her, limping slightly, through the living room and dining room and into the big, old-fashioned kitchen, lecturing himself silently. He'd get a lot farther by charming Annie than by fighting with her.

The kitchen distracted him. For the first time since he'd driven into town yesterday, he had a sense of homecoming. He'd spent a lot of hours in this room. "This hasn't changed much. The floor is new, but it's almost the same shade of green as the old one."

Annie set the bags down on the scarred oak table. "The floor was new five years ago. You haven't been here in a long time, Jack."

"Has it been that long?" Strange, he thought, it didn't seem like it, not with memories crowding up as close and friendly as puppies. He moved over to the table and automatically began helping her unload the groceries, just as he'd done a thousand times before at this house.

Annie stood on the other side of the grocery sack. Close enough for him to touch...if he'd thought his touch would be welcome. She was frowning. "You're limping."

"I had an accident a couple weeks ago, banged up my knee. Nothing serious."

The quick flash of concern in her eyes pleased him. "What happened? You're a good driver."

Yes, he was—which was why the accident had been minor. It could have been a lot worse. He was going to have to tell her about that and a lot more, but not yet. Not yet. "Hey! Jalapeños." He grinned as he took out the plastic bag holding two of the small, potent peppers. "Is Ben planning to fix some of his chili?"

"Yes." She grabbed the milk and butter that he'd unloaded and carried them to the refrigerator.

"What are the chances of me getting an invitation to

supper?'' He hadn't had any of Ben's stomach-burning chili in a long time.

She glanced at him quickly over his shoulder. ''Good grief, Jack, don't you think that might be a little awkward under the circumstances?''

His brief fling with nostalgia thudded to an end. ''I guess he doesn't know we're married.''

''No.''

''So why haven't you told anyone about Vegas?'' Was she ashamed of him? The idea added another layer to the anger he was trying to ignore.

''I—I didn't know what to say. It's not like we had a real marriage. I was here and you were thousands of miles away, in Timbuktu—''

''Borneo,'' he said, temper lending a lash to the word.

''Whatever. You were off building things, and I was here. I didn't know what to tell people. You never answered my letter.''

''I'm here, aren't I?''

''Jack.'' She sounded exasperated. ''I'm not talking about that note I scribbled two weeks ago. I'm talking about the four-page letter I wrote after you left.''

''I answered that, too.'' She'd written him four pages, all right—four pages about how confused she was, how she cared about him, but she didn't want to leave everything she knew unless he could make a real commitment to her. Which had made about as much sense as skinny-dipping in January. He'd *married* her. How much more committed could a man get?

''A one-way plane ticket is not what I'd call an honest effort at communication,'' she said dryly.

''You knew what that ticket meant. I wanted you to join me. But you were too busy hiding here in Highpoint, fixing people's roofs and plumbing, to live up to your promises.'' He moved closer. ''Did you keep our marriage a secret because the marriage wasn't real to you? So you would be free to date? I hear Toby Randall has been sniffing around lately." Ida had mentioned that last night.

She rolled her eyes. "Get real. Toby Randall? He's a nice guy, I suppose, but for heaven's sake! His mother still irons his Jockey shorts."

"She does, huh?" A smile tugged at his mouth in spite of his mood. Jack couldn't believe Annie knew about the condition of the man's underwear for the obvious reason. "How would you know that?"

"He told me. He wanted my advice on how to get her to quit. Honestly, Jack, you're being ridiculous. I've always had a lot of guy friends, you know that. I can't believe you thought I took my ring off because I wanted to fool around on you." She turned away, getting very busy with unpacking the last of the groceries. "I thought you knew me better than that."

He sighed. "Hell, Annie, I'm sorry. This is all new territory for me." Brand-new. Until this morning, he would have sworn he'd never been jealous of a woman—not since the seventh grade, anyway, when Charlie tried to cut him out with Mary Wolfstedder. He wasn't even sure what he was feeling *was* jealousy. Whatever it was, he didn't like it.

Dammit. Annie kept making him feel things he didn't want to feel. "So where's your ring?"

"Upstairs, in my jewelry box." Apparently putting the groceries away was more important than talking to him, since she didn't glance his way again as she bustled around the kitchen. "Why are you making such a big deal about it? You didn't want to wear a ring yourself. You said you'd probably lose it, since you'd have to take it off whenever you were working. And it's not like it was a real marriage, so—"

"Don't." His voice came out edgy. "Maybe you didn't think our marriage was real, but I did."

She froze, a can of beans clutched in one hand, her other hand reaching for the door to the pantry—then falling to her side. "I'm sorry. I was going to tell my brothers, at least, but I wanted to wait until I knew what you were going to do. With the way things were between us when you left... You just took off, leaving me that stupid note. 'When you come to your senses, you can join me.' Geez."

She shook her head and vanished into the pantry. "You're supposed to be so good with women, Jack. Did you really think that note was going to make me decide to fly off to the ends of the earth to be with you?"

"You're not like other women. You're *Annie*." Annie, his friend, who had stood beside him in a gaudy little wedding chapel and promised to be with him forever...but forever had only lasted two hours. Long enough for him to be called out of the country on an emergency. Long enough for Annie to change her mind about him. "I was angry when I wrote that note. You refused to go with me."

She came out of the pantry. "I wasn't expecting to leave the country practically the minute I got married! Good grief, I wasn't expecting to get married at all. I thought there would be time to adjust...but then you got that call. Everything happened so fast. Too fast. I'm not proud of the way I reacted, but if you hadn't—oh, damn. I'm doing it again." She grimaced. "I promised myself I wasn't going to pick up our argument where we left off. We did each other enough damage that night."

He remembered. More clearly than he wanted to, he remembered the ugly words he'd said as their argument had taken on a life of its own, and the words she had flung back at him. Words that had shocked her into silence and sent him down to the casino that night and halfway around the world the next morning. Words like *liar* and *selfish* and *for God's sake, grow up.*

And the ones that had stuck to him for two months and seven days, a scab that refused to heal and peel away. *"Marrying you was the biggest mistake of my life."*

"Is that why you didn't tell anyone, Annie? Because you didn't want to admit what a terrible mistake you'd made?"

"I've been a coward, all right? Is that what you wanted to hear? I didn't want to face everyone's questions because I didn't have any answers. At first I was waiting until you answered my letter, but you never did. The more time that passed, the harder it was to say anything."

Jack rubbed his face. She was the one who hadn't answered, not him. He'd sent her that ticket and she'd ignored it. "Let's not argue about whether I answered your first letter or not. I'm here because of your second letter."

She stared at him. "My second letter? You ignored the four-page letter I wrote you and came tearing back because I got mad about what some idiotic ex-girlfriend of yours did when she stopped taking her medication?"

He grabbed her shoulders to keep her from moving away. "You said you got an anonymous letter. That it threatened you. What did it say, exactly?"

"A bunch of nonsense about how I'd be sorry that I'd married you. For goodness' sake, Jack, it wasn't important."

"Did you keep it?"

"Of course not." She tried to shrug his hands off. "I can't believe this. Is that letter the reason you're here?"

"It's one of the reasons. Look, Annie, we've got to get some things settled, and I'd just as soon do that before your brothers get home."

The freckles that were scattered across that cute little nose stood out in stark contrast to her sudden pallor. "All

right. All right, I know what you mean. You want a divorce.
I won't protest. I just hope we can handle it...quietly."

"Divorce?" Anger rose, quick and hard, a thick snake
wrapping its coils around him and squeezing. "I'm not here
to ask you for a divorce, Annie. I'm here to claim the wedding night we never had."

Chapter 2

Annie fell back a step. "I can't believe you said that."

"What's so hard to understand? You keep saying our marriage wasn't real. A wedding night ought to change your mind. And you owe me that much. You didn't keep your other promises."

Annie stared at the man she'd thought she knew as well as she knew anyone in this world. She didn't recognize him.

Oh, she knew the face. Jack had one of those charmingly irregular faces made for crooked smiles and wicked suggestions, a collection of roughly matched features that somehow added up to be a whole that's more appealing than the static gloss of standard good looks. But the look in his dark chocolate eyes turned that familiar landscape foreign and frightening. She'd never seen them so hard. Even on the terrible night when they'd hurled words at each other like grenades, his eyes had been hot with temper.

Now that anger seemed to have aged and hardened, twisting his thoughts into alien shapes.

"Oh, Jack," she said sadly. "Is this what we've come to?"

"What do you mean? We're talking, aren't we? Working things out." He moved closer. "You ought to be happy. From what I can tell, women are nuts about talking and working things out."

"What is there to work out? You don't even like me very much anymore." And that was her fault. She'd known better than to give in to the attraction she'd always felt for Jack, because she knew Jack. He was a great friend—fun, funny and loyal. But he was hell on any woman foolish enough to care about him.

The alien anger vanished in a flash of surprise. "Of course I like you. You're Annie."

"You keep saying that as if my name were some sort of explanation!"

"Well, isn't it? We've been friends for a long time."

"We should have stayed friends. *Only* friends."

"There's no reason we can't be friends and be married, too."

She shook her head. "You don't understand." Probably he couldn't understand, and because of that she had hurt him. She had put that calcified anger into his eyes, and that made her ache. "Jack, I want more than friendship from marriage."

"It's you who doesn't understand." Frustrated, he ran a hand over his hair. It was too short for his gesture to mess it up. "Look, if I'm willing to forgive you for running away, you ought to be willing to meet me halfway."

His gesture distracted her...or maybe she just wasn't ready to get into a discussion that she knew was going to hurt.

The last time she'd seen Jack, his hair had been long, shaggy, intriguingly streaked by the blistering sun of Paraguay. She'd touched those pretty streaks, tangling her fingers in his hair. But now it was too short to run her fingers through. Now the best she could do would be to pet it, stroke all that soft brown hair along the curve of his head....

Her lips tightened. She couldn't afford those kind of thoughts.

"What's wrong now?"

She said the first thing that came to mind. "You let the barber scalp you again."

He gave her an irritated glance. "I'm trying to have a serious talk, here, Annie. Do you think we could save the comments on my appearance for later?"

"It's not just your hair. You're looking thin, too, and you're limping. You need to take better care of yourself, Jack."

He cocked his head to one side. "I know what you're doing. The question is—do you?"

"I'm not doing anything except offering you a little advice."

"You're trying to go back to pretending you're my sister. It won't work, Annie. Not anymore. Not when I've held you in my arms and felt you turn to fire."

Her face went hot and tight. She turned away. "I'm not going to go to bed with you."

"Want to bet?"

Something dark and ominous in his voice made her whirl—but as fast as she moved, he was faster. He seized her shoulders and jerked her up against him, and she almost cried—at the harshness of his face, at the impossibly dear feeling of his body against hers. Her heart pounded. "Let go of me."

His lip curled. "I don't think so."

He was looking at her mouth, and the throb of her pulse alarmed her more than the taunting arousal of his body. She tasted that dark rhythm in her throat. And elsewhere. "I don't want this."

"You know, I don't think you ever lied to me before you married me."

She'd been wrong. She *had* seen a hardness like this in Jack's eyes before—when he was competing. Jack was easygoing most of the time, but there was a buried edge to him that surfaced when he set himself to win, and she had become a challenge to him. Something to be won.

"I'm going to kiss you, Annie."

No, she thought. But she didn't move. No, she stood there, stiff and trapped by his hands and the hammer of her pulse. *Maybe if I let him kiss me, he can stop trying to win.* Maybe then he'd let her go.

His head lowered—but he didn't kiss her. Instead, the tip of his tongue painted one long, sweet sweep of temptation on her lower lip. She jerked her head back, but his hands on her shoulders tightened, holding her in place. Her breath hitched as he used his tongue to tickle along the line of her throat.

She pushed at his chest. "Dammit, Jack, don't do this. Don't play with me."

"Who said I'm playing?" This time his mouth didn't tease. It claimed. Hot, hard, ruthless, it asked nothing of her and demanded everything.

Heaven help her, she wanted to give him all that he demanded, and more.

There was heat, a rich current of heat urging her to let go of common sense and heed the clamor of her senses. There was taste, the heady taste of Jack, a shock of familiarity in spite of the time that had passed since she'd learned it on the night he married her. Just before he left her.

She shuddered and managed to wrench her head back. "Jack—" She shoved at his chest. He didn't move. His body was hard and urgent against hers, his scent filling her nostrils until she wanted to howl with the unfairness of it all. "This isn't right."

"It's right." His eyes were hard, his voice soft. "Let me show you how right it can be with us, Annie."

"What the *hell* is going on here?" a deep, gravelly voice demanded from behind her.

Annie closed her eyes. Great. The only thing worse than having her brother walk in on a clinch between her and Jack would be if Jack—

"Not much, Ben," Jack said, his eyes never leaving Annie's face. "I'm just saying hello to my wife."

Yep. That was it. Now her day was complete.

The storm had passed, leaving the air still and cold, the sky crowded with stars, and the porch swing wet. Annie ignored the dampness seeping through the seat of her jeans and pushed gently with her feet, listening to the creak of the chain and trying not to think. There were no good thoughts to keep her company tonight, none at all.

But she did have company from the one member of her household who wasn't upset with her. Twenty pounds of cat sprawled warmly across her lap. Samson's version of offering comfort meant allowing her to minister to his pleasure by lifting his chin so she could scratch underneath. As she did, his inaudible purr vibrated beneath her fingertips.

Ben always said the animal was too blasted lazy to purr out loud.

She sighed. Her oldest brother was barely speaking to her. Charlie had actually yelled at her—an event almost as rare as for Samson to purr out loud—and Jack...well, if Jack didn't exactly hate her, he sure didn't like her very much right now. Everyone she cared about was angry and hurt, and she was to blame.

Not that Jack didn't share some of that blame. He'd dropped his bombshell as casually as if he were talking about the weather, knowing full well what the effect would be. He'd done it that way on purpose, to get back at her, and that hurt. In all the years she'd known him, Jack had never set out to hurt her.

But everything was different now, wasn't it?

Was taking her to bed supposed to pay her back, too? It would be a tidy sort of revenge, she supposed, to claim the wedding night she'd denied him and then be off to Timbuktu—this time without inviting her along for the ride.

Until that afternoon, Annie would have said Jack wasn't capable of using sex as a weapon. Now she wasn't sure.

"So what else is new?" she muttered at Samson. It had been so long since she'd been sure of anything that she'd forgotten what it felt like. Not since she quit her job and married her best friend. Of course, she hadn't originally intended to marry Jack. At first she'd tried to get away from him. Then she'd decided to go to bed with him.

How had she managed to accomplish what she hadn't set out to do, and failed at what she thought she wanted?

Jack, she thought. Jack was what had happened to her plans. Of course, they'd been pretty screwy to start with....

Denver, last July

Annie pulled the last of the books down and set *Early Childhood Development* in the box with the others. She straightened, grimacing. Her ribs were still sore. She wouldn't be able to carry any of the boxes she was busy filling, but her brothers would be down in a couple of days to help.

She looked around at the clutter of boxes and clothes filling her formerly tidy apartment. So many dreams were being packed away along with her textbooks. But she was still going to teach, she assured herself. Just because Denver hadn't worked out didn't mean she couldn't still be a teacher. It was all she'd ever wanted.

No, she thought. Be honest. Teaching wasn't *all* she'd wanted. But it was an attainable goal, unlike the foolish longing that was sending her away. The doorbell rang. She threaded her way through the boxes to the door, wondering which of her friends from school had dropped by. She'd be glad of some company. Packing was a melancholy business.

But it was an old friend, not a new one, she opened the door to.

His hair was shaggy, his shirt was wrinkled and his jeans were old. He looked wonderful. She wished with all her heart he was still on the other side of the world. "Jack! I—I wasn't expecting you. I didn't think you were due back for another few weeks." She'd been counting on that.

"What do you think you're doing?" he demanded.

"Packing." She turned away, going back inside. "As I'm sure you can see." She hadn't expected him to be angry. It disconcerted her.

"Dammit, Annie. Why didn't you tell me?" He followed her into her apartment that had pleased her so much when she first moved in, the first place of her own she'd ever had. The complex had been brand-new then. After living in an old house all her life, followed by an old dorm while she was at college, she'd thought she would enjoy the newness. That was yet another thing she'd been wrong about.

After a while the new apartment had seemed cold and impersonal instead of fresh and exciting.

She moved to an open box, and began wrapping a glass bowl in newspaper. "You weren't here, Jack. How could I tell you?"

"Your brother managed. He called me the day before yesterday. I chewed him out for not calling me sooner and got here as quickly as I could."

She stopped, her back to him. "Which brother? Charlie?"

"Of course. Ben doesn't like me." He put a hand on her shoulder and turned her around, studying her face intently. "Aw, hell. Annie." He lifted a gentle hand to her cheek.

She managed not to flinch. The bruising had faded, and the swelling was mostly gone. But it was still tender. "I'm okay."

"You don't look it." He sounded grim. "And if you were really okay, deep inside, you wouldn't be moving back home. What happened?"

"I thought Charlie told you." She moved away, unable to bear his scrutiny for long, and tucked the bowl into a box.

"He said you were beaten. Two weeks ago. By a couple of punks at your school." The words came out flat, staccato. "And you've quit your job because of it and plan to move back to Highpoint."

The attack wasn't the only reason she'd decided to move home, but it had clarified some things for her. "That's pretty much what happened, though the attack wasn't the only reason I quit. I haven't been happy here."

"I know you haven't been crazy about the large classes and all the paperwork, but I hate to see you chuck it all in. After all the years you worked to get your teaching certificate, it doesn't make sense!"

"I'm not planning to give up teaching. I just don't want to do it here. Not anymore."

"Don't tell me you're still homesick." He shook his head. "You've been away from that stupid town for years now, what with college and then your job here. You can't still be pining for Highpoint."

She felt a familiar pang. Jack would never understand how deep her roots went in the small town where she'd grown up, the town he'd been only too happy to leave after high school. He didn't understand roots. "That's part of it, too. But only part. I don't like the big city, Jack. You know that. And…" She hesitated. But he was her friend. He would understand. "I just don't feel safe here anymore."

"I hate what happened to you. I really hate that it happened while I was gone. If I'd been here—"

"It still would have happened. But I'm okay now. A little sore still, but everything is mending. Only…you know how news reports always say, 'the victim was treated and released from the hospital'? That's what happened. Nothing broken, just a cracked rib and a lot of bruises. But I always thought that 'treated and released' made it sound as if no one was really hurt." She tried to smile. "Wrong!"

He frowned. "Would you quit trying to be brave and plucky? It's annoying the hell out of me."

That surprised a laugh out of her—which she suspected was what he'd intended. They looked at each other for a moment in silence before he spoke again, his voice carefully level.

"Charlie said that the attack wasn't sexual."

"I wasn't raped. I—oh, good grief." Her eyes irritated her by filling with tears. For days after the attack she'd wanted nothing more than to have Jack there, holding her. But he'd been in Paraguay. "I don't know what's wrong with me. The doctor said it could have been a lot worse. He said I was l-lucky.''

"The doctor's an idiot. No one needs that sort of luck. Come here." He put his arm around her and urged her over to the couch, which was covered with neat piles of clothing she had yet to pack. He dumped one of piles on the floor.

"Jack! My clothes—"

"Never mind your clothes." He tugged her down onto the couch beside him. "Annie, I'm so sorry. So terribly sorry."

He just held her then, unspeaking, his body warm and hard and comforting. She rested her head on his shoulder and let his warmth soothe her, let herself cherish this moment. She'd needed this, needed it badly. Too badly. That—although she would never tell anyone—was the main reason she'd decided to leave Denver. She couldn't afford to need Jack Merriman.

After a moment she made herself straighten. She didn't pull away entirely, though. He still had one arm around her. His body was still warm and solid along her side. "I really am all right. I had no idea I was such a wimp until this happened."

"You're not a wimp." There was a strange look in his eyes, one she didn't recognize. "Can you tell me how it happened? What were you doing at the school in the summer?"

"Teaching summer school, of course. I'd stayed late grading papers, but it should have been okay. I mean, I'd done everything right." That was what kept eating at her. She'd done everything right, and still she hadn't been safe. "I was parked near the door in a well-lit area, and there were people around. Not a lot, but the kids in the theater group had been rehearsing and were leaving at the same time. The security guard was there. I thought I was okay.

Even when the two of them came up to me, I thought I was safe enough.''

His mouth tightened. ''There were two of them?''

She nodded. ''One grabbed at my purse. I yelled at him. I was so mad…I should have just let him have the purse, but I was mad, not scared. I—I knew him. He was one of my students.''

Jack stroked her hair. ''That made it worse, didn't it?''

''Yes.'' She blinked the sting out of her eyes. ''He yelled back at me, called me filthy names. Then h-his friend slapped me. I wasn't expecting that, but I still wasn't scared, not really. I hit him back. I didn't think. I just hit him, punched him right in the stomach. I hit him hard, too. But he was high on something. He didn't feel it. It just made him more angry. And then they…they both started hitting me, and I couldn't…I couldn't…''

''Where was the guard?'' Jack's voice was tight. ''Where was the damned security guard while all this was happening?''

''He got there as fast as he could. He'd been walking some girls to their cars, but when I yelled he came running. The two of them—my assailants, to put it in police jargon—ran away before he got there. And then it was all over.'' Except for the police reports, and the 'treated and released' part, and the bad dreams. She shivered, and Jack rubbed her shoulder.

He meant to comfort her. She knew that, but the slow, insidious warmth seeping into her had little to do with comfort, and everything to do with her reasons for leaving. She pulled back. ''I really wasn't badly hurt. I was sore all over and shook up, but that's all.''

''You were beaten,'' he said flatly, ''and scared half out of your mind. You're still scared, or you wouldn't be running away like this.''

That stung. "I'm not running away. If I had been happy here in Denver, satisfied with my job, I wouldn't let one unpleasant incident chase me off."

He looked away. "The thing is, Annie, I'm going to miss you. It's been nice, knowing you would be around when I was between jobs."

Nice? She didn't say anything. She couldn't.

Jack worked for a private, nonprofit organization headquartered in Denver. International Construction Aid built schools and clinics in developing nations all over the world. When Jack was between assignments he was in Denver, too. Though Annie was amazed now at her foolishness, that had actually been one of the reasons she'd chosen to live in the Mile-High City after getting her certification. She had thought it would ease her homesickness to have an old friend around part of the time.

And at first it had helped. Whenever she and Jack had gotten together to eat pizza and argue over what movie to rent, or to drive into the mountains for a day's hiking, she hadn't been homesick. But she'd begun to depend on those flying visits too much. Instead of easing her homesickness, the times she'd spent with him had left her feeling more alone than ever after he left.

And, of course, he'd been gone most of the time.

"Listen," Jack said. "I can see why you want to leave Denver. But why go back to Highpoint, for God's sake?" He gave her his most beguiling smile.

That smile put her on her guard. "I miss Highpoint."

"But there are lots of small towns close to Denver where you could feel safe—Shawnee, Longmont, Boulder, Bennett—half a dozen others. I'll bet some of them are crying out for teachers with your qualifications. If you lived nearby, it would still be easy for us to get together when I'm in the country."

"Highpoint isn't that far from Denver. We can get together if you're willing to drive a little farther." He wouldn't do it, of course. Not often, anyway. Jack hated Highpoint as much as Annie loved it.

Abruptly he stood and started to pace. "You could try compromising a little. What about Colorado Springs? If you lived there you'd be able to see your brothers every weekend if you wanted, and it still would be simple for me to drive down for a visit."

She watched him pace, exasperated. "Are you suggesting I should shape my life and my career around your dislike for our hometown?"

He stopped. That odd look was back in his eyes when they met hers, a strange hardness she wasn't used to seeing on her old friend's face. "No, I'm suggesting you shouldn't shape your life around fear."

Her heart jerked in her chest. "You think I'm running away. That I'm a silly, scared fool."

"I don't blame you for being frightened by what happened. Hell, my hands shook for half an hour after I heard. But running home isn't the answer."

"I'm not 'running home.' I like it in Highpoint, Jack. I like it better there than anywhere else I've been. Why wouldn't I want to live there?"

"You've never really been anywhere, Annie. You've never cut the ties. You keep the past knotted up around you like a rope. It's familiar, it's comforting, and it's keeping you from following your dreams."

She shook her head. "I'm not giving up my dreams. I'll still teach—"

"Forget about teaching. I'm not talking about that. What about travel? What about all those places you always wanted to see someday?"

"Travel is your dream, not mine."

"You teach English as a Second Language because you're fascinated by other places, other peoples."

"I—you're wrong. There's a great demand for ESL teachers—it made sense to go where I'd be needed, that's all."

His lips thinned. He paced over to the box she'd just finished filling and started digging around in it.

She came to her feet. "What do you think you're doing?"

"I know they're here somewhere." He moved to another box, one she'd already sealed, and pulled the tape off.

"Stop that." She moved over to him, shoving at his hand.

He ignored her, ripping open the box and grabbing a handful of the contents—her collection of old *National Geographic* magazines. "How many back issues do you have, Annie? How long have you been dreaming about faraway places?"

"Oh, good grief! Millions of people read *National Geographic* who don't have some secret yen to take off for Tunisia!"

"But most of them weren't abandoned by parents who preferred those faraway places to staying home and raising their kids. Parents who died in one of those faraway places."

She froze. How *could* he? How could he throw that in her face? "My mother didn't abandon us. And my father had to work."

"You mother was gone almost as much as your father, from what Charlie has told me."

"She felt that her place was with her husband, whenever possible," she said stiffly. "She knew we'd be fine with Nana." Hurt throbbed through her. She turned away. "I had no idea you were building some kind of a fantasy based on my reading material. There's no deep, dark secret here, Jack. I like to read about distant places. It doesn't mean anything.''

''Doesn't it?'' He shook his head. ''Maybe I've got some selfish reasons for not wanting you to move back to Highpoint, Annie. But not all of my reasons are selfish. I don't want to see you bury yourself there.''

She turned around. He was close. Too close. He stood only a hand's breadth away now, his bitter-chocolate eyes intent on her face, his long, perfect body near enough that she could feel the heat from it. Her heart began to pound out a strange, erratic beat. ''You're seeing me through the lens of your own compulsions, Jack. I'm not the one who feels trapped if I stay in one place for too long.''

''No, unfortunately you don't feel trapped in Highpoint. You feel safe.''

''What's wrong with feeling safe? What's wrong with wanting to be around people who know me, people I've known all my life?''

''I hope there's nothing wrong with wanting to be around people who know you.'' His crooked grin was familiar. The look in his eyes wasn't. ''Since that's one of the things I like best about you. You know me better than just about anyone. Annie, don't go back to Highpoint. Come away with me, instead.''

''What? What did you say?''

''Come with me when I leave on my next job. You can teach. There will be plenty of people who want to learn, believe me, and I'll take care of you. I can make you feel safe, Annie.''

''I can't believe you said that.'' Jack had never been overprotective the way her brothers were. He'd been the one who taught her rock climbing—he had insisted on it, in fact, showing her how planning and knowledge mini-

mized the risks. Annie could handle almost anything if she
knew what the risks were and could plan for them.

But you couldn't control some risks. She licked her lips
nervously. "You're looking at me funny. I wish you'd quit
it."

His eyes drifted to her mouth. "Funny?" he said ab-
sently. "I guess so. I've always liked your mouth, Annie."

"What?" Alarm had her heart jumping into her throat.
She raised one hand to where her pulse throbbed, as if she
could force her heart back where it belonged. "What are
you talking about?"

"Your mouth. Maybe..." he murmured, and she had the
feeling he was talking to himself, not her. "Maybe it's
time." He started to lower his head.

She jerked hers back. "What are you doing?"

His grin flashed. "Isn't it obvious? Here. I'll show you."
And his mouth came down on hers.

The shock of it held her still for a moment too long.
Long enough for the pleasure to catch her, a shimmering
loop of pleasure that settled over her in one quick shiver.
Long enough for a thrill to chase itself up and down her
spine as his lips moved on hers...oh, such smooth and
clever lips. She had wondered. For years she'd wondered
about Jack's kisses as much as she'd feared them, fighting
the need and the curiosity with her too-complete knowledge
of the man. One taste, and wonder overtook fear in a burst
of heat. His hand was at her nape and his fingers were as
clever as his mouth, drawing chills across her flesh, making
her ache. It was too much.

It wasn't enough.

That thought made her turn her head away from his lazy,
maddening mouth. "Jack, this is stupid. You don't think
of me this way—you know you don't!"

Turning her head hadn't saved her. It only left other

places available to him. When his mouth skimmed along her cheek to the sensitive skin just under her jaw, she shivered. He chuckled, damn him. "Of course I've thought of you 'this way' from time to time. I'm a man." He nibbled at her earlobe. "I just never let myself do anything about it before, because we're friends."

"Then why—oh, stop that!" She got herself together enough to push away the hand that had wandered up her side, nearly reaching her breast.

He obeyed, straightening to look at her. "You're trying to leave me, Annie. I don't want you to go." His eyes were dark and unreadable—magician's eyes, capable of raising both heat and hope in a woman who welcomed neither.

The hope was impossible. She knew that. The heat was all but irresistible. And why not? she thought suddenly. Why not let herself have this one time, this one memory? Surely being with Jack one time wouldn't make the hurt that much worse later, when he was gone.

He raised one hand and deliberately cupped her breast, those magical eyes fixed on hers. Her breath caught and her eyes closed and she knew she was losing her mind. Giving herself to Jack would only make the pain worse. Much worse.

But maybe it would be worth it. Maybe…

When his mouth caught hers again, she wasn't ready. How could she have been ready for the need in him, the hunger? It amazed her, swept her under, taking her to a dark, private place where sensation ruled and no hope seemed truly impossible. He wrapped himself around her— his arms, his scent, his hunger—and when he pulled her down with him, she went.

When she finally broke the kiss, they were tangled together on the floor. He'd kept most of his weight off of her, but her ribs ached dully. The pain was an insufficient distraction when Jack's hand was beneath her sweater, hot and demanding on her breast.

"Don't leave, Annie," he murmured against her neck.

"Jack," she gasped. "Jack, I'm not the one who will leave. You will. In a few weeks you'll be off again, building something on the other side of the world."

"So come with me." He lifted his head. His eyes were bright with impulse and delight. "Why not? The timing is perfect, Annie. You're at loose ends right now. You want to feel safe, and I want to make you safe. Why not come with me on my next job?"

"Why not?" The question was so foolish that her mind went blank for a moment. "Why *not?* Are you crazy? Do you really think I'm going to travel halfway around the world with no ring on my finger, no promises, nothing but a casual 'why not?'"

"All right." He sat up suddenly. He was grinning. "All right, that's fair. We'll get married first."

Chapter 3

She had crumbled, Annie thought, giving the porch swing another desultory push. As humiliating as it might be, that was the truth. One hint that Jack needed her—one more long, passionate kiss—and all her good sense had been burned away. She had agreed to fly to Las Vegas with him that same night.

Another creak joined the one from the porch swing as the front door opened, spilling light across the darkness for a moment. The door closed again, renewing the darkness.

"You hiding out here, or holding a one-woman pity party?" Her next-oldest brother's voice was deep, but not the bass rumble of Ben's; Charlie was lighter than their oldest brother in every way.

"Neither one. I'm brooding over my sins."

"Ben wants to know if you've got your jacket on. The wind's starting to pick up again."

She sighed. Ben might not be speaking to her, but he was still looking out for her in his own overbearing way.

"Yes, I'm wearing a jacket. Have you come out here to yell at me some more?"

"Maybe." He moved toward her, a lean, rangy shape in the darkness. "Scoot over."

"It's wet," she warned him, sliding to one side.

"I'm tough. I can take it." His weight added another creak to the quiet night as the wooden swing settled under him. "That was quite a bombshell Jack dropped."

"Wasn't it, though." Jack hadn't hung around to deal with the aftermath of his revelation. He'd given Annie one more quick kiss and announced that he'd be seeing her soon. Ben, who'd had that "pound now, talk later" look showing in his eyes, had grabbed Jack. Fortunately, Charlie had shown up then and had stepped between the other two men.

Jack had told Charlie to keep an eye on her, and left.

"So," Charlie said. "Which of your sins are you brooding over?"

"The sin of silence."

"Ah. You know, I think I understand why you didn't tell us you'd married Jack. It's a stupid reason, mind you, and I'm still mad. But I can understand."

"Really?" Annie gave a small, mirthless laugh. "Tell me, then, because I don't understand myself anymore."

"You hate to make mistakes. Either marrying Jack was a mistake, in which case you didn't want to tell anyone until you fixed it by getting divorced. Or letting him go was the mistake, and you didn't know how to fix that." He pushed off with his foot, and they swayed gently. "Which was it?"

"Both. Neither."

"You still don't know, huh? Okay. How about telling me how you ended up marrying Jack Merriman in the first place, then?" He slanted her a glance. "According to that lame excuse for an explanation you gave us, Jack showed up unexpectedly at your Denver apartment one afternoon, and that night the two of you flew to Vegas and got married. He got a call from his boss about an emergency with some project of his, you panicked, the two of you argued, and the next day he flew to some godforsaken corner of the world and you flew back to Denver, where you finished packing and then came home to Highpoint.''

"That about sums it up.''

"I think you're leaving a few things out,'' he said dryly. "I can picture Jack deciding to get married at five o'clock and tying the knot at midnight, but you aren't exactly the impetuous type.''

"If you think that's funny, try this—it was more or less my idea.''

He dragged his foot on the porch, stopping the swing. "You're kidding.''

She shrugged. "I was the one who mentioned rings. I just didn't expect him to jump on the idea.'' Annie had always found it easier to talk to Charlie than to Ben, but she couldn't imagine explaining exactly how the subject of marriage had come up—with Jack's hand on her breast and her mouth wet from his. "I wasn't myself. I was still shaken from the assault, I'd just turned in my resignation, and when Jack showed up I was packing.''

"That's another thing I don't understand. Why aren't you teaching?''

How could she explain what she didn't understand herself? "I *am* teaching. The evening classes at the community college are enough while I figure out what I want to do. I don't want to make another mistake.''

"So...you were confused when Jack showed up, and being confused naturally made you propose?''

She had to smile. "Not exactly. I indulged myself with the idea of fate. The timing seemed so...I mean, Jack wasn't supposed to be back in the country for another two or three weeks, but suddenly, on almost my last day in the city, there he was. And there I was, newly unemployed." She shook her head. "Fate seemed like a reasonable explanation at the time."

"Seems like you're still leaving out something pretty important. Like your feelings, and why you would jump to the conclusion that Jack Merriman was your fate."

"Sheer, unadulterated stupidity?"

"You were infatuated with him when you were fifteen."

"I'm not fifteen anymore."

"No, you're old enough to know the difference between infatuation and love. Which is it you feel for Jack?"

She didn't want to say it. Not to Charlie, not to herself. So she pushed against the wooden floor of the porch with her toes, getting the swing moving again, and didn't answer directly. "Did I mention that we were married by an Elvis impersonator?"

Charlie gave a bark of laughter. "An Elvis impersonator? Was he wearing one of those glittery costumes?"

"Complete with a cape and jet-black hair falling in a little curl on his forehead. And a potbelly."

"How did you wind up getting married by Elvis?"

"It was Jack's idea, of course. We landed in Vegas about nine, and it took a while to get the license." Long enough for Annie's common sense to wake from the sensual daze caused by Jack's kisses, but every time she'd been about to change her mind, he'd kissed her again. Jack had swept her to the altar—or in front of a caped Elvis—on a tide of hormones, humor and muddled misgivings. "We drove around a long time, arguing about where to do the deed. It was nearly midnight when he spotted the Elvis chapel and that was it for him—the perfect place to tie the knot."

It had been so tacky. And so much fun. In spite of the nerves that had made her half-sick by the time they spoke their vows, she'd giggled when the King's look-alike had drawled out the ceremony. "My favorite part was when 'Elvis' crooned, *Do you promise to love this man tender, love him true, in sickness and in health...*'" She grinned, remembering.

"But you stopped laughing at some point."

Not long after the promises she'd made that midnight, in fact. Annie looked away, turning her face into the wind. The cold air made her eyes sting. "We were in the hotel elevator on our way up to the honeymoon suite when I found the courage to ask what I should have asked before we left Denver."

"What was that?"

"I asked him if he loved me." She closed her eyes. She could see the expression on his face as clearly as if it had happened only seconds ago. "He looked at me as if I'd suddenly started speaking Martian. Then he gave me one of those lopsided grins and said, 'Sure. Of course I do.'"

That's when Annie had known herself for a fool. It would have hurt less if he had been upset or angry, because then she would have known that the words meant something to him. Instead, it had been painfully obvious that he'd said what he thought she wanted to hear.

Charlie spoke quietly. "A man couldn't ask for a better friend than Jack. But for a woman...well, he doesn't mean to be hard on the women in his life, but he often is." He paused. "Do you remember his senior prom? He had three dates that year."

She sighed. "He ended up going with Ellen Baxter."

"The weird thing is that none of them hated him afterward."

"Weird, but not surprising." Part of Jack's charm was his kindness. He could be impulsive, thickheaded, careless enough to end up with three dates to the senior prom—yet he hated to hurt a woman's feelings. He'd taken Ellen because he'd known that the other two girls would be able to replace him easily—and they had. But Ellen had been new in town, and shy. Jack had worried aloud to Annie that Ellen would end up staying home if he didn't take her. That was why he'd asked her, in spite of the fact that he was slightly overbooked for the occasion. He hadn't treated Ellen like a pity date that night, either. He'd done everything he could to make her feel special.

Then he'd never asked her out again.

Annie doubted that Jack had any idea how much poor Ellen had hoped that he would want to see her again. And because she knew Jack, she couldn't help wondering…had he had married Annie because he'd guessed how she felt about him? Because he'd felt sorry for her?

It was possible. Oh, yes, it was only too possible.

You want to feel safe, he had said, *and I want to make you safe.*

Charlie stood. The swing groaned, swaying from the sudden loss of his weight. "You've gotten yourself in one hell of a mess, half pint. I don't think you'll be able to straighten it out until you figure out what you want." His footsteps were quiet as he headed for the door.

"I know what I want. I just don't think I can have it."

Charlie's voice was gentle. "What, then?"

"I want to have Jack back." She swallowed the quick stab of pain. "I want things to be easy and comfortable between us the way they used to be. I want us to be friends again."

"Then why are you still married to him? Seems like you would have changed that at some point in the last two months if you really wanted to just be friends." Her brother opened the door without waiting for an answer. Light spilled onto the porch, then was swallowed up by the night once more as the door closed behind him.

It was the third thud that did it.

Normally Jack could sleep anywhere. He'd slept in

shacks, sheds, hotels, tents and palaces; on feather beds, cots, couches and a pile of smelly hides tossed on the earthen floor of a herder's hut. But he'd had trouble falling asleep last night.

Seeing Annie again had been part of the problem. Being in his aunt's house was the rest of it. Memories that were gentled by daylight often came out to prowl at night, and he had felt trapped from the moment he'd lain down on the bed he'd slept in as a teenager. After tossing and turning, even getting up to pace a couple of times, he'd abandoned his old bedroom and gone downstairs with a pillow and a blanket.

Jack had never been allowed to lie down on the long sofa in the parlor; it was for sitting, his aunt had always said, and for company. He liked to think it was the novelty of stretching out there that had made it possible for him to finally fall asleep, rather than some lingering trace of adolescent rebellion.

Once he had dozed off, though, he'd slept like the dead. So the first series of knocks didn't rouse him. He just worked the sound into his dream.

Whoever was there knocked again. This time he managed to get his eyes open and glance at the clock on the wall. Good God. It was barely 6:00 a.m. Who could be so blasted eager to see him at this hour?

But he didn't respond until a single loud, forceful thud landed on the front door.

He flung back the blanket, dragged himself upright and limped to the entry hall.

There he zipped up his jeans, opened the door and frowned at the man who had been his friend since the sixth grade. "I figured it had to be either you or Ben. I hope you haven't come here to beat me up. I'm not awake yet."

"I haven't decided if you need beating up or not. Here."
Charlie handed him a foam cup.

Belatedly Jack's nose caught the scent of freshly brewed
coffee. He took the cup, pulled off the plastic lid and
stepped back, inhaling the aroma and watching warily as
Charlie came inside. "You're not going to punch me while
I'm distracted by caffeine, are you?"

"Spoken like a man with a guilty conscience." Charlie
hadn't been here as often as Jack had been at his house
when they were younger, but he knew his way around. He
headed for the living room, flipped on the light and glanced
at the couch. "Camping out?"

"Something like that." Jack sipped at his coffee and
watched his friend.

Charlie had been a tall, lanky teen, a forward on the
basketball team in high school. He'd added muscle to his
inches as he got older, but he was still long and lean, standing three inches over Jack's six feet. He didn't look much
like his sister. His hair was redder, and he had a craggy
face with a nose that would have done a Roman emperor
proud. "I've got some questions to ask you."

"Figures." Jack took another sip of coffee. It was hot
and bitter and just might be strong enough to jump-start his
brain. "I don't suppose you've got any doughnuts to go
with this coffee?"

"I ate them on the way here."

Jack grimaced. "That figures, too." He took another sip.
He needed to be alert in case Charlie changed his mind
about pounding him. "You might as well go ahead and ask
whatever you came here to ask."

"Did you marry Annie because she's pregnant?"

Jack choked, coughed and managed to clear the coffee
from his windpipe. "What kind of question is that?"

"A pretty obvious one, I'd say." Charlie set his cup
down on the coffee table and moved restlessly over to the

window. "This marriage happened awfully damned quick."

Jack sipped his coffee and watched Charlie pace as if the floor were covered in hot coals instead of bland beige carpet. Charlie was certainly uncomfortable with the idea of his little sister having had sex. "I don't know why you woke me up to ask such a stupid question. Even you aren't dumb enough to believe Annie would lie to you about something like that."

"I, uh...I didn't ask her."

"You didn't ask her. You thought your sister might be pregnant and had somehow forgotten to mention it, and you didn't ask her." Jack shook his head. "You're an idiot, you know that? I hate to be the one to break this to you, Charlie, but Annie is twenty-six years old. I don't think she's a virgin anymore."

Charlie stopped moving. "No, she's married. To you. And if I find out that she *had* to get married—"

"Calm down. I didn't touch her. Well, no, I did touch her, but not enough to get her pregnant."

Charlie glowered at him. "And just when did this touching take place—before the wedding, or afterward?"

"Would it make you feel better if I said we've never been to bed together?"

"No. That would be downright weird. You *are* married."

Jack took a healthy swallow of coffee. Obviously he needed more caffeine, or he was going to say something stupid and mess up an important friendship. Jack didn't fool himself that he came first with Charlie—or anyone else, for that matter. Including Annie. With the McClains, family came first. Always. And however many hours Jack might have spent in the McClain kitchen when he was younger, he wasn't really family.

Though he *was* Charlie's brother-in-law now. Funny. That hadn't occurred to him before. He liked the idea.

"Okay, so I'm acting like an idiot." Charlie scraped his hair back from his face. "I didn't really think you'd gotten her pregnant. You've got your flaws, but you wouldn't have left her to handle things alone if she'd been carrying your child, no matter what kind of emergency came up with your job."

"Thanks for that much."

"She might have gotten pregnant by someone else, though. Someone who couldn't or wouldn't marry her. I thought maybe she told you about it, and you married her to give her child a father."

A peculiar feeling stole over Jack when he thought about Annie being pregnant by another man. It wasn't jealousy. At least, he didn't think it was, since it was nothing like the nasty twist of anger he'd felt when he'd heard that Annie might be interested in Toby Randall. No, this was a quiet feeling—quiet, but not gentle. Not soft. A stinging gray feeling, like an acid fog. "Have you taken to watching soap operas? That's the screwiest idea you've come up with yet."

"But it's just the sort of thing you *would* do, Jack. Or are you going to tell me that if Annie were pregnant and unmarried you wouldn't offer to marry her?"

"Well..." Jack rubbed a hand over his face. Charlie was right. He'd do just about anything for Annie. "That wasn't how it happened, though. Annie wasn't—isn't—pregnant." And his reasons for marrying her had been wholly selfish.

"Yeah? So why did you two get married, then?"

Jack didn't know what to say. He wasn't going to lie to Charlie. He'd already lied to Charlie's sister, and that had felt bad enough.

When the inspiration to get married had first hit Jack, it hadn't occurred to him that Annie might want the empty trappings of romance slicked over the very real friendship they shared and the passion they'd just discovered. He'd thought she was too sensible to buy into all those pleasant lies about love that so many women wasted their lives on. On their wedding night he'd found out he'd been wrong.

They had been alone in the elevator, on their way up to the honeymoon suite, and Jack had been skimming his mouth across hers, teasing himself with a taste of the feast waiting for them. All of a sudden she'd pulled back, her eyes serious and scared. She'd asked him if he loved her.

Jack had felt sucker punched. He'd taken a couple of seconds too long to answer. Oh, he'd managed to smile and say what she wanted to hear, but his hesitation had hurt her. He hated that as much as he'd hated lying to her.

"Well?" Charlie demanded. "Is it that hard to come up with a reason?"

"I was hoping to think of a way to phrase it that wouldn't make you want to punch me." Jack rubbed a hand across the back of his neck. It felt odd. He was used to having hair there. Annie had accused him of having let the barber scalp him. He smiled. At least she noticed him. She didn't want to admit it, and she would have liked to push him back into his not-quite-a-brother place in her life, but she did notice him. And *not* as a brother.

Charlie eyed him for a moment, then shook his head. "Maybe I don't want to know. If it has something to do with sex—"

"You don't want to know."

Charlie scowled and moved over to where he'd left his coffee. He took a sip, grimaced and set it down. "Damned stuff is cold."

"Serves you right for eating all the doughnuts. Why did you come hassle me so early, anyway?"

"I've got a load of pipe that's supposed to be in California tomorrow and I wanted to talk to you before I hit the road. Which reminds me—why did you tell me to keep an eye on Annie until I talked to you?''

Jack frowned. ''Damn. I wish you didn't have to leave town right now.''

''Curiouser and curiouser. If you're looking for me to play matchmaker—''

''No, it's nothing like that.'' Jack ran a hand over the top of his head. No way to lead into this gradually, he decided. ''I think someone tried to kill me. There's a chance that Annie is in danger, too.''

The sun was up, but Annie wasn't. Normally she was out of bed as soon as she was awake, which was always early. But today she didn't want to get up. She didn't want to sing with the radio or talk to her brothers. She didn't want to face the decisions this day was likely to bring. Most of all, she didn't want to face Jack.

Pulling the covers over her head and staying in bed for the next few weeks sounded like a great plan, she thought wistfully as she watched dawn chase the shadows from her room. But she'd played the coward too long already. With a sigh, she threw back the covers and left the warmth of her bed.

Charlie's car was gone, she noticed when she glanced out the window, but Ben's pickup was still in the driveway. No doubt she had an uncomfortable discussion waiting for her.

Annie showered quickly and dressed in jeans and an old beige sweatshirt. To bolster her spirits she pulled on yellow socks—yellow turned up on high, a blindingly cheerful color she hoped would give her a visual punch of optimism whenever she glanced at her feet. Then she gritted her teeth and went downstairs.

Her big brother sat at the kitchen table, scowling at his coffee.

Ben was the oldest, the largest and the darkest of her brothers, both in appearance and outlook. He was a seriously stubborn man with a passion for the outdoors, a quick temper and a huge heart. Some people were intimidated by him. Many underestimated him, thinking a man as big and gruff as he was had to be all brawn and no brain.

Annie knew better. She mentally girded up her loins for battle and stepped into the kitchen. "Good morning," she said brightly, heading for the coffeepot. "Why aren't you down at the yard making your secretary's life miserable, or out browbeating a flunky or two at one of the sites? It's nearly eight o'clock."

"I need to talk to you."

"Maybe you could yell at me instead. It usually makes you feel better." Ben's temper didn't bother her. His brooding did. It meant he was blaming himself for something.

"You're not having breakfast?" he said when she sat down across from him.

She shrugged. "Didn't feel like it."

He studied her over the rim of his cup as he sipped his coffee. "One of my crew on the Baker job called in sick. If you're not already booked up, I could use you. I want to get the drywall finished today."

Was that all he'd wanted to talk about? "Sure," she said, relieved, though hanging Sheetrock was one of her least favorite construction jobs. The only one she liked less was laying insulation. She always itched for days after handling that, no matter how careful she was. With Sheetrock she just sneezed a lot from the dust.

"All right, then." He set his cup down, squaring his shoulders as if he were about to heft some unpleasant burden. "Annie, I think you should move out."

Hurt jolted through her. Her hand jerked, and coffee spilled. "I—I thought things were working out okay, but if there's a problem..." Her voice twisted into silence before she could get control of it. "If that's what you want, then, sure. I'll move out. It may take me a little while to find a place...you know what that's like around here, especially with skiing season coming up, but—"

"Hold on. I didn't mean it that way. The house is yours as much as it's mine. Hell, I'm not doing this right." He scowled. It was the expression Ben used for almost any strong emotion. "I've been selfish. I like having you around, but it isn't right. You should be living your own life."

"But I *am!* Maybe you try to interfere with that from time to time, but I don't let you. So there's no problem."

He shook his head. "You're married, but you're living at home with your brothers. That doesn't sound to me like living your own life."

Uh-oh. She'd bumped into one of Ben's walls. He was usually fairly reasonable in a pigheaded sort of way, but there were a few subjects on which he was stone-hard, granite-solid. Rigid, in other words.

Marriage was one of them. "I realize my situation is unusual, Ben, but this marriage isn't—" *Real,* she almost said, but she remembered the way Jack had reacted when she'd said that yesterday. "This isn't exactly a normal marriage. We haven't lived together. We haven't..." No, she didn't want to tell him what else she and Jack hadn't done. "It's complicated."

"Either you're married or you aren't. If you are, your place is with your husband."

That had certainly been what their mother had believed. She'd followed her husband all over the world, leaving her children with their grandmother—until she'd left them in the most permanent way possible. Annie's mouth tightened. "This isn't the nineteenth century, and even you aren't that black-and-white. There are all sorts of reasons that a woman might not stay with her husband...infidelity, cruelty, abandonment—''

Ben's hand fisted on the table. ''If he's hit you—''

''No. Oh, no! I didn't mean that! Good grief, Ben, you know Jack. You might not like him, but you know he would never hit me. Or any other woman.''

''Was he unfaithful?''

She opened her mouth—then closed it again. She had no idea. It was something she'd tried not to think about. Logically she knew that if Jack hadn't been faithful to their hasty, unconsummated marriage, she couldn't blame him. All they had really shared was a few kisses and some impulsive promises spoken in front of an Elvis impersonator. But she felt absolutely wild at the thought of Jack being with another woman.

Annie licked her lips and answered with careful honesty. ''Not as far as I know.''

''Then you should be with him. Not here.'' He leaned back in his chair. ''And I don't dislike Jack. It may take me a while to get used to the idea of having him as a brother-in-law, but I don't dislike him.''

''You hit the ceiling yesterday when you heard he was in town.''

''That was a knee-jerk reaction. I thought you were keeping something from me the way you used to when you and Jack and Charlie were up to something.'' His eyebrows drew down. ''As it turned out, I was right.''

The ringing of the doorbell was a welcome interruption. ''I'll get it,'' she said quickly, pushing her chair back and standing.

''Wait a minute.'' Ben's hand clamped around her wrist. ''You should know that I'm going to send a notice to the paper today, announcing your marriage.''

''You're *what?*''

''You heard me.''

"It isn't up to you to make a decision like that!"

"Now that I know that you're married, it would be lying for me to pretend otherwise. I don't like lies. A notice to the paper is the simplest way to handle things."

"It must be nice to be so perfect," she said bitterly. "So sure of yourself and what's right."

"I'm not sure of much this morning. Obviously I made some major mistakes when you were younger, if you didn't think you could tell me that you'd gotten married."

More than lectures, more than scowls or yelling, she hated it when Ben started blaming himself for her mistakes. That was one of the reasons she hated making mistakes so much.

The doorbell rang again. She jerked her hand free, hurried through the living room to the front door, flung it open...and groaned.

Jack's grin came slow and packed with wicked suggestions. "Good morning."

She slammed the door shut.

Chapter 4

Ben came up behind her, turned the knob and stepped out on the porch. "She's upset," he said to Jack.

"I got that impression."

"I told her that I'm sending a notice to the paper about your marriage."

"Good."

Ben paused, looking Jack over. He was half a head taller and forty pounds heavier than the younger man. "If you hurt her, I'm going to break parts of your body. I haven't decided which ones yet."

Jack looked wary, but nodded. "Fair enough. You've got the right to look out for her." He glanced at Annie, then back at Ben. "I need to talk to you about that, actually. Later."

Annie considered closing the door again and locking it against both of them, but Ben probably had his key with him, which would really detract from the effect.

"There's something I need to know," Ben said.

Jack's eyebrows went up quizzically. "And that is...?"

"Have you been faithful to Annie?"

Jack straightened. "I think that's something to be discussed between Annie and me. So—do you want to arm wrestle? Bloody my nose? Or can I go inside now and talk to Annie?"

Ben's hands closed into fists. "You can damned well answer me first."

If anyone was going to hit Jack, it would be her. She stepped outside and put her hand on Ben's arm. "No. This is between me and Jack."

It wasn't easy for her brother to back down. She knew that. Ben needed to fix things. It might drive her crazy when he tried to fix her, but he also wanted to fix things *for* her. She knew that his instinct now was to shake the truth out of Jack.

For the first time, she wondered if her brothers had spoiled her. Oh, not in a material sense. After her parents died there had been money enough for the necessities and an occasional treat, but that was about it. But Ben and Duncan and Charlie had always been there for her. Their love was a constant in her life, something she could depend on, no matter what. Maybe that had made her expect too much. Maybe no man would ever love her the way she wanted to be loved.

After a moment she felt the tension ease in her brother's arm. "All right. I don't like it, but all right. I need to get to work. Annie, I need you on the site at eight. We'll talk more about you moving out when I get home."

Jack's eyebrows went up again, but he didn't speak until he'd followed her into the house, closing the door behind him. "You're moving out?"

She shrugged. "Ben's suffering from one of his attacks of uprightness. You want some coffee?"

"Well, I'll be damned." Jack shook his head. "Uprightness? Ben thinks you should be living with me, doesn't he?"

She felt her face heat and spun around, starting for the kitchen. "I want coffee, whether you do or not."

He followed her, still marveling. "Who would have thought that Ben McClain would turn out to be on my side?"

"Remember that he also threatened to break various parts of your body," she said as she grabbed a mug from the cupboard.

"Only if I screw up. I don't intend to do that. Annie?"

Something about the way he said her name made her turn, the empty mug in one hand, her back against the counter.

He was too close. He came even closer, stopping a hand's breadth away and trapping her by leaning in, his hands braced on the counter on either side of her. "Why did Ben ask if I'd been faithful? Were you afraid to ask me yourself? Or do you just not care?"

Her heart made a nuisance of itself, pounding out a quick distress signal against the skin of her throat. "Back off, Jack. If you want to talk, you need to give me some space."

"It is hard to talk when we're this close," he agreed, and lifted one of his hands from the counter. But that gave her no relief, since he used it to play with her hair. He didn't touch her. He just sifted his fingers through her hair, holding it slightly away from her head, studying it as if there were something fascinating about hair that was as straightforward and lacking in mystery as the rest of her.

It shouldn't have made her knees weak. It shouldn't have made desire coil low in her belly, an electric snake pulsing its neon message throughout the rest of her body.

His gaze slid back to hers. "So—are you going to ask? Do you want to know?"

She tipped her chin up. "Have you been with another woman?"

"I haven't been with *any* women since we flew to Las Vegas, Annie." That slow, wicked smile dawned. "Not even you, unfortunately."

Relief hit her hard, getting tangled up in her brain with hope and colliding in her middle with the pulse of that hungry snake. "Why are you smiling? You were furious before."

He shrugged and gave her hair a tug. "It's hard to seduce a woman when I'm yelling at her."

"I—" She stopped and cleared her throat. "I don't want you to seduce me."

"Don't you? I thought you liked it pretty well."

Annie hadn't known that heat could raise goose bumps the way cold did. That it could make her shiver. "What I like and what's good for me aren't always the same thing."

"You want me, Annie. Don't try to convince either of us otherwise."

"And what do you want—a wedding night, or a real marriage?"

"If I married every woman I'd ever wanted for one night, I'd be in deep trouble. I want *you,* Annie."

Oh, damn. How could he twist her heart into a knot and make it sing at the same time? She put her hands on his chest and pushed, and he let her shift him back a step. "Don't pretend you can't keep your hands off me. You managed to do that for years with no trouble."

He smiled and shifted to lean against the counter, all lazy good nature once more. "Weird how things change, isn't it?"

She carried his mug over to the coffeepot, which put her

back to him. It was easier to talk to him that way. "Look, this is how we got into trouble before. We let ourselves get all hot and hasty and didn't talk about what we wanted from marriage. From each other. Then, when our expectations had a head-on collision, we hurt each other. I don't want to do that again."

"Okay. Move in with me, and we'll talk about our expectations."

She froze with the coffeepot in midair. After a second, she poured his coffee. Her hand was admirably steady. "Now, that's a sensible solution. I can move in with you for a couple weeks, we can have lots of hot sex, and by the time you have to leave the country again you ought to have worked me out of your system. You know how quickly you lose interest, Jack." She turned around and held out his coffee. "Thanks, but no thanks."

"Annie." He took the mug in one hand—and lifted the other to touch her cheek. "I like the part about lots of hot sex, but I don't want to get you out of my system. I *do* want to make sure nothing happens to you."

"You aren't talking about that stupid anonymous letter again, are you?"

"Sort of." He ran a hand over the top of his head. "Look, there are some things I haven't told you."

She looked at him in disbelief. "You really *do* have a crazy ex-girlfriend."

"I don't know. Someone sent you that letter. Someone who knew we were married, and you didn't tell anyone. There's a chance that it's connected to…some things that happened on my last job. So I really need to know exactly what the letter said."

"I don't remember word for word." Distracted, she went over to the table and sat down. It seemed like a good idea to have plenty of solid oak between her and Jack. "Something about how I'd be sorry for taking you away from her, and you'd be sorry for treating her so badly. It was childish—the phrasing, the sentiments, even the spelling. Whoever wrote it didn't bother with a spell checker.''

''So it was either typed or done on a computer.'' He frowned and brought his mug over to the table, sitting beside her. ''How about the envelope? Was it hand-addressed?''

''No, it was done with a printer on one of those white labels. I noticed because I was curious and I was mad, and that's why I sent you that note about it. I thought she must be someone you knew pretty well, well enough that you had to break the news of our marriage to her yourself. She had my address.''

''Annie, I haven't been in touch with anyone I used to date—not in person, not by mail, not at all. And there's no reason for any of them to have your address.''

''Well.'' She cleared her throat. ''There wasn't any return address on the envelope, so I tried to read the postmark, but it was smeared. It had U.S. postage, though. It didn't come from Borneo or Paraguay or wherever.'' She put her cup down. ''Jack, what's going on?''

''Unlike you, I did tell people about our marriage. But not my old girlfriends. I notified ICA headquarters. You're covered by my insurance now.''

''I am?'' The thought jolted her. ''Jack, I—I'm sorry.''

His mouth quirked up. ''You don't want to be covered by my insurance?''

''I'm sorry I kept saying our marriage wasn't real.'' She toyed with the handle of her mug, not looking at him. ''I didn't think you took it seriously.''

''You've got a pretty strange opinion of me, then.''

''What was I supposed to think? The last time I talked to you was when we had that terrible fight. You didn't call or answer my letter...when you showed up here, I expected you to ask for a divorce or an annulment. I didn't understand.'' But she was starting to.

"We're back to the letter I didn't write, are we? I'm not good at that sort of thing. I thought you'd understand what the ticket meant. That still I wanted you to join me.''

She kept running her fingers over the mug's handle. "I guess I knew that, but I was hoping for something about your feelings.''

"I *felt* mad as hell. It didn't seem like a good idea to put that in a letter.'' He sighed. "Look, we're getting off the subject. Annie, there's something funny going on, and it's connected with my last job.''

"The emergency that took you away the day after we got married, you mean?'' Jack's beeper had gone off the moment they entered their hotel room. Annie hadn't wanted him to answer it. She'd been even more upset when he announced he had to leave the country the next day. He'd assumed she would go with him. She'd tried to persuade him to let someone else handle the emergency. She'd known he didn't love her, but part of her had hoped he cared enough to give her time to adjust—that he cared more about her than his job. But mixed with the anger and the hurt had been a sly, shameful sense of relief, because another part of her had hoped he would go away and they could pretend Las Vegas had never happened.

"Hey—are you with me still, or have you wandered off?''

"Sorry.'' She shook her head, trying to clear it of the past. "You said the man who had been in charge was in the hospital. Some kind of complications from an appendectomy, I think it was. But what has that to do with the anonymous letter I got?''

"Bear with me a bit. The complications weren't all medical. Metz—that's the man I replaced—was supposed to be building and stocking a rural clinic. Well, he had the structure mostly finished, but there was a problem with the supplies. Or the lack of supplies. The drugs he'd planned to stock it with were not what ICA had paid for. They were virtually useless.''

"Oh, no. Had he stolen the others?''

He nodded grimly. "Sold them on the black market, probably. Dammit, Annie, people die from the lack of antibiotics in places like that! The ones he was going to use were expired. Degraded tetracycline can cause a kidney disease instead of curing the illness it's prescribed for.''

"What did you do?''

"I notified the government inspector, for whatever good that did. If he wasn't in on it, his boss was. Then I went to the last two sites Metz had been responsible for. He'd pulled the same crap at both of them.''. He started pacing. "I also notified Amos Deerbaum, of course.''

Annie nodded. Deerbaum was the nephew of ICA's founder, and the current director. He'd been something of a mentor to Jack professionally. "What did he say?''

Jack grimaced. "He was encouraging, but he's been gone most of the time on a couple of those hunting trips he's so crazy about—first in Alaska, then a safari in Africa. He told me to find out what I could, but he left Herbie in charge at the main office.''

"Herbert Bickham? The one you called a living embodiment of the Peter principle?''

"That's Herbie, all right. All he's worried about is keeping things quiet. He doesn't want to blacken ICA's reputation and possibly dry up some of our sources of funding.''

"That's wrong, but a lot of corporations do have that attitude about white-collar crime. They don't want to be embarrassed by having it made public.''

"He did fire Metz," Jack said grudgingly. "But he refused to press charges, didn't even want me to investigate. So I did it, anyway."

That sounded like Jack. Damn the bureaucrats and full speed ahead. Annie's fingers went back to playing with her coffee mug. "So, is that what you've been doing the last two months? Investigating?"

"When I could. Metz had cut some corners in getting the building up, so I had to redo a lot of it. And there were problems with the other two clinics he'd built, too. But I was making progress. I spent as much time as I could in Singapore—that's our closest regional office—trying to find out how he'd rigged the substitution and what had happened to the original shipment." He hesitated. "Three weeks ago I heard that Metz had killed himself."

"Oh, no." She touched his hand. "You don't blame yourself, do you?"

"Hell, no. The bastard sold out innocent people, the people he'd been sent there to help. But his death put an end to any hope I had of learning more from him about who else was involved."

"You think there were others in on it?"

"I didn't know, not for sure, but it was a possibility. Then…a week after I learned of his death, someone ran me off the road."

"Someone—oh, my God. Your accident."

He nodded. "Right after it happened, I found a note in my room, warning me to 'leave well enough alone.' I figured it was from the black market people in that area. Then, two weeks later, your note finally caught up to me, and from what I could tell, you got your threatening letter about the same time I got mine."

Someone had threatened Jack's life. Someone had tried to *kill* him. Annie couldn't take it in. "But there isn't any connection. The letter I got was a silly attempt to cause trouble between us, nothing more.''

''Maybe. But the timing...'' He shook his head. ''At any rate, as soon as I got your note I booked a flight home. I'm not taking any chances. You have to move in with me so I can protect you.''

Had she thought, for even one moment, that Jack had suddenly decided he didn't want to live without her? No, he wanted to protect her. He'd flown thousands of miles, not to work things out between them, but to protect her from a threat she couldn't believe existed.

She shoved her chair back. ''Jack, turn this over to the police. Let them do their job, and then no one will have any reason to be after you.''

His face hardened. ''I'll talk to the police, but there's only so much they can do. There are strong indications that someone else with ICA was involved, and whoever it was has to be stopped.''

For lack of anything better to do, Annie grabbed her mug and moved to the sink. ''You will be careful, won't you?''

''Hey, I'm always careful.'' She heard his chair scrape against the floor. ''If you move in with me, though, you can make sure of it.''

''I can't decide something like that so quickly.'' She rinsed the mug and slid it into the dishwasher. ''Even if there is a threat to me, which I don't believe, I'm already living with two men who are nuts about protecting me, whether I like it or not.''

He moved up beside her. ''Charlie's gone more than he's here, and Ben has to be at work during the day. I'm on leave. I can be with you twenty-four hours a day.''

''I have to work, too. I—uh-oh.'' She glanced at the clock on the stove. ''In fact, I'm supposed to be hanging drywall right now.''

"You'd better go, then. But think about what I said. And think about this, too." He cupped her cheek with one hand, smiling down into her eyes, his intentions as easy to read as if he'd spoken them aloud.

Her heart stuttered. "Keep your hands to yourself."

"Okay. He dropped his hand and smiled. "No hands, Annie." Then he bent and kissed her.

There was no anger in his kiss this time. His mouth settled over hers as easily as dawn settles over morning. She made a small sound deep in her throat. She thought it was a protest, but she couldn't blame him if he didn't take it that way. Not when even to her own ears she sounded more urgent than angry.

Jack wasn't urgent. No, he took his time, kissing her as if he had the whole day ahead with nothing more important to do than to learn how their mouths fit, checking first one angle and then the next. He smelled of soap and coffee. Morning smells. Annie's mind dimmed, rolled and went under, seduced by a pleasure that owed nothing to the past or future. The heat came, a warmth so quiet and simple it made her want to stretch like a cat in the sun—and to stand still, holding herself motionless in the moment.

She didn't know she'd closed her eyes until his mouth left hers and she found herself alone in the darkness behind her closed lids. Slowly, with an effort, she opened them. His eyes were bright and hard—bright as sunshine on snow, hard like the middle of winter, long before the thaw. His heavy eyelids and taut jaw spoke of arousal, but those eyes... Confusion stole through her. Her hand lifted in a question she didn't have words for. "Jack...?"

His hand fell away from her cheek. As if he'd flipped a switch or drawn a curtain, the hardness in his eyes vanished behind his familiar crooked smile. "I'll see you in the

morning, Annie.'' He gave her hair a friendly tug, turned
and left.

And Annie stood in the kitchen for a foolishly long time,
unable to move, trying to understand. There had been no
threat in his kiss, no demands. So why was her heart pounding now with alarm?

The day was cool and nearly windless, the sun bright—
a good day for construction work. Annie had only worked
with one of the men on this particular crew before, and she
was the only female on the site. But she was used to that.
It didn't take long to have the others comfortable enough
with her to spit and cuss when they felt the need. If there
was one thing she was good at, she thought gloomily, it
was being one of the guys.

She spent the first part of the morning cutting Sheetrock
and trying to talk herself into her usual calm good sense,
but her heart kept pounding out a confused message of heat
and hope and fear. She couldn't forget the look in Jack's
eyes after he kissed her. There had been intent there, a hint
of calculation. While she'd been wholly caught by the moment, by the pleasure he offered and the promises she'd
thought she sensed behind that pleasure, he had held
enough of himself back to plan the kiss and its effect.

It hurt.

She'd become a goal to him. Someone to rescue, to protect. Once Jack set himself to accomplish something—
whether it was winning a track meet back in high school,
or building a school in Tunisia—he didn't let anything
stand in his way. And once he'd accomplished a goal, he
moved on. Always.

Yet he had been faithful to her. At least, that's what he'd
said. Of course, he'd been acting strange since he came

back—hard and edgy at times, angry when she least expected it, switching back to lazy humor unpredictably.

But when has Jack ever been predictable? she asked herself as she measured Sheetrock amid the racket of construction, the hammering and talking and the occasional loud whine of a saw. He might have changed in some ways, she thought, sticking the tape measure back in her pocket. But he hadn't changed so much that she couldn't trust his word. If he said he hadn't been with another woman, he hadn't.

He'd also said that someone had tried to kill him.

A cold chill chased up Annie's spine. She didn't for one minute believe Jack's assurance that he would be careful. The man didn't know the meaning of the word. As for his suggestion that she should move in with him so she could protect him—she snorted. She wasn't about to fall for that blatant attempt at manipulation.

Although, if he was busy protecting her—or thought he was—he'd be alert, aware of possible dangers. Jack would be careful for her sake even if he wasn't careful for himself.

Dammit. He wouldn't have to talk her into anything if she kept thinking that way—she'd talk herself into it. Annie forced herself to concentrate on what she was doing.

Maybe it was time to grow up. Time to put away her unrealistic dreams of what love should be. Maybe she'd been expecting too much from Jack—from life in general—and she ought to be thinking in terms of compromise. Some people did have long-distance marriages these days. If Jack would settle for that, she could be with him when he was in the country, and when he was gone...

When he was gone, she could be miserable.

Annie shook her head and slashed off the end of the Sheetrock with her knife.

Maybe she'd better stop thinking.

* * *

The Merriman house had been built around 1940 by a man Jack had never met—his grandfather. It was typical of what Jack knew of the man that he had chosen to build a Victorian-style home long after the era was over, complete with gables, gambrel roofs, gingerbread and a pixie-hatted turret. Waldo Merriman had been a rigid old devil with a passion for the past and the good opinion of his neighbors. He hadn't had much feeling left over for his two daughters.

One daughter had run away from home at the age of seventeen with a musician. The other had stayed and grown into a rigidity as complete as her father's.

The house had twelve rooms, including five bedrooms and the servant's quarters by the kitchen, where Ida had retired to watch the movie of the week. Jack had considered appropriating another of the bedrooms, since he couldn't sleep in the one that had been his. In the end, he'd decided to move into the parlor. His laptop computer rested on the marble-topped center table, and his pillow and blankets occupied the griffin-armed sofa.

It wasn't as if this was his favorite room, but he'd spent very little time here. There were fewer memories to set him to pacing.

The sudden pounding on his door startled him. He swung his legs off the sofa. Maybe it was Annie. Maybe she'd decided to move in and couldn't wait to tell him so.

He grinned ruefully at his imagination as he walked into the tiled entryway. Most likely it was Ben. They hadn't been able to talk long when Jack had stopped by his office earlier.

Jack liked Annie's oldest brother. Benjamin McClain was a hard man in some ways, but he was the rock who had held his family steady through some rough times, and Jack admired him for that. In fact, Ben was one of the reasons Jack had chosen the career he had. He'd seen the satisfaction Ben took in building homes, churches—things that lasted.

Of course, he'd always known that Ben didn't think much of him. Until today he hadn't thought that it bothered him. But when he'd realized that Ben had told Annie she should live with her husband, not her brothers, he'd felt a surprising pleasure. Ben must have changed his mind about Jack somewhere down the line. He must have decided that Jack was okay.

Whoever was at the door knocked again, harder. Jack grimaced as he unlocked it. He had more than one reason to hope Ben hadn't changed his mind about him again. The man could pound him into the ground if he wanted to.

He swung the door open. "Annie!" A pleased smile broke out.

Annie wasn't as happy to see him as he was to see her. She put both hands on the middle of his chest and shoved. He fell back a pace and she stormed past him into the parlor.

He closed the door behind her, his eyebrows lifting, and followed. "When I heard someone trying to beat my door down I thought it was Ben. Charlie's already had his turn at that."

Annie was wearing jeans and a denim jacket. Under the jacket was the same oversize top she'd had on earlier that nearly hid the existence of her breasts. It was a nice color for her, though, a soft caramel shade that went well with the angry flush on her cheeks.

He didn't think this was a good time to tell her that she looked pretty when she was mad.

She put her hands on her hips. "You sicced my brother on me."

"Not exactly." Her hair was braided tonight—a practical style, he supposed, since she'd been hanging Sheetrock all day. But he had a sudden yen to see it loose around her face. "I don't think I've seen your hair down since I got back. I like it pulled back, but maybe you could wear it loose tomorrow?"

"Forget about my hair! You went to see Ben, didn't you?"

Of course he had. Jack had gone straight from telling Annie about the situation to Ben's construction office. Her big brother had not been happy to hear that Annie might be in danger. "What gave me away?"

"Do you know how many times he stopped by the site today? At first I was furious at him, because I thought he didn't trust me to handle a simple drywall job. Then I figured out it was you I needed to be mad at. You told him I was in danger, didn't you?"

"I told him you *might* be. Stopping by the site was his idea." One that Jack had heartily approved. Until he persuaded Annie to move in with him, he'd have to rely on her brothers to keep her safe.

"This is going to be horrible. Ben's overly protective at the best of times, but now..." She seemed at a loss for words.

"If he gets too bad, you can always move in with me."

Her cheeks flushed in renewed fury. "You told him just so he'd drive me crazy, didn't you? You're trying to force me to move in with you!"

"No." All levity left him. "I told him because you may be in danger, and he needed to know. Aside from the question of protecting you—and I know you see that differently than Ben and I do—if you're at risk, he might be, too. Since you live with him."

Her eyes went wide. "I never thought of that."

His conscience twinged. Honesty could be a real pain sometimes. "There probably isn't much danger to him."

"But if he's in danger because of me..." After a moment she shook her head. "I just can't believe it. Jack, it's not my safety that's an issue here. It's yours."

She was wrong, but her concern made him smile. "You're a good friend, Annie."

She looked down. He saw her throat move when she swallowed.

"Look." He crossed to her and took her hands. "I know you don't believe friendship is a good basis for a marriage. But I think you're wrong. I want a chance to prove it to you. Come on." He let go of her hands and turned to look for his jacket.

"What the—where do you think you're going at this hour?"

He spotted his jacket on the chair. "It's where *we're* going, not where I'm going." He grabbed the jacket with one hand and her hand with the other and towed her out of the parlor. She protested, but there was laughter mixed in with her protests until she realized what his goal was.

"Oh, no." She dug in her feet, forcing him to stop at the foot of the stairs. "I am not going up there with you."

"I'm not dragging you off to my room for sex," he assured her.

"I know that. If you were trying to seduce me again, you'd be taking clothes off, not putting your jacket on. But I am *not* climbing out on the roof with you. Good grief, Jack, we're supposed to be adults now."

"You still like to climb."

"Mountains. Not roofs."

"Don't you want to see 'God's freckles'?" Annie's hair was more brown than red, but she had a redhead's complexion and had been much-afflicted by freckles when she was younger, before she started using sunblock regularly. She'd told Jack that when she was little her mother had

tried to reconcile her to her speckled face by telling that
the stars splattered across the night sky were God's freckles.

"I can see them fine from the ground. Jack, it's forty
degrees outside."

He ignored that. They had jackets. "C'mon, Annie. The
sky is supposed to be clear tonight. The stars will have
already come out to play. You aren't going to turn them
down, are you?"

The sudden white flash of her grin gave the lie to the
huge sigh she heaved. "I can tell you're not going to give
up. I suppose I'd better go with you so you can get it out
of your system."

Chapter 5

The east window in Jack's old bedroom opened onto a narrow, sharply sloping patch of roof. It wasn't the easiest route, but it was the one he'd always used when he lived here and the one he wanted to take tonight.

Annie was the only one who had ever gone with him to his special spot on the roof. He'd never asked anyone else to join him there, not even Charlie, and he wondered now why that was.

The first time he'd persuaded her to follow him out his window he'd learned something important about her. Annie had no fear of heights. Once he'd realized that, he'd stopped taking "no" for an answer about teaching her rock climbing. Her brothers all climbed, or had back then, and he'd seen her fascination with the sport, even though she refused to try it. She had associated climbing with dare-deviltry—something she wanted no part of.

Her brothers hadn't pressed her to change her mind. Jack had.

Annie had taken to climbing as if she'd been born to do it. Jack climbed for the sheer physical exhilaration of the sport and because it was a natural outgrowth of his love for the outdoors. Annie shared that love, but he suspected that she needed the challenge in a way he didn't. Climbing was a well-planned risk, one she could control and triumph over.

Hidden behind those cautious fences of hers, Annie possessed an adventurous soul. Even if she didn't know that, Jack did.

They scrambled up the steeply sloped roof to their goal—a snug, shingled valley between two pitches that rose like miniature mountains to either side, cutting off the wind and the sight of everything but what lay directly ahead.

And up. Oh, yes, he thought, settling his back against the steepest side of their roof valley. The stars were making a spectacle of themselves tonight, scattered like glowing confetti across an inky black sky. Jack tilted his head back, ready to enjoy the show.

Annie settled beside him. He wanted to reach for her hand, but for some reason laced his fingers together on his stomach instead. The conflicting urges made him frown. He wondered if she was remembering the other times they'd climbed up here, if she felt safe and comfortable with him the way she used to. Or if she felt the way he did.

It wasn't the same. He'd thought that getting Annie onto the roof would remind them both of the friendship they'd built over the years, a relationship they could depend on. But nothing felt the same tonight.

Jack liked stargazing for some of the same reasons he liked climbing or hiking. Nature on a grand scale had a way of shrinking a man. When he hiked in a forest or rappelled down a cliff or stared at the sky, whatever was eating at him shrank right along with the rest of him, clear-

ing his mind of the self-important snarls that could bog him
down.

But tonight he couldn't lose himself in the vastness overhead. He was too aware of the woman beside him. When
she shifted, he heard the rustle from her clothes. When she
sighed, he wondered why. When he inhaled, he breathed in
the scent of her, a wispy scent that was apples and Annie.
And he felt her. All along his side, he felt her—a subtle
warmth that was her body heat and something more, something that came from inside him.

Sex. It lay between them now, shimmering with possi-
bilities, distracting him. Changing things. Maybe it wasn't
going to be easy to turn a friend into a lover, and still keep
her as a friend. The thought had him shifting restlessly.
"You wearing some kind of perfume?"

"You know perfume makes me sneeze."

So did Sheetrock. He smiled, wondering if she'd been
sneezing a lot that day. "Then I must be hallucinating,
because I could swear I smell apples."

"Oh. That's my shampoo."

He sat straighter, bringing one knee up to rest his arm
on. He wanted to kiss her. Hell, he wanted to do a great
deal more than that, but kissing would be a start.

If he could just *have* her, surely he could feel comfortable with her again. He reached for her hair and tugged a
strand loose from her braid. She had such silky hair. Fun
to play with. He wanted to wrap it around his hand and
pull her face toward his, so he started to do just that.

He heard her breath hitch. "Jack, you've got to stop
trying to get me into bed every time we're together."

"Why?"

That stumped her for a moment. Then, low-voiced, she
said, "Because sex alone isn't enough. Not for me."

Anger flickered to life. He dropped her hair. "Do you
really think that's all I'm after? If sex was all I wanted

from you, Annie, I would have already had it. In fact, if
that was all I wanted, I could have you right here. Now.''

"Here?'' She made a disgusted noise. "Arrogant. Stupid,
too, if you think I'd make love on a rooftop.''

Swift and smooth, he rolled. In one click of a second he
was on top of her, his weight forcing her to slip down until
they were as close to horizontal as their little rooftop valley
would let them be. Oh, yes, she was warm, deliciously so,
with her breasts pushed up against his chest, but the parts
of their bodies he most wanted to meet, didn't.

The roof was a challenging spot for this sort of thing.

"You get off me right now!'' Her words were firm. Her
voice wasn't. "I didn't come up here to fool around.''

He snuggled his leg in between hers. Maybe he couldn't
have the heat and the pressure where he wanted it right
now, but she could. "In a minute, sweetheart.''

She gave a mighty, whole-body heave. Annie was strong;
her move was almost enough to send him sliding down the
splintery slope of the roof. But he was stronger, and he
outweighed her by fifty or sixty pounds.

That, he thought with a flicker of amusement, was going
to infuriate her. But sometimes anger lay only a heartbeat
away from other passions, close enough that the right touch
could flip a person from one to the other before they knew
what was happening.

Jack took her mouth without asking because he knew
what the answer would be, but he took it carefully, licking,
coaxing, nibbling. He didn't want to force Annie. He
wanted to prove that she did want him, that he could be
enough for her, even without the words she believed in.
And while his mouth persuaded, while his body held hers
trapped if not accepting beneath his, he slid his hand between her legs and cupped her firmly.

Annie wasn't the only one who tripped between anger
and need.

She went still. Faster than he could have guessed, she stopped fighting him, and with her response the dull force of anger that had moved him flared into something else. Something hot and unsteady. He drew a ragged breath and groped for control, pressing his palm up against her, rotating it slowly. A long shudder went through her.

Just that fast, he went under.

He had meant to show her technique, to use his skill to dazzle her with her own hunger, to prove…something. What? He couldn't remember. Not with Annie coming alive beneath him, her hands suddenly speeding over his shoulders, his back, racing across his body as if she had to touch him everywhere at once. Not with the promises her mouth made, causing his heart to pound against his ribs.

Not with need kicking him in the gut, a sudden clawing need like nothing he'd ever felt before.

Jack had wanted before. He'd wanted Annie so much he'd married her. His desire hadn't been purely physical, either, though that had been a big part of it. He'd just plain wanted her with him. Permanently. Once the idea of having Annie with him wherever he went had been planted in his mind, it had been irresistible.

But even then, he hadn't wanted like this.

Even as he tugged her sweatshirt up so he could feel her breast, he was trying to stop. He didn't want to need this way. But her mouth was sweet and avid, her breast was warm and perfect, and he had to taste her first. Just one taste. Just once, and then he would stop.

He bent and suckled her through the thin material of her bra, and she cried out. His hand continued to knead her, but he was caught now, too enthralled by the primitive rhythm pounding through his blood to remember technique. He had to touch her harder, deeper.

The denim of her jeans was in his way.

He would strip them off her. But the shingles beneath

them were too rough. They would hurt her skin. It was only
a wisp of a thought, but it was enough to make him act,
putting his arms around her and rolling, intending to reverse
their positions so he was on the bottom.

They slid. Willy-nilly, they slid several feet down the
roof before he managed to stop them with his feet.

Jack's breath came fast and panicky as sanity seeped
slowly back. He'd almost sent them both plunging off the
roof. He'd forgotten everything in his need to have her, and
that wasn't right, wasn't sane or safe or anything he wanted
to feel.

Annie's breath shuddered through her in long, heated
gasps. After a moment she tucked her face into his shoulder
and said in a small, disgruntled voice, "I was going to stop
you."

How could she make him want to laugh when hunger
still ripped at him? He leaned his forehead against hers.
"Sure. If you say so." Had he wanted to prove that she
was susceptible to him? What an incredibly stupid idea.

"Just because you can make me hot doesn't mean I
wasn't going to stop you."

"Okay." He raised his head. Her face was a pale oval
in the darkness. "But I did have a point I wanted to make,
before testosterone took over and made me crazy. I wanted
to show you that sex is simple." At least, it always had
been before. He didn't know what had gotten into him tonight.

"No, *men* are simple. Simple-minded." Her words were
sharp. Her breathing was still unsteady.

"Maybe so. But sex really isn't all that complicated.
Even when it blows the top of your head off, it's a natural
reaction. But friendship...a friendship takes time, compromise, attention. It isn't always easy, but it matters. A friendship like ours is worth a lot more than any pretty promises

made in the dark by people who don't like each other the next day. I don't just want sex from you, Annie."

Her voice was soft, almost inaudible. "The way you describe friendship sounds almost like...love."

He swallowed. "I do care. You know that. If you need the words—"

"Don't. Don't say you love me if you don't mean it. That makes everything worse."

He didn't speak for a moment, remembering other words—words she'd flung at him on their wedding night. *"You don't mind saying you love me because the words don't mean anything to you! How many times have you said them to other women? How many times have you used them to get what you wanted?"* Jack looked Annie in the eye. "I don't say those words to get a woman to go to bed with me, and that's sure as hell not why I would say them to you."

"No. You'd say them if you thought they would make me feel better." She sounded terribly sad. "Jack..."

"What?"

"Do you believe that love isn't real, or do you just not want to feel it?"

He released her and rolled onto his back. He hated this sort of discussion. This whole "in love" business mattered to Annie, though, so he made himself answer. "It's real enough while it lasts, I guess, but it never lasts. Once the fire dies, there isn't much left." He turned his head to look at her. "I know you said you wanted more than friendship in a marriage, Annie. But friendship is a lot better basis for marriage than love." He intended to prove that to her.

"Do you feel that way because of your mom?"

"For God's sake, don't get all Freudian on me!"

She sat up, hugging her knees to her chest. "That wasn't what I meant. I know you loved her, and that she loved you, too. But she wasn't perfect. No one is. And she did move around an awful lot, didn't she?''

''Yeah, but that's not such a bad thing. Not many kids get to see as much of the country as I did.'' Until his mother died. Then he'd ended up with his aunt, who had been duty-bound to take him in, and he'd been stuck in Highpoint for the next seven years with no hope of reprieve or parole. When he'd graduated from high school, the prison doors had swung open.

''Didn't you get tired of all the moving, though? It seems like an uncertain way to grow up, never sure where you'll be living next week.''

''I'm not like you,'' he said sharply. ''I don't need to latch onto one spot as if it were the only place on earth that mattered.''

Annie fell silent.

''Hell, Annie, you know this is a touchy subject for me.'' His aunt had only disapproved of one person more than she did Jack—his mother. As she'd made clear in countless ways over the years.

''I know.''

''It's better to be a dreamer like my mom was than to be dead from the heart down the way my aunt was.'' Privately, Jack admitted that his mother's dreams had sometimes led her to do foolish things, like giving up a good job to follow a rodeo cowboy across the country, or packing up on a moment's notice because she'd decided her true love must be waiting down the road. That didn't mean she'd been wrong to dream. She'd just picked the wrong dreams to chase.

''I've wondered sometimes if your aunt was jealous of her sister, and that's why she always put her down. I never met your mom, but she sounded like the sort of person everyone likes.''

''She was.'' Therese Merriman had been a laughing,

spontaneous woman, warm and open and loving. Too loving, in some ways. Too eager to believe in the happily-ever-after that was sure to come once she found the right prince.

Wasn't Jack a living, breathing example of how foolish it was to place too much importance on love? His mother had told him often enough that he'd been conceived in love—as if that was supposed to make up for never having set eyes on the man who'd fathered him, the man his mother had been so deeply, if temporarily, in love with. A man who had been married to another woman.

Jack's father had only wanted one thing from Therese when she made the mistake of getting pregnant. He'd wanted his lover and his illegitimate child to disappear and not trouble his narrow little life. Therese had given him what he wanted. That was what love meant, according to her—sacrificing your own needs for the sake of the one you loved.

It had never seemed to occur to her that she might have sacrificed Jack's needs, too.

The stars were still bright overhead, but Jack was no longer in the mood for stargazing. The air was getting colder and the wind was picking up. But his hand was warm. At some point while his mind had drifted along the useless corridors of the past, Annie had taken it.

He gave her hand a squeeze as he got his feet under him, crouching to keep from skidding any farther down the roof. "Come on, we need to get moving before Ben comes looking for you. It's getting late."

"Good grief, Ben doesn't come looking for me anymore. I'm all grown up."

Jack wasn't sure Ben realized that, but he and Annie had disagreed on enough subjects for one night. He kept his opinion to himself.

They didn't go back through his window, but took the

easy path down, which included a short drop onto the roof over the veranda. From there it was a simple matter for the two of them to swing down onto the wide railing that enclosed the veranda.

"I'll walk you to your car," Jack said.

She was amused. "Jack, my Bronco is right there in your drive, in plain view."

"I'll go with you." Annie had been attacked once in a place where she should have been safe. He didn't know if she still had bad dreams about that, but he did. She might or might not be in danger now, but he wasn't taking any chances with her. She was too important to him.

She didn't argue. Nor did she protest when he put his arm around her. It felt good, walking with Annie snuggled up against him this way. "I have to go to Denver tomorrow."

"Is this something to do with investigating the theft of those drugs?"

"Partly. I do intend to see what I can find in the records at headquarters. But I'm also sort of AWOL."

"What do you mean?"

"I'm not officially on leave yet. I called my boss and told him I was taking time off, but I haven't done the paperwork." Herbie hadn't exactly agreed to let Jack take a leave of absence. He'd blustered his way through a few vague threats about "termination"—*firing* was too direct a term for the prissy little man—but Jack wasn't backing down on this. "There's a form I have to fill out. Herbie is nuts about forms. And I need to talk to the Denver police."

"That's good." She nodded encouragingly. "I'm glad you're turning this over to them."

He wasn't exactly turning it over to them, but someone official needed to be aware of what he thought was going on. "I want you to go with me."

"I—I don't know. I've got a painting job tomorrow—"

"See if you can postpone it. I want you to tell the police about the letter you received. It may not be connected, but they should have all the facts."

"You could tell them about it. And wouldn't it be outside their jurisdiction? I don't live in Denver."

"We aren't asking them to prosecute whoever wrote the letter, but they should know about it, and they should hear it from you. They're trained and experienced in this sort of thing, Annie. I'm an amateur. The cops may be able to draw something out of you that I've missed."

"I guess, if there's even a slim chance it would help the police find whoever threatened you, it's worth a try."

"Great." Relief broke over him in a wave. He grabbed her hands again. "That's great, Annie." He needed to keep her with him—to keep her safe, yes, but also to keep from making the same mistake he'd made with her before. He'd screwed up big time when he'd allowed anger and hurt to send him away from her the day after their wedding.

"Are we going to drive back tomorrow, too?" she asked suspiciously.

"We'd better plan on staying there overnight. I need to pick up a few things at my apartment, anyway."

"I'm going to stay at a motel."

"Now, that's silly. I know you don't have much money. Why pay for a room when you can stay with me for free?"

"Because you've only got one bed."

"Well, I'd rather you slept with me, of course. But if you insist on separate bunks, there's nothing wrong with my couch." In fact, the image of Annie on his couch—rumpled and flushed and well on her way to being naked—appealed to him strongly.

"Jack, you have a studio apartment! Your couch is in the same room as your bed. I'd like a little more privacy than that."

He scowled, not liking what she was forcing him to do.

"Okay, okay. I promise I'll keep my hands off you while you're at my place. It won't be easy, but I can handle it for one night."

"You can promise to keep your hands to yourself the whole time."

"The whole time?" He sighed heavily. "All right. I promise. You do trust me to keep my word, don't you?"

Apparently she did, because her last protest was so feeble it hardly counted. "Your couch is too short. You wouldn't be comfortable on it."

"No problem." He grinned. "You can take the couch. Little as you are, you should fit just fine. I'll even let you use my favorite pillow."

She blinked—then laughed. "Okay, okay, you've talked me into it. But I expect you to behave yourself."

That wasn't going to be easy, but he'd promised. And it was more important to keep Annie with him than to get her into bed. At least, that's what he told his unruly body. "Can you be ready to go by eight tomorrow morning?"

"Sure," she said. "You know me. I'm always up early."

Annie overslept. Last night, images of Jack in danger had followed her into her dreams. After dozing and waking for hours, she'd given up on sleep, propping herself up in bed with pillows so she could read. It had worked so well that she'd fallen asleep with her light still on—then hadn't woken until Jack rang the doorbell.

As a result, she slept the whole way into Denver. When she blinked herself awake, the land had flattened into lumpy hills and traffic had thickened around them. The man-made peaks of Denver's skyscrapers were growing ever larger in the windshield of Jack's sporty two-seater, while the natural peaks fell behind.

The city was almost upon them.

When she stretched, Jack glanced over at her. "Is this

the first time you've been back to Denver since you quit your job?''

''Yeah. It feels funny. Especially since I won't be going to my old apartment.''

''Nope. You'll be staying with me.''

He looked much too cheerful for a man whose life had been threatened, and entirely too gorgeous for her peace of mind. He was wearing a crisp blue shirt today with his faded jeans—Jack's version of business attire. ''Don't worry.'' He gave her what he probably intended to be a reassuring grin. ''I remember my promise.''

But she hadn't promised not to touch *him*. And she wanted to. Annie's heart drummed out a renewed beat of panic that had nothing to do with the congested traffic.

Was she crazy for letting him talk her into this trip?

She fiddled with the ring on her finger, a shiny gold band she'd impulsively slipped on last night before going to bed. When was she going to learn that acting on impulse never worked for her? Jack hadn't even noticed the ring. Annie felt foolish. She'd expected some kind of reaction from him. It had seemed like a pretty big deal when she'd put it on for the first time since waking up alone on the morning after her wedding.

It was hard to forgive him for that. Understand, yes— she knew she shared the blame for the fiasco of their wedding night. But understanding and forgiveness weren't the same thing.

The silence between them was making her uneasy, something that never used to happen. Too much lay between them now, weighty and unresolved. When they left I-40 for Sixth and headed north, she grabbed at the direction as an excuse to speak. ''You're heading for LoDo.''

''That's where I work when I'm in the U.S.''

''I know that, but I thought we'd go to the police station first.''

"We'll do that this afternoon. I want to check a couple of things first." The downtown skyscrapers loomed up on either side of them now. "I thought we might go to lunch with some of the folks from the office. Give them a chance to meet you, and let you get to know them a bit."

"Do they know about me, then? That we're married?"

"I'm sure they do. Becky—she's the one I contacted to get you added to my insurance—is a darling, one of my favorite people, but she's also a major gossip. She'll have spread the word."

Annie fiddled with her ring and wondered what Jack's co-workers thought of his sudden marriage. She wondered about the darling Becky, too.

"Which direction are we headed?" she asked as they left the dimness of the parking garage for the sunny and crowded sidewalk.

The wind was up that day, blowing skirts and hair, snaking between buildings to surprise pedestrians with a sudden hard gust. Annie put up a hand to hold her hair out of her face. She'd worn it down—not because of what Jack had said, she told herself. There just hadn't been time to do anything with it when she'd overslept so badly.

"To the left. You can see the building from here. It's the four-story red brick with the elaborate cornices."

How odd, she thought suddenly, that she had never been to Jack's office. She hadn't even known what building it was in. She frowned and started in that direction.

Jack stopped her by taking her hand. Her left hand.

He held it up between them, turning it palm down. The gold ring on her third finger caught the sunlight. His face was very serious. "I'm glad you wore my ring today, Annie. But I wondered...is it just for today, so I won't be embarrassed?"

"No," she answered in a low voice. "Last night it just seemed right to put it back on."

He lifted her hand, touching his lips to her knuckles just above the ring. "I'm glad. We made promises to each other that night in Vegas, Annie."

To have and to hold, in sickness and in health, until death do you... She closed her fingers around his tightly. Someone had tried to part them permanently. "I've been thinking."

"Uh-oh."

"No, this is serious. Your accident and that warning you received—they both happened on the other side of the world. If the black market people over there were trying to scare you away, maybe they're satisfied now. You left, after all."

He shrugged. "That's possible."

"The only reason we have to think that the danger might have followed you here is that anonymous letter I received. So it's really important to find out who sent it. If it came from an old girlfriend of yours, like I think, we won't have to worry."

He looked at her quizzically, as if he'd listened to her words but heard something she hadn't said, and squeezed her hand. "Let's not think about that right now. Let's just enjoy the day and the great fall weather."

Since the wind chose that moment to slap her hair in her face, she laughed. "It's gorgeous, all right. If we don't blow away."

His face lit in a sudden grin. "As little as you are, you might. I'd better keep hold of you."

He held her hand the rest of the way.

Annie had dressed for warmth, but she'd also wanted to feel feminine, so she'd decided on tailored slacks in a rich bronze with a creamy sweater set. The cardigan fastened with tiny copper buttons. She felt rather pretty in the outfit until an acquaintance of Jack's stopped them just outside the ICA building.

A very blond acquaintance in a very short skirt.

"Jack!" she cried, her perky little face lighting up. "I haven't seen you in *ages!* Will you be in town long? You've just *got* to come to Wynkoop's tonight. Everyone will be there!" She wrapped one small hand around Jack's arm. Her nails were long and painted pink to match her sweater. What there was of her sweater. Which wasn't enough, in Annie's opinion, to counter the heat loss from exposing her entire legs to the current windchill factor.

Was this Becky, the darling?

"I won't be able to make it this time," Jack said. "Millie, this is Annie, my—"

"Annie?" Millie let go of Jack and turned her cheerleader's enthusiasm on Annie. "I have a *cousin* named Anna, but she always *hates* to be called Annie—I don't know why, such a cute name!—so if I slip up and call you Anna, *do* forgive me!" She beamed. "I am *so* glad to meet you. Do tell Jack he has to take you to Wynkoop's Brewery tonight! The whole gang will be there, and it will be tons more fun if Jack is, too! *Everything* is more fun with Jack around!"

Annie couldn't help smiling. The girl was obviously *terribly* fond of Jack—and terribly young. "I don't think tonight will work out, but thanks for the invitation."

Jack managed to detach them from his cheerful friend. They were stopped again, though, in front of a small coffee shop just inside the building—this time by a dark-haired woman wearing an elegant pinstriped suit and an irritating smile that hinted at either past intimacies or the hope for future ones.

Jack introduced them. "Laura, good to see you again. I'd like you to meet my wife, Annie Merriman. Annie, this is Laura Caprello."

Both of the woman's eyebrows scooted up to hide beneath her neatly trimmed bangs, but Annie was too busy dealing with her own reaction to be bothered by the other woman's shock. It was the first time she had heard herself introduced as Annie Merriman.

The woman recovered quickly and congratulated them both before excusing herself, and Jack and Annie made it to the elevator without further interruptions. It was a small, richly paneled box with the look of an old-time elevator. They had it to themselves.

Annie faced straight ahead. "I thought everyone knew you were married."

"I'm sure everyone at ICA knows, but Millie and Laura work for other firms here in the building. I guess they haven't heard."

Annie watched as the arrow on the dial that indicated their floor moved slowly from two to three. "An insecure woman might have a problem with her husband being constantly accosted by other women."

He winced. "They're just friends. Friendly acquaintances, I mean. Well, Laura and I did go out a few times, but I, ah…" His voice trailed off and he rubbed a hand over the top of his head. "How much trouble am I in?"

Annie couldn't keep a straight face any longer. She laughed. "Relax, Jack. You've been a magnet for females ever since I've known you. I'm not mad. It would take more effort than it's worth to get upset over every woman you've charmed over the years."

"A magnet for females, huh?" he said, his sudden grin breaking out. The elevator creaked to a stop, and he took her arm. "I like that."

She snorted.

The elevator doors opened—onto a party.

Or was it a wake? The small reception area was crowded with women in all shapes and sizes—women who called out "surprise!" in a chorus of feminine voices as Jack and Annie stepped out of the elevator. Women who were, one and all, dressed in black. Black crepe paper dripped from the ceiling, spiderwebbing between tables and chairs. A banner behind the receptionist's desk proclaimed in bold black letters Our Hopes Are at an End. A poster taped to the wall read Our Loss Is One Woman's Gain.

Jack froze. Annie, too, stopped moving. Silence fell. Then a voice at the back of the room said clearly, "Oh, crap."

Annie glanced at Jack. He looked horrified. She cleared her throat. "You were right. Obviously everyone here at ICA knows about our marriage."

Chapter 6

"I am very, very glad you have a sense of humor."

The woman talking was Rebecca Reeves, the office manager—also known as Becky. Jack's "darling" was a sixtyish woman with soft white hair and a figure twenty pounds beyond plump. Her dress was crisply pressed cotton, nicely tailored. And black. "I forget whose idea it was," Rebecca said, "but when Mr. Bickham mentioned that Jack was coming into the office today, we thought we should give him a hard time about—" She cleared her throat. "We decided to surprise him."

"I think you succeeded," Annie said dryly.

"Giselle Brown—she runs the coffee shop on the first floor—was supposed to let us know when he reached the building so we could all be waiting when he got off the elevator." She shook her head. "She did that, but she failed to mention that you were with him."

"Please don't worry about it. I've known Jack for years. Teasing him about his sudden marriage must have been irresistible."

"I must say that the expression on his face was something I'll never forget."

Annie grinned. "He looked like he wished the floor would open up and swallow him, didn't he?"

"That he did." Mrs. Reeves patted Annie's arm. "You're a dear to take it so well. All that nonsense about being in mourning—well, that's all it is, Mrs. Merriman. Nonsense. Jack has never dated anyone from ICA."

Mrs. Merriman. The name created a ball of warmth in Annie's middle and confusion in her mind. She'd been Annie McClain all her life. It felt strange to be called by another name, as if she were no longer the person she'd always been. "Call me Annie."

"Then you must call me Rebecca." She chuckled. "Jack is the only one who calls me Becky. Anyway, Jack's rule about not dating anyone from the office has become something of a standing joke. Everyone knew about it. That kept him safe, you see."

"You mean it let him flirt like crazy without anyone taking him seriously?"

"Exactly. Jack does love to flirt, and he's terribly good-looking, of course, which makes it fun. It could also have made him something of a target, if he had ever singled anyone out—but he never did. When he was here he'd tease everyone about quitting and running away with him. Even me." She turned a delicate shade of pink. "It's amazing, really, how something like that can brighten a person's day."

The perfect fantasy man—charming and sexy and never, ever to be taken seriously. Yes, Annie thought, that had undoubtedly made Jack feel safe. "He likes to make people feel good."

She glanced over at Jack, who was thoroughly surrounded. A pretty redhead and a dark-haired woman about Rebecca's age were laughing at something he'd said. So was a skinny older man. There *were* a few men at the "wake." Annie just hadn't seen them at first because of the overwhelming female presence.

"We all…oh, dear." A frown drifted over Rebecca's. "There's one in every office, isn't there?"

"One what?"

"A troublemaker. Come on, dear. Let's go rescue your husband."

Annie followed Rebecca, who was heading for Jack.

She noticed the expression on Jack's face before she saw the cause. He was trying not to lose his temper. Then she saw why. Another woman had joined the group clustered around him. She was very small, even shorter than Annie, with dark hair so long the ends brushed the tops of her thighs. She had sharp, dramatic features and a sallow complexion, and she'd latched onto Jack's arm with both hands.

"I am so curious about your new little bride, Jack," the woman was saying just as Annie reached them. "I can't wait to meet her."

"Good thing you won't have to, then, isn't it?" Rebecca said briskly. "Annie, this is Leah Pasternak. She works in Accounting."

"Nice to meet you, Leah." Annie held out her hand.

Leah didn't let go of Jack's arm. She looked Annie up and down in a way that was meant to be insulting. "*You're* Annie?" She sounded incredulous.

"To my friends, yes." Annie smiled sweetly. "But you can call me Mrs. Merriman."

Someone nearby made a choked sound that sounded like muffled laughter, but quickly turned into a fake cough. The tiny beauty glared at Annie, then turned and left without another word.

"Goodness," Annie murmured. "I don't think she likes me."

"Don't pay any attention to Leah," Rebecca said. "I'm

afraid she considered Jack's 'hands off' rule with the office staff a challenge. She's made something of a pest of herself.''

Jack grimaced. "She likes to stir up trouble."

Annie turned to him, her eyes widening. "She might be the one who wrote the—"

"Later, Annie," he said hastily.

Rebecca's bright, inquisitive gaze went back and forth between them. "The one who wrote what?"

"Becky, my love," Jack said with an easy smile, slipping an arm around her substantial waist to give her a hug, "you are the worst gossip in this place. I'm not telling you a thing."

She frowned at him. "Shame on you, Jack. You can't tell me there's something worth gossiping about and then refuse to say more."

"Good heavens," a fussy male voice exclaimed. "What's going on here? What is all this?"

Much of the chatter died down, and people looked self-conscious. Annie turned to see who had spoken. A small man with thick glasses and a long upper lip covered by a double helping of mustache had just stepped out of the elevator a few feet away. He was frowning.

So was Rebecca. "We're having a little party, Mr. Bickham."

"A party? With black crepe paper, and on company time? This is in poor taste. Very poor taste. Everyone should get back to work."

"Now, Herbie," Jack said, "you can't object to people giving me a party to celebrate my marriage, can you?"

"Celebrate? With black crepe paper? Not appropriate. Not at all."

"I suppose that depends on whether you have a sense of humor or not. Which reminds me." He reached out and drew Annie to his side. "This is my wife, Annie Merriman. Annie, this is Herbert Bickham, senior engineer for ICA."

When Bickham came up to them, Annie found herself looking him right in the eye, which was an unusual experience for her with a man. He was exactly her height. She felt a twinge of sympathy. Being short was a nuisance for her at times, but it could be a real disadvantage for a man. "How do you do?"

"Very well, thank you, Mrs. Merriman. And now, if you'll excuse me, I really must shoo my people back to their offices. We're on company time, you know." But instead of shooing, he looked at Jack. "I assume you are here about your application for leave. I have decided to grant it, once you fill out the correct form. After all, this is your first opportunity to spend time with, ah, the new Mrs. Merriman." Bickham's mouth twitched into a tight smile beneath that overhanging mustache. "I quite understand."

Jack's eyebrows went up. "Are you feeling well, Herbie?"

"I hope I am not unreasonable," he said testily. "You wish to spend time with your new bride. I quite understand. And there is no reason that you cannot begin work on the Nairobi project while you're, ah, out of the office. You have a laptop. I'd like to see the specifications in a week."

Jack shook his head firmly. "No new projects for me yet. I've got an old one that isn't finished."

"I assume you're referring to the unpleasantness in Borneo. There is no point in pursuing that any further. The chief malefactor is dead, and the government inspectors who were involved are beyond our authority. We must consider the possible damage to ICA's reputation. It was quite unpleasant when Metz killed himself. The man didn't have the courtesy to leave a suicide note."

"Damned inconsiderate of him."

"He did it to cause trouble, I am sure. The police were

forced to investigate. They came around several times, disrupting everyone's work." He sniffed. "Fortunately, we were able to keep the matter out of the papers."

"Metz's death was inconvenient, all right. It made it harder to discover who else was involved in the theft."

"I am aware of your theory. However, you have presented no conclusive evidence to support it. The matter is closed."

"No. It isn't."

A muscle in Herbie's cheek twitched again. "That determination is mine to make."

"We'll see if Amos Deerbaum agrees with you. I've sent him a copy of the report I faxed you."

Herbie's eyes, enlarged by the thick lenses, gleamed with malice. "We'll discuss this later. I have work to do."

"Whew," Annie said when the little man moved away. "He likes you about as much as your pint-size girlfriend likes me."

Jack gave her an irritated glance. "Leah is not, and never has been, my girlfriend."

Rebecca shook her head. "Jack, I know Mr. Bickham can be difficult. He and I have rubbed each other the wrong way often enough. But are you sure you want to go over his head with this? He's not going to take that well."

"Herbie can take it however he wants. As a matter of fact, he can take it and shove it—" He paused. "Shove it where the sun doesn't shine."

The party broke up after that. Jack needed to talk to someone in Accounting about the invoices for the stolen supplies, so Annie waited for him in his office.

It wasn't what she had expected.

She'd been to Jack's apartment a few times. The comfortable approach to clutter she'd seen there fit what she knew of him. But here, in his office, she didn't see the near-chaos she'd expected—no tottering piles of files, no crumpled papers or missed tosses near the trash can. No debris. It was rather Spartan, in fact, except for the collection of framed photographs that covered one wall.

Of course, he'd been out of the country for months, she reminded herself as she drifted along one wall, looking at the pictures. Even Jack would want to leave things tidy when he was going to be gone for a long time.

Still, it was unsettling. As if she didn't know him quite as well as she had thought.

She paused to look at one of the photographs. It reminded her of a picture from one of her *National Geographic* magazines…and of the exotic places her mother used to write her about. Jack was standing in front of a small building in an African village, surrounded by a grinning crowd of natives. One of them held up a startlingly colorful snake.

"I wonder where this was taken," she murmured.

"On the Kenya project, I think," a voice behind her said.

Annie turned, smiling because she recognized the voice.

Rebecca Reeves stood in the doorway. "I hope you don't mind my barging in. I thought we might get better acquainted while Jack is busy. I can ask you nosy questions, and you can tell me to mind my own business."

Annie laughed. "Sure, as long as I get to ask nosy questions, too. Who's the man standing beside Jack?" She gestured at the photo.

"Oh, that's Mr. Deerbaum. He flew out there for the dedication. He was very proud of Jack—the Kenya job was his first big solo project, you know."

Rebecca started talking about Jack's various projects, using the photos on the wall to give a guided tour of his career. As Annie listened, she had the jarring thought that she really didn't know much about Jack's job. Oh, he talked about people he'd met, about customs in other countries.

He'd told her any number of funny stories. But he hadn't talked about the important things—about the details, frustrations and triumphs of his work, or what the job itself meant to him...other than a way to stay on the move. As she listened to Rebecca describe a man she hardly knew—an organized, dedicated man who took his responsibilities seriously—some strange, sharp feeling kept tugging at her heart.

"Thanks for the tour," she said when they'd looked at the last of the photos. You must be wondering...I've known Jack for so long, yet I don't know that much about his work."

The older woman smiled at her kindly. "Sometimes it's the people we think we know best that we have the most to learn about, isn't it? We become used to seeing them a certain way and stop really seeing them at all. And then, Jack does have a habit of tucking the rest of us into a slot and keeping us there."

"What do you mean?"

"He likes to assign the people in his life a role, doesn't he? His rule about not dating anyone from the office is a good example, but it goes further than that. He doesn't talk to those of us he works with about the other people in his life—the women he dates, his family, his nonwork friends. Like you."

She was right, Annie thought in surprise. Jack did keep the relationships in his life tidy by assigning everyone a role—and her role was "friend." Only she wasn't Jack's friend now. She was his wife.

Annie kept her voice light. "Is that a subtle way of leading into some of those nosy questions you mentioned?"

Rebecca laughed. "You're on to me. So, how did you and Jack meet?"

"My brother brought him home from school one day,

after they'd been assigned detention for getting into a fight on the school grounds.''

Rebecca was easy to talk to. She was nosy, yes, and did like to gossip, but her curiosity rose from a genuine and unquenchable interest in the people around her. Annie enjoyed their conversation...but part of her mind wasn't on it.

What was the sharp-sad feeling that kept building in her?

''You know,'' Rebecca said suddenly, ''you really don't have to worry about Leah.''

''I'm sorry, what did you say?'' Annie had been so sunk in her own thoughts she wasn't sure she'd heard right.

''More than I should have, apparently,'' Rebecca said ruefully. ''You seemed preoccupied, and I thought—but obviously I was wrong.''

Annie smiled. ''Now I'm curious. What were you going to say to reassure me about if I *had* been worrying?''

Rebecca leaned closer, her body language announcing that this was particularly juicy gossip. ''I don't think Leah will be here much longer.''

''Really? You, ah, plan to dismiss her?''

''Oh, no. Difficult as she is, she's always done her job. But she's been seen socially with someone quite important in the organization.'' Rebecca nodded wisely. ''A woman like that won't spend her days inputting data if she's spending her nights with a wealthy sugar daddy.''

Annie had to smile at Rebecca's old-fashioned language. ''So you think she'll be quitting soon?''

''Not that you'd have anything to worry about, even if she stayed,'' Rebecca assured her. ''I just thought you'd like to know.''

''I appreciate that. You know, I am getting thirsty now. Could you show me the way to the Coke machine?''

''Nonsense. I'll get you one.''

Rebecca wouldn't listen to Annie's protests. Annie suspected she was still trying to make up for Annie's rather startling first impression of Jack's co-workers. When Rebecca left to get her something to drink, Annie went back to looking at Jack's photographs. They were pictures of exotic places, yes, but the ones that meant the most to Jack, the one's he'd framed and kept, were pictures of *people*. People he had helped. People whose welfare he cared about.

Suddenly she knew what feelings kept tugging and cutting at her.

Pride. She was so proud of Jack it hurt—and so ashamed of herself. She'd never known. All these years she had thought of Jack's job as an excuse to wander the world...as something that took him away from her. But it was more. So much more. Annie felt small and petty and close to tears.

She faced one more truth she had been hiding from. What she had wanted—what she had truly and selfishly wanted—was for Jack to love her enough to stop wandering and stay in Highpoint. But he wasn't going to do that. He loved his work. How could she ask him to give up what he loved?

She'd spoken no more than the truth when she told Rebecca she wasn't worried about Leah—or any woman, she realized. But she was jealous as hell of his job.

"I can't believe you got anchovies," Annie said, frowning at her slice of pizza. It was seven o'clock, and she'd just paid the delivery boy for the pizza Jack had ordered. "You know I hate anchovies."

"If you can rent a chick flick for us to watch, I can have anchovies. Just pick yours off like you do the onions." Jack slid a huge slice of pizza onto a paper plate, leaned back and propped his feet on the coffee table.

She started removing bits of onion. "It didn't sound like

that detective is going to do much." They'd seen the police that afternoon, just like Jack had promised. But the results hadn't been what Annie was hoping for.

"Hmm?" He balanced the paper plate on his stomach so he could sort through the debris on the end table. "Oh. Yeah, I was hoping for a little more enthusiasm myself, but as far as they're concerned, Metz was the guilty party and he's dead. I guess there isn't much they can do until I can come up with evidence that someone else was involved. At least he's going to look into the anonymous letter."

"For whatever good that will do."

"He'll talk to Leah. If she wrote the letter, that ought to put a little fear into her."

"Maybe." And maybe she'd be delighted to know she'd worried them enough to consult the police. Annie sighed and started picking anchovies off.

Jack's apartment was a typical bachelor quarters in many ways. The cluttered coffee table doubled as a dining table, and the king-size bed in the corner was unmade. There was a big-screen TV and a stereo system with more gauges and LEDs than the cockpit of a small plane.

But some things weren't typical of anyone but Jack, like the books that nearly crowded out the gadgets on the shelves of the entertainment unit, or the huge brass elephant near the door, or the prayer bowl from Tibet. Or the end table whose clutter Jack was currently sorting through. It was an enormous drum from Kenya that he'd topped with a heavy circle of glass.

"Dammit." Jack straightened and put his paper plate on the coffee table. "Where is it?"

"What?" She finished disposing of the anchovies and took a bite.

"The remote."

She chewed, swallowed and answered. "Oh, that. I hid it."

"You *what?*" He sat up straight. "Annie, a wise woman does not come between a man and his remote control."

"Ha! I'm not about to let you get your hands on it. You'd fast-forward through all the good parts." She settled back smugly. Let the man have his stupid little fishes on the pizza. Hers was the greater victory.

He headed for the entertainment unit and started looking behind books.

"You won't find it. Listen, while you're up, why don't you go ahead and get the movie started?"

He shook his head sadly. "Using the controls on the VCR itself instead of a remote goes against a man's deepest instincts." But he did manage to perform that unnatural act, then came back to sit on the couch with her—but leaving a couple of feet between them. He'd been careful not to touch her all day.

Sharing a pizza and a movie, arguing over what they would watch, sitting on the couch together while Annie pretended her heart wasn't beating faster, that her skin didn't tingle or her body ache at his nearness…oh, yes, she thought glumly. This was almost like old times.

A couple of things had changed. There was a ring on her finger, and Jack knew that she wanted him. She glanced at him. The knowledge didn't seem to be driving him into a frenzy of lust. He sprawled beside her, his feet on the coffee table, his attention on his pizza.

"What kind of evidence were you looking for at the office today?"

"Shipping stuff. Listen, do you want to get into this right now? You've never wanted to hear about the nitty-gritty before."

Maybe not, she thought. But Jack had avoided talking about his job, too—just like a guilty husband who never discussed his mistress with his wife. "You've never had someone try to kill you over your job before."

"That does make a difference." He took a bite of pizza, looking thoughtful, as if he were organizing his thoughts. "Mostly I'm concerned with how Metz set up the switch. Supplies are tracked pretty carefully, and I don't see how he could have done it without someone else in ICA helping him. He should have had the routing information in his files, but his files were a mess. I checked the Singapore office already, because most supplies for that region are routed through there. But they didn't have any record of those shipments."

"And today?"

"I checked the main files. Everything any of the regional offices handle, along with everything on-site personnel receive, is supposed to be tracked and reported to headquarters. There are some of Herbie's beloved forms for that sort of thing."

"What did you find?"

"Everything was in order—forms filed, destinations logged in. But the files show the shipments as having gone through Singapore, and they didn't."

"Do you think the problem might be at the Singapore office? A clerk who conveniently lost the records?"

"It's possible. Hell, all sorts of things are possible. I'm not an investigator, and the paperwork end of the job has never been my strong point. But I went through the records pretty thoroughly in Singapore. They have a good system there—Herbie's doing, probably. It would be hard for a single clerk to circumvent it." He shook his head. "I wish I could get Herbie to take an interest. If anyone could sort through the paperwork jungle and figure out what went wrong, it's him."

"I had the idea you thought he was incompetent."

"He's a petty tyrant, a pain in the butt, but he's a whiz at systems. Hell, the man lives to see that every *t* is crossed—in triplicate. He's a born bureaucrat."

''Maybe it's him.'' She sat up, excited. ''Maybe he's the one who helped Metz.''

''Herbie?'' Jack was incredulous.

''Whoever did this obviously knows how to get around the system. Who would be better at that than the one who knows it best?''

''It's logical, but…'' He shook his head. ''I don't know. It doesn't feel right. The only things Herbie is passionate about are his forms and procedures. I can't see him sabotaging them.''

''But if he were desperate for money, he might have. Maybe he's a secret gambler or something.''

''The man doesn't have any vices. It's one of the things that's so irritating about him.'' Jack didn't look happy. ''I guess I have to consider the possibility, though.''

She tilted her head, puzzled. ''I thought you didn't like him.''

''I don't, but I've always thought he was dedicated to ICA in his own twisted way.'' He glanced at the TV, where three women were hugging one another and laughing, then at his plate. ''You've kept me talking too long. I have no idea what's happened in the movie, and my pizza is cold. Here.'' He offered her his plate, along with a winning smile. ''Why don't you warm it up for me? It's the least you could do after making me ramble on so long.''

She laughed. ''You don't really think that's going to work, do you?''

''It was worth a try.'' He stood and carried the plate into the tiny kitchen, which was separated from the rest of the room by a breakfast bar.

Annie looked back at the TV, but her mind wasn't on the show. She had a lot to think about. Jack had behaved himself all day. It had been a lot like old times, exactly what she'd told Charlie she wanted. She ought to be happy.

She wasn't. She'd been fooling herself. She wanted

more, much more, from Jack, and it was time to stop pretending otherwise. Why else had she been stuck in idle ever since Las Vegas, unable to decide on a direction for her life? Deep down, she'd been hoping that Jack would decide he wanted the same things from her that she wanted from him: Passion. Commitment. Love.

Well, she could count on Jack for passion. For mindblowing sex, anyway, and if they ever did go to bed together, there would be real passion on her side. Commitment? Well, the way he'd talked about friendship last night had sounded like the very essence of commitment. But love…Jack didn't want any part of it. And somewhere in the middle of a mostly sleepless night, Annie had stopped fighting the words that named a truth she'd long known.

She wasn't addicted to Jack. She wasn't infatuated, or physically attracted to him. No, she was crazy, head over heels in love with him.

Should she settle for two out of three? *Could* she settle for that?

Annie glanced at her ring and thought of the promises she'd made when Jack put it on her finger. He was right. She hadn't honored those promises. She'd panicked, as frightened by her feelings as she had been of leaving the safety of her familiar world.

She was still afraid. Loving Jack was a risk she hadn't wanted, but it didn't seem to be something she could stop.

Annie glanced at Jack, who was staring as if entranced at the changing numbers on the LED of the microwave. He wanted to keep her in her current slot—that of friend—and to add a new role. Lover. Annie didn't want to be lovers when the love was so one-sided, but if she kept insisting on more than he was willing to give she might lose everything—their marriage and a friendship that had sustained her for years.

Fear coated the back of her throat. She lifted a hand to where her pulse pounded.

Not yet, she thought. She wasn't ready to give him everything yet. But she wasn't going to give up on what she wanted, either. Somehow she had to find a way to make loving Jack less of a risk. She had to find a way to make him love her back—or at least accept the possibility of love.

Jack scowled at the numbers blinking their way down to zero on the microwave's LED. This "hands off" business was killing him.

Annie had been right when she'd said they didn't have a real marriage. That was his fault. He'd made a big mistake on their wedding night by letting anger and hurt send him down to the casino instead of doing what he was supposed to do. What he'd sure as hell *wanted* to do. Annie took sex seriously. If she had gone to bed with him, she would have felt committed to him.

At the very least, if he'd taken her to bed then, he wouldn't have to pretend now that they were still buddies.

The microwave dinged, but Jack didn't hear it.

He and Annie would always be friends, he assured himself. He would do whatever he had to do in order to make that so. But they weren't buddies. Not anymore. Not when he knew the taste of her, the scent of her skin in the hollow of her throat where her pulse throbbed, the feel of her hips lifting to press against him. Sex lay between them now, a temperamental beast too full of whims and uncertainty for Annie's taste. She liked to feel in control. He knew that, just as he knew that whenever he touched her she lost control. Like an idiot, he'd made a point of proving that to her on the roof.

Jack didn't mind the loss of control. That was temporary. He didn't like the *need*. Friends relied on each other, but they didn't burden each other with needs as strong and shattering as he'd experienced last night.

"Hey," Annie called from the couch. "Could you get me a glass of water while you're in there? I've had enough caffeine for the night."

"Sure." He remembered what he was supposed to be doing and got his pizza out of the microwave.

Maybe Annie was right about waiting, he thought as he filled a glass with water. Maybe they weren't ready to ride that uncertain sex-beast together yet. He glanced at the big bed in the corner of the room.

Hell, no. *He* was ready. But Annie wasn't—or she didn't think she was.

If he pressured her into bed before she was ready, she would panic. Just like she had on their wedding night.

Jack gave her a smile and her water when he returned to the couch, then sat and pretended to be absorbed by the movie. He had to be patient. When they finally did go to bed together—and he hoped to heaven it would be soon—she needed to feel it was her decision. That would make her feel more in control. He also had to keep her with him. The more they were together, the stronger that sex-beast would grow, and the less she'd be able to think of him as her buddy.

"So," he said casually after he'd finished his pizza, "have you thought some more about moving in with me?"

She slid him a suspicious glance. "What made you bring that up?"

"I'd like you to move in with me. You know that. I want to make sure you're safe." Actually, Jack was beginning to think that Annie was right—the letter she'd received probably wasn't connected to the warning he'd gotten. She didn't have anything to do with what he was investigating, and harming her wouldn't protect the culprit, whoever that was. She might be right about the danger to him being over now that he was back in the States, too, though he didn't intend to relax his guard completely.

But he didn't think it would be wise to tell her that he wanted her around twenty-four hours a day because he hoped that constant exposure would cause her to jump his bones.

"I'll think about it," she said grudgingly.

"That's what you said before." He sighed and played his ace. "Look, would you feel better about it if I gave you the same promise I did for this trip? That I'll keep my hands to myself?"

She didn't look reassured. In fact, she didn't look as if she liked the idea very much. "I'll think about it," she said again.

Jack smiled and went back to pretending to watch the movie. He was making progress.

Chapter 7

The tiny café was crowded. Noise, dust and smells from the nearby bazaar competed with the pungency of strong coffee, the spicy steam from the stew being served that day, and the less savory smells of some of the café's customers. Water was at a premium in the small oasis town. Not everyone cared to waste such a valuable commodity on bathing.

Two men sat at one of the outside tables. One was small, dark-skinned like the men at the other tables. Unlike most of them, he wore Western-style clothing—khaki trousers, a plaid shirt and dark glasses to guard against the fierce desert sun. The other man wore khakis, too, but his slacks looked custom-tailored and his shirt had come from Italy. He was a big bear of a man, perhaps sixty years old but very fit for his age. His thick, steel-colored hair was the exact color of the frames of his sunglasses.

The waiter brought them coffee, a murky brew served in tiny cups. The smaller man spoke as soon as the waiter moved away. "My employers are not happy." He spoke English with a slight accent.

"Damned if I know what their problem is." The American's voice was deeper and much louder. "Didn't I get Merriman back to the U.S. and out of their hair like I said I would?"

The smaller man frowned. "Please speak more softly."

"None of these asses understands English. Why do you think I picked this dump?" The big man took a sip of the coffee and made a face. "Nasty stuff. I'd rather have met you at the hotel, where I could get a decent glass of whiskey."

The smaller man spoke quickly, keeping his voice down. "Delays are not good for business. If you are unable to begin processing shipments, your partners will have to make other arrangements."

The big man might be loud and arrogant, but he wasn't stupid. The people he was doing business with had an abrupt and permanent way of dissolving unwanted partnerships. He felt a twinge of regret for what he had to do, but business was business. "I'll have things cleared up at my end within a week."

"I do not know if they are willing to wait another week."

The big man stood. "Bull. It would take them a lot longer than that to move the shipments without me. They know it, and I know it. I'm a reasonable man, though. I know the delay is costing them, so I'll move the first batch at no charge."

"And the...impediment?"

"I took care of Metz, didn't I? Greedy little bastard. I'll take care of Merriman, too." It was a pity, though. He'd always liked Jack. Tried to warn him, too, with that accident. But the stubborn fool wouldn't give up.

The smaller man tilted his head back so that his dark glasses were aimed at the other man. "Why does this require a week?"

"Because it would be damned inconvenient to get the police involved. No one's going to buy suicide a second time, and the cops in the U.S. aren't as easy to buy off as you might think. It needs to look like an accident." He had a man picked out for the job. No one he knew, of course. He wasn't acquainted with that sort of scum. But his contact in Denver had found someone and made arrangements.

He had the groundwork laid for an alternative plan as well, if anything went wrong. But that plan would require his personal involvement. Better if the professional could handle things.

Besides, he hadn't finished his vacation.

"One week." The smaller man stood at last. "That is all the time you have to settle things."

The big man hated dealing with some of these self-important little asses, but business was business. "I said a week, didn't I? Damnation. My word is good." He nodded and left the café, forcing a path through the crowded bazaar. He would call his contact when he reached the hotel and put things in motion.

Well, Jack, he thought as he headed for the tiny hotel at the edge of the bazaar, I hope that new wife of yours is plenty hot. Be nice if you could spend the last days of your life in bed with her.

Chapter 8

It was wonderful the way a good mad could clear a person's mind.

The day after she and Jack returned to Highpoint, Annie had an unprecedented flurry of phone calls from people wanting handyman work...among other things. By the time she pulled into the driveway that night, she'd left confusion way behind. She was well past ticked off and headed for steaming mad.

Ben wasn't home yet, but Charlie was back, she noted as she turned the ignition off. Good. She could use a sympathetic ear—or someone to fight with. At the moment, she didn't much care which. She paced up the walk onto the porch, jerked the front door open and slammed it behind her.

Her brother was in the living room, watching the news. "Your turn to cook," he said without taking his eyes off the tube.

"Fine," she snapped. "If the phone rings, tell whoever it is that I'm pregnant with alien triplets."

"Aliens, huh?" He turned to look at her. "Maybe I should call the newspaper."

"Good idea. If they're going to print stuff about me, we might as well make it interesting." She pulled off her jacket. "And obviously no one cares whether a story is true or not."

"I take it the notice of your marriage was in today's paper."

"I knew people would make a three-day wonder out of it when they heard, but this is ridiculous. You'd think no one in Highpoint had ever gotten married before!"

Charlie came near death at that moment, though he didn't realize it. He laughed. "Not the way you did it. And not to Jack Merriman."

She threw her jacket at him and headed for the kitchen. "If you knew what my day has been like, you wouldn't say things like that."

He followed her. "My guess would be that the phone has been ringing off the wall, and you've been busy on a bunch of trumped-up repair calls from people who wanted to pump you for details about your secret marriage."

She paused in the doorway. "You've been listening to my answering machine."

He grinned. "Two people want you to call as soon as you get home, and a couple others want you to stop by and give them bids. And Phoebe Peyton wants to pay you ten dollars to get her cat out of the tree."

"To get her—" She growled and spun around. "Phoebe doesn't have a cat."

"Maybe it was her neighbor's cat."

"Maybe she wants to know if I'm pregnant." She yanked open the refrigerator door and scowled at the contents. "You would not believe how many people assume that I *had* to get married. Everyone I saw today stared at my stomach."

"Well…it wasn't a strange notion for them to have. Under the circumstances."

She found a head of cabbage in the vegetable bin and grabbed it. Coleslaw. Whatever else she fixed tonight, it would have to go with coleslaw, because she intended to hack that head of cabbage into teensy shreds with a nice, big knife. "How stupid do people think I am? If I'd gotten married because I was pregnant, wouldn't it defeat the purpose to keep the marriage a secret?"

"Ah…"

She glanced at him as she carried the cabbage over to the sink. He was rubbing the back of his neck and looking shamefaced. "Charlie," she said reproachfully. "Not you, too."

"I did wonder."

She turned on the tap and started rinsing the cabbage. "So why didn't you just ask me when you were yelling at me that first night?"

"I, uh…because I'm an idiot?"

"Good grief." She took out a knife and set the cabbage on the cutting board.

"Of course, you're not the only idiot. This whole town is populated with them." *Whack.*

"Hey." He came up behind her and laid a hand on her shoulder. His voice was sympathetic, even if his words weren't. "What did you expect? You kept the marriage a secret. Secrets imply that you've got something to hide. Add to that the fact that the two of you aren't living together…" He shrugged. "Folks are bound to be curious."

"I knew people were going to talk. I just didn't realize…do you know what Suzy Watkins said?" *Whack.* "She couldn't decide if she envied me or pitied me, because Jack is such a hunk—" *whack* "—but everyone *knows* he can't be faithful to any one woman."

"Suzy still in one piece?" he asked interestedly.

"Yeah." Though she'd been tempted, sorely tempted. The knife came down again on the helpless cabbage. "She was more blunt than most, but everyone—*everyone*—had the same basic script. Some just tried harder to hide it than others. First, Jack wouldn't have married me or anyone else if he didn't have to. Second, I must have been desperate or crazy, because everyone knows Jack is wild and irresponsible."

"That's pretty much the way people remember him."

"I suppose." And for the first time Annie saw why Jack hated Highpoint. Why hadn't she noticed before now how narrow people's attitudes about him were? "But Jack isn't like that! I suppose he's not what you would call obvious husband material, since he doesn't want to stay in one place." And he didn't want to fall in love, but Annie wasn't going to bring that up. "But he's not some wild kid anymore, for heaven's sake. He takes his job very seriously." The pile of shredded cabbage was growing larger. "He's responsible for helping an awful lot of people all over the world."

He gave her a strange look. "So he is. What did you say to Suzy?"

"I told her that just because Jack hadn't made a commitment to her didn't mean he was incapable of commitment." Suzy had been one of the three girls Jack had asked to the prom—and then hadn't taken. "I said that she needed to get over what happened back in high school and get on with her life. She didn't like that," Annie finished with satisfaction.

She looked down at the cutting board. The cabbage was thoroughly destroyed. She opened the cupboard and reached for a bowl. "If you're going to hang around, you may as well be useful. Get the chops from the refrigerator, would you? And a couple carrots."

"You're not going to put raisins in the coleslaw, are you?"

"I like raisins." When he didn't move, she said, "Oh, all right. Get the chops and the carrots and I'll leave out the raisins this time."

"You know, Annie," he said as he went to retrieve the requested items, "it sounds like you've changed your mind about Jack."

"Why do you say that?" She dumped the cabbage into the bowl.

"You're talking about how responsible he is. I don't think that's been a big part of your picture of him before." He handed her the carrots, but kept the package of meat. "You grate, I'll fry. It's more manly."

"You and Ben think anything with grease is manly." She frowned as she started shredding the carrots. "Have I really given the impression I thought Jack was irresponsible?"

"Not exactly. I didn't think you saw him much differently from the way everyone else around here does." He got out a frying pan. "Probably my mistake."

But Annie couldn't shake off what her brother had said. Today she'd had a good, clear look at how people in her hometown saw Jack. Some of the things they'd said circled in her mind now, detached from the speakers so that only the surprise, the curiosity—and the implicit criticism—remained.

"Jack Merriman? You married *him?"*

"Are you two planning to start a family right away?"

"Of course I'm happy for you. Really."

"I like Jack. Who doesn't? He's incredible fantasy material, and he'd be perfect for a hot, torrid affair. But I sure never pictured him getting married."

"I am so jealous. He's just the sexiest thing."

"You've got more guts than I do."

Fun. Likable. Great fantasy material. Hot.

It all sounded familiar. Too familiar. She'd said things like that to herself about Jack, hadn't she? Yet when she'd heard others speaking of him that way, it had made her furious.

So what had changed? And when?

"Jack thinks I'm staying in Highpoint because I feel safe here," she said abruptly. "But he thinks I've got some secret yen to take off and see the world like he does."

"Hmm." While she'd been miles deep in thought, Charlie had started the pork chops cooking and gotten a beer from the refrigerator. He sat at the table now, sipping it and watching her.

"Is that all you have to say? You don't think he's right, do you?"

His voice was gentle. "Well, honey, there was a time when you wanted to see the world pretty badly. Before Mom and Dad died."

"That was a long time ago." She added the shredded carrots to the cabbage. "People change." When she was a child she *had* wanted to travel, to see the exotic places that her mother wrote her about. But even more, she'd wanted to be with her parents. To be part of their world for a while.

"Hmm."

She shot him an annoyed glance as she moved to the refrigerator. "Would you stop that? If you've got something to say, come out and say it."

"Okay. I think that if Mom and Dad hadn't died the way they did—and *when* they did—you'd be in Borneo right now. With Jack."

Annie stirred the dressing into the slaw. "I guess their deaths did make me lose whatever wanderlust I had."

"So you think it's gone? Vanished, kaput, no more?"

"Of course. Why would—" The phone rang. Annie felt

oddly relieved. "Get that, would you? And be sure to tell whoever it is about the alien triplets."

Charlie grinned and stood. "Remember—you told me to say it." He ambled over to the phone on the wall and picked it up. "UFOs "R" Us," he said cheerfully. "You spot 'em, we…" His voice trailed off. When he spoke again a moment later, he sounded utterly neutral. "Yes. How long?" Another pause. "I'll take care of it. We'll be there in two shakes."

Annie had turned around the moment Charlie's voice turned cool and careful. She watched him now as he hung up, anxiety skittering up her spine. "What is it?"

"It's okay," he said reassuringly. "Don't get all upset."

"Damn it, don't soothe me—just tell me!"

"There's been an accident."

Annie entered the emergency room of the small county hospital with her brothers flanking her. She and Charlie had been leaving the house when Ben pulled up. Charlie had opened the passenger door before Ben could get out, urged Annie inside with a hand on her back, climbed in after her, and told Ben he'd explain where they were going and why on the way.

Annie had been here before. Plenty of times. It should have looked familiar. It looked alien. Frightening. She headed for the desk where a woman dressed in a pale blue uniform was seated. Beyond the desk lay the wide hall whose walls were lined with crash carts and medical paraphernalia. The doors in those walls led to the examination rooms.

Jack was in one of those rooms.

"I need to find Jack," she told the woman. "Jack Merriman. They said he was in an accident. That he was unconscious." Probably a concussion, Charlie had said. She clung to that. She'd had a concussion once. It had hurt like crazy for a day, but it hadn't been serious. Not serious like a skull fracture would be. Blood clots. Hemorrhaging inside the brain...

"Merriman," the woman said. "Ah, yes. Are you family?"

"I'm...his wife."

"Good. I need to get his medical history and the name of his insurance carrier. He was unconscious when they brought him in—"

"I know that! Where is he?"

"The doctor is with him now," the woman said soothingly. "If you'll just have a seat so we can get the admission forms taken care of—"

Ben's gravelly voice broke in. "I'll do that. You go on, Annie."

She started to move past the desk.

"Wait a minute—"

"What room is he in?"

The woman sighed. "He's in 4-A. Now, sir, if you can just tell me who his insurance..."

Annie didn't hear the rest. She was halfway down the hall.

Jack was sitting up on one of those narrow beds on wheels, scowling at a chubby man in a lab coat whose back was to Annie. "No way am I—Annie!"

She stared at him stupidly. A clear tube snaked from an IV machine beside the bed to the back of his hand. He was pale, but other than that he looked unhurt. "They said you were unconscious."

"I'm okay. You know me. I've got a hard head." He gave her what he no doubt thought was a reassuring grin. "Now, if I could just get this doctor to stop talking crap about keeping me here overnight—"

"You must be kept under observation for twenty-four

hours,'' the man in the lab coat said firmly. ''That is not negotiable.''

''No way.'' Jack pushed to his feet—and went from pale to dirty-snow white.

The doctor pushed him gently back onto the bed. ''Mr. Merriman, I believe you've got a concussion. There are no lateralizing signs to indicate a skull fracture or hematoma, but you were unconscious for at least twenty minutes. I want a CAT scan to check for fracture, and I need you under observation for twenty-four hours. You cannot go home yet.''

Color seeped slowly back into Jack's face. ''I wasn't planning on driving. I'm sure Fred wouldn't mind giving me a lift.'' He looked behind Annie. ''How about it, Fred?''

''Not until the doctor releases you.''

Annie jumped, startled by the presence of someone else in the room. She looked over her shoulder and saw a tall man with a vaguely familiar face and a patrolman's uniform standing in the corner. He'd been two years ahead of her in high school, which put him in Jack's graduating class. ''Fred,'' she said. ''Fred Bergstrom. What are you—oh, you must have responded to the accident.''

''Yes, ma'am.'' He took out a small pad. ''You're Annie Merriman?''

Jack rolled his eyes. ''You know who she is, Fred.''

He ignored Jack. ''Could you tell me where you were between five o'clock and now, ma'am?''

It felt strange to have Fred Bergstrom calling her ma'am. She supposed it was a cop thing. ''Why? Did you try to reach me on my cell phone? I always turn it off when I'm through for the day.''

''Would you quit playing investigator?'' Jack sounded angry.

"It's procedure," Fred said stiffly. "I have to ask these questions."

"You're not a detective, you're a traffic cop. Also an idiot, if you think Annie could have had anything to do with it!"

Anything to do with... Annie suddenly felt sick. "The accident. What happened?"

Jack didn't answer. The cop with Fred Bergstrom's face did. "At six-oh-two the caretaker at Peaceful Gardens found your husband near the foot of the cliff at the western end of the cemetery. He was unconscious, having apparently hit his head on a rock when he fell."

"Dammit, I didn't fall!"

Annie's brain went flat. Empty.

"You don't have any memory of the incident."

"Use some common sense, will you? I didn't have any climbing equipment with me. I don't have to remember what happened to know I'm not stupid enough to free-solo that cliff in the dark."

"Seems like I remember you saying something once about how the only equipment you needed for a night climb was a flashlight."

"I said and did a lot of stupid things in high school that I wouldn't do now."

Fred tucked his notebook back in his pocket. "Well, we'll check it out. It's a shame you can't remember what happened. It would help if you could identify your assailant. If there was one."

"I damned sure didn't crack my own skull open."

Annie met Jack's eyes and saw there the same grim knowledge that had just revealed itself to her. The "accident" had been intentional. Someone had tried to kill Jack.

He looked away. "How about a compromise, Doctor?" he said in his most reasonable voice. "You can run your CAT scan, and I'll stay here and let you observe me for a couple hours. Then, if my head doesn't swell up like a balloon or something, you'll let me go home.''

"If you're concerned about whether your insurance or HMO will pay for an overnight hospital stay, Mr. Merriman, you needn't be. This is standard procedure.''

"Dammit, I'm not worried about the bill. I just don't like hospitals.''

Annie knew how true that was, and why. When Jack was eleven his mother had suffered a bad reaction to medication. He'd called the ambulance when she grew dizzy, but they hadn't let him go to the hospital with her. He'd had no one to go to, no friends of the family, because they were new in town. He'd ended up waiting at a group home, surrounded by strangers, for his mother to come home from the hospital. She'd died there.

The doctor shook his head. "Not when you don't have anyone at home to keep an eye on you except a housekeeper.''

"But he does," Annie said. "I'll be there.''

Life, Jack thought, has a mean sense of humor sometimes. He'd been trying to get Annie to move in with him ever since he got here. Now he had to keep her away. He frowned, then winced. His head felt like an explosion about to happen. "No.''

"What do you mean, 'no'?'' She moved closer. "This is just what you've been wanting me to do. Okay, you win. I'm moving in.''

"Things have changed. I can't protect you now.''

"You're the one someone hit over the head, not me.''

"Exactly. You're better off with your brothers.''

Annie's lips tightened. "So are you.''

"What?''

"Better off with my brothers. At least for now.''

"Wait a minute. I'm not—''

Ben's deep rumble sounded behind her. "All right. What's going on here?"

Right behind him came a woman in a nurse's uniform. She sounded flustered. "I'm sorry, Doctor. I tried to stop them, but they wouldn't listen."

"Our sister is here," Charlie said reasonably as he crowded into the room behind the nurse.

Ben put an arm around Annie, but spoke to Jack. "You look like hell."

"Thanks." Jack watched, bemused, while the nurse ordered two oblivious McClain brothers to leave; Charlie greeted Fred, who had been backed up into the corner by the influx of McClains; Annie told Ben that someone had tried to kill Jack…and the doctor lost his patience.

"Out! Everyone! Now. Before I call security."

Ben scowled. "Right. Charlie, you and Fred clear out of here. Nurse Whatever-your-name-is, you probably need to go pester someone else about their insurance company. Annie—"

"I'm staying."

"All right," he said as if he, and not the doctor, were in charge. "Jack, you'll need to straighten out the billing later. I didn't know who your insurance company was, so I had her bill it to me so she'd quit yapping at me. Doctor, when you get ready to release him, let me know. He'll be coming home with us."

Jack stared. "No, I'm not. Don't you get it? Annie shouldn't—"

"Damned fool," Ben growled. "We'll watch out for Annie—and you, too—until we find out what's going on." He looked around. "Well? Didn't I tell the rest of you to get out of here? Man's been hurt. He needs it quiet."

Jack wasn't surprised when everyone did as instructed. Ben had that effect on people. Ben himself was the last one out, and he closed the door behind him.

"Well," the doctor said, his eyebrows raised. "That's quite a family you have, Mr. Merriman. Now, as I was about to say—since you do have people who can keep an eye on you, I may be able to release you earlier. We'll see. I still want that CAT scan, and I want you to stay here awhile longer. And I want you to lie down. Now."

Jack opened his mouth to say that no one got everything they wanted, but Annie put her hands on his shoulders. And pushed. "Lie down."

He had to, with her pushing on him that way. He eased down, turning his head carefully to avoid touching the knot on the side of his head that felt about the size of a basketball.

The doctor went to the door. "Someone will be by to take you for that scan shortly. Keep him lying down, Mrs. Merriman."

"I will."

Jack's eyes wanted to close the moment he was on his back. He gave in and let them. In the silence that followed the emptying of his room of McClains, doctor, cop and nurse, the pain eased so that it only hit unbearable at the crest of each pulse, then receded to hurts-like-hell.

Annie's hand closed warmly around his.

After a moment he spoke. "That *was* your brother Ben who was just here, insisting I go home with you, wasn't it? Not some alien shape-changer?"

"You know anyone else who gives orders that way?"

Jack had been certain that Annie's brothers wouldn't want her anywhere near him once they knew someone was really trying to kill him. Especially Ben. It wasn't safe, dammit. "I didn't agree to go home with you."

"You don't have any choice. Ben is bigger than you are."

"You didn't even ask him about it. He decided that by himself."

"Jack." She squeezed his hand. "You have a family now. Mine. They can be irritating as the devil, but they aren't going to let you deal with this alone."

Ben and Charlie wouldn't agree with her, Jack thought. In-laws weren't real family...were they? It was getting harder to push thoughts through the blanket of pain wrapped around his skull. Annie's brothers must have done it for her sake, he decided. So she wouldn't worry about him.

"Fred said it happened out at the cemetery," she said.

"Yeah."

"Were you taking your mom some flowers?"

"Yeah." He always did. Annie knew that. Any time he came back to Highpoint, he took his mom flowers. Daffodils if it was spring, poinsettias in the winter, roses for summer, mums in the fall... But he'd had nothing for his aunt. "I saw her at Christmas."

"Who?" She sounded startled.

"My aunt. Her grave is beside my mom's, you know." He opened his eyes, but he didn't really see the small, overly bright room. "I didn't have flowers for her." And it had bothered him. Looking down at the two graves, one old but brightened by the mums and asters he'd brought, one new and bare, he had felt strange. Sad. It hadn't occurred to him to bring flowers for his aunt.

And why should it have? he asked himself. Aunt Sybil hadn't appreciated flowers. He'd given her some once. A little over a year after he'd come to live with her, he had given her a bouquet for her birthday. She had thanked him, put them in a vase and given him in return a lecture on the value of money and the foolishness of spending it on something as ephemeral as flowers.

But that hadn't mattered when he'd stood there looking down at the two graves. He'd wanted to cry. Stupid as it was, he had actually felt like crying because he had no flowers for his aunt. "She tried," he said suddenly. "She didn't know what to do with me, but she tried."

"Your aunt?"

He started to nod, but the small movement made the pain squeeze his brains out his ears, so he closed his eyes again. "I don't know why you keep talking. It makes my head hurt."

"Sorry."

Jack's thoughts drifted. Annie had said her family was his now, but she was wrong. He didn't have any family, save for the two women who rested side by side in that small cemetery. But it had been a kind thought, offering to share her family with him.... "Did I just snap your head off?"

"No more than a quick nip. I'm sure you'll do it again before your head feels better."

He probably would, since it seemed he was going home with Annie and her brothers. Just until he felt better. Then he'd take Annie with him...back to his aunt's big, empty house? Or should he try to talk her into leaving Highpoint entirely? Or was she better off nowhere near him, now that the danger was increased?

He tried to think about that, to decide where Annie would be safest, but his mind was balky. It drifted stubbornly to images of the cemetery, and the two graves he'd visited.

Sybil and Therese Merriman had been sisters, but it was easy to forget that. They had been so different. Jack had the sudden bizarre notion that maybe he'd never really met his aunt, never seen the person behind the platitudes.

Wasn't it a shame, he thought fuzzily, that love and the ability to do what was right never seemed to come packaged together. One sister had never loved, never married. The other had loved too easily, but she, too, had never married. How odd. They'd had that in common, at least. Both had been single all their lives.

Jack wasn't single, not anymore. He was married. To Annie. She sat by his bed now, holding his hand. It felt right. It felt...important. He had the sense that there was some piece he was missing, some thought he needed to connect with another thought, but his head hurt. He couldn't keep his thoughts together. They scattered, bringing up snatches of other times, other places.

He remembered the time he *had* thought of bringing his aunt flowers, and the lecture she had given him. *Flowers fade,* she'd said, and *Waste not, want not.*

She couldn't lecture him anymore, could she?

He would take her flowers, he decided. Before he left Highpoint again, he would take his aunt a small bouquet. She couldn't argue about it this time.

The house was as quiet as a big old house ever is, with no more than an occasional wooden mutter of complaint to disturb the silence as beams and boards settled into the small hours of the morning. Annie sat on the floor beside the couch where Jack lay sleeping. The light from the hall was dim, just enough for her to see that his eyes were closed, that his chest rose and fell shallowly, evenly...that he slept, but he was still with her. Damaged, but alive.

The doctor had released him shortly after midnight. They'd brought him here—pale, shaky, unsteady on his feet—only to confront the barrier of the stairs. All of the bedrooms were on the second floor. Jack couldn't tackle the stairs in his condition, but Ben could have carried him to bed without much trouble. But Jack had been thoroughly offended by the idea of being toted around. He'd ended up on the couch in the family room.

Men, she thought, fond and exasperated. They were such babies sometimes. Babies with man-sized egos.

She would have to wake him soon. She remembered the nurses waking her over and over when she'd had a concussion, and how much that had irritated her. But the doctor had said to wake him up every two hours and make sure he was responsive, so she would do that.

Of course, she didn't have to sit on the floor for those two hours, watching him sleep. But she wanted to. Needed to. Here in the near-dark, with the house quiet and her body exhausted, Annie couldn't stop thinking. Jack had been so surprised that Ben and Charlie had wanted to bring him home. Shocked. It had obviously never occurred to him that they would do that.

Had anyone ever really *been* there for Jack? One hundred percent on his side, no matter what?

His aunt hadn't. Oh, maybe Sybil Merriman had tried to do right by him, as Jack had said. She'd paid for his clothes and his meals and his college. But she'd never attended a track meet to watch him compete or bought him something just because he wanted it. Or praised him. Or hugged him. Maybe she hadn't known how to do any of those things. Maybe the only way she'd been able to express caring had been with an endless series of lectures, but she'd held so much of herself back that only her disapproval had come through clearly.

His mother hadn't been there for him, either. Not really. She'd loved him, yes—Annie believed that, because Jack did. But Therese Merriman had been too needy herself to truly place her child first. Though Jack never said so, Annie knew his years with his mother had been uncertain, even scary at times. And then she'd died. Annie knew well how little difference there was to a child between death and abandonment.

It was no wonder Jack didn't trust love. The people he'd loved, the ones who had loved him—or who should have loved him—had let him down.

Including her.

There in the darkness, Annie admitted the truth. She

hadn't stood by Jack. She'd been too busy protecting herself, loving him but holding herself back, hunting for ways to make what she felt safer, less risky…less total. She'd married him, then refused to leave with him because it was too sudden. Too scary. Because she hadn't wanted to have her whole heart on the line.

Foolishness, of course. She hadn't been able to put nice, safe limits on love. She'd just managed to convince them both that her commitment to him came with strings.

He stirred restlessly, making a small sound of discomfort, but didn't wake.

She stroked his jaw lightly. The skin there was rough with beard and his muscles felt tight, as if even in sleep he couldn't escape the pain. Slowly, she drew her fingers down his cheek, cherishing the feel of him, wishing she could draw the pain out and fling it away. Then she gave in to the curiosity she'd felt ever since he came back and touched his hair. It felt soft and straight and thick, warmed from his skin, like an animal's fur.

Maybe her touch felt good to him, too, on some level. When she stroked his jaw again, it wasn't as tense.

I love you.

Annie wanted to whisper the words to him while he slept. This time, it wasn't fear that held her back. She understood so much more now than she had two months ago when she ran off to Vegas, dizzy with lust and love and fear. Jack didn't need words of love. He needed to *believe* in love, needed someone he could believe in and depend on. She had let him down. Badly. It amazed her that he still wanted her, but he did. He didn't love her, but he wanted her.

I won't let you down again, she promised him silently.

There was darkness here, and silence, except for the soundless scream of pain in his head. But there was soft-

ness, too. A gentle brush of fingers along his cheek called
Jack up from the deeper silence of sleep.

Annie. He knew her touch, even in the half-aware place
where he drifted. He didn't open his eyes; it would take
too much effort, and he didn't need to see her. It was
enough to know she was there.

Memories rumbled in, a noisy crowd clamoring for his
attention, pulling him closer to full consciousness. Nothing
about the attack came to him, though. He couldn't recall a
single moment beyond the one when he'd turned away
from the two graves he'd visited. But he remembered
enough.

Someone had tried to kill him. Again.

Before, Jack had been troubled by conflicting urges. Now
his deepest instincts were at war. He had to keep Annie
safe. That was as an absolute. And it wasn't safe around
him, not now.

But he needed to *keep* her, too. He wanted her with him
all the time. He wanted her nearby in the day so he could
tease her and irritate her and watch her face when he kissed
her in the sunlight. He wanted her in his bed at night, where
they could delight each other with the magic their bodies
made. And he wanted her with him the way she was now—
in the darkest hours of the night, the empty hours when
loneliness howled at a man's soul.

Jack lay awake in the darkness with his eyes closed and
his mind troubled, waiting for Annie to touch him again.
Somehow he had to find a way to satisfy both needs—for
Annie's safety, and for Annie.

Chapter 9

"We've got problems, sweetie."

"What?" He held the phone close to his ear to better hear the female voice on the other end and sat up. The woman beside him stirred sleepily. "Damnation. Do you know what time it is here?"

"I didn't stop to figure out time zones. This couldn't wait."

He sighed. "Hold on a minute. " He slapped the round bottom of the woman he'd hired. "Out. *Vas-y. Tu t'en vas.*"

She protested in a sleepy mixture of French and some bloody incomprehensible native tongue, but the sight of a few extra bills soothed her feelings. It sure as hell didn't soothe him. Whores were always greedy. He'd already paid her for the whole night, and now he was paying her to leave.

As soon as the door closed he picked up the receiver again. "This better be important."

''I know not much is as important to you as getting laid, but this is business.''

''What's wrong?'' he demanded. ''Are the police suspicious?''

''No, everyone thinks it was an accident.'' She paused. ''Including Jack.''

''What the hell? Merriman's alive?''

''A little blurry about some things, apparently, but definitely alive.''

''Dammit to hell, you hired some two-bit street punk, didn't you? If I find out you pocketed the money you were supposed to have spent on a real professional, you're going to be sorry you ever thought of cheating me!''

''I saved you a bundle! I thought—''

''I don't pay you to think.'' He was breathing hard. It took him a moment to get his control back. ''Tell me what happened.''

''Johnny—that's the name the guy I hired goes by— called me half an hour ago. He said he'd followed Jack out to the cemetery last night. The place was deserted, and it was nearly sunset. It looked like the perfect opportunity. He got Jack to follow him over to the foot of a cliff with some nonsense about a lost dog, distracted him and bashed him on the side of the head with the length of steel he carries. Remind me to tell you where he keeps that, sweetie. It's a hoot.''

''Tell me about your damned sex life later,'' he growled. ''Why isn't Merriman dead?''

''He turned just as Johnny was whacking him and ducked—not completely, but enough. Johnny had just knelt to see if he was dead or not, when he saw headlights pull up. He cleared out.''

He exploded, describing the hit man's incompetence and Leah's stupidity and greed in language drawn from the gutters of several countries.

She let him rant for a while, then said coolly, "Your instructions were to make it look like an accident. If Johnny had been found on the scene with a length of pipe in his hand—or in his pants—no one was going to assume that Jack went climbing and fell."

"All right," he said, sitting heavily on the bed. "All right. But you said everyone *does* think that was what happened? Even Jack? Your man didn't have time to plant the climbing gear on him."

"Jack doesn't remember the attack. Apparently that happens a lot with head trauma. The cops assume he went climbing without any gear."

He was calmer now. He was a realist, after all. Employees screwed up all the time. A smart businessman allowed for the possibility. "If this happened last night, why did you wait until now to call me?"

"I called as soon as I heard from Johnny. He hung around Highpoint until he could be sure Jack didn't remember what had happened."

"You know what you have to do now, don't you?"

"You want me to send Johnny after him again? I guess he could arrange a fire—"

"Hell, no! What are you using for brains? We can't stage another accident without tipping our hand. Plan B, woman, plan B!"

She was silent a moment. "You want to go with the betrayed wife bit, then. That's going to cost extra, sweetie."

Women. They were all whores. Everything cost—smiling, staying, going, screwing—whatever you wanted 'em to do, it cost. "You aren't going to have to kill him yourself."

"I know what I have to do." She sounded irritated, as if *he* were the one with compost for brains. "Make it obvious to everyone that he's fooling around on his sweet little wife. Honey, that much I would do for free, especially if I can turn appearance into reality. It's the rest that will cost you.''

Her silence, in other words. The little bitch had every intention of blackmailing him. He smiled grimly. ''I expected that, Leah. Just do your job well, and you'll get everything we agreed on.''

Chapter 10

Two days later, Jack was still on the couch in the Merriman's family room. At least, when Annie was around, he was on the couch.

"The doctor wants you to rest for forty-eight hours," she'd said last night when he started pacing. "You'll mend faster if you give your body what it needs" she'd told him when he wanted her to loan him her weights. When she'd caught him doing stretches after lunch, she'd been less tactful. "Get back on that couch, Jack. Don't make me hurt you."

He grinned, remembering, and swung his legs off the couch. Annie wasn't here now. There were shadows under her eyes and she'd been yawning all afternoon, so he'd talked her into taking a nap.

He stood up. He was never going to get his strength back by lying flat on his back, and he needed to get better, fast. He had a plan. Yesterday he'd wired Amos Deerbaum about recent events, including the attack. With any luck he'd hear from ICA's director in a day or two. He would need Deerbaum's backing to get any cooperation from Herbie in tracking down whoever had been Metz's partner...especially if Herbie *was* that partner.

Today he'd made three phone calls—when Annie was out of the room—one to Sergeant Parks of the Highpoint Police, one to Becky in the Denver office, and one to Fred Bergstrom.

Sergeant Parks wasn't going to be any help. Jack had suspected as much when the sergeant had questioned him yesterday, and today's phone call confirmed it. Parks didn't plan to waste any effort looking for Jack's assailant because he didn't believe there had been an assailant. Like so many others in Highpoint, his opinion of Jack was frozen in time. He'd heard too much about Jack's younger, wilder days, including the time Jack had free-soloed a cliff that only an idiot—or a teenager—would climb without bolts and rope. *Not that I fell, even then,* Jack thought with a trace of offended pride.

He walked across the room slowly. The nausea was gone, thank goodness, but he still got dizzy if he moved too fast. His head still hurt, too, but the pain was dull, more like a bad hangover than the monster headache that had squeezed his skull on the first day. He could do what he needed to do. He just couldn't do it quickly.

Jack put his palms against one of the walls and began some simple stretches to warm up his muscles.

Fortunately, he had options other than the skeptical sergeant. Fred, for example. Jack's old track teammate had wanted to play detective at the emergency room, so Jack had told him about his plan and Fred had agreed. He seemed excited, in a sober, cautious sort of way, about the part he would play.

Jack would have liked a little more backup. He wasn't exactly in prime condition, and while Fred was steady and dependable, he wasn't the brightest bulb on the Christmas tree. Charlie would have been a perfect partner-in-crime, but Charlie wouldn't be back for two days. He'd stayed in town as long as he could, but he'd had to either make his scheduled run today or forfeit the job.

What about Ben?

Jack frowned. There was no denying Ben would be a good man to have at his back right now, and the man *had* insisted that Jack come here when he was released from the ER. He supposed he could let Ben know what was going on. That way Ben could offer his help—or not. It would be up to him.

Jack headed for the hall. Ben had said he'd be in the kitchen battling with his quarterly taxes if Jack needed anything, so that's where Jack headed. Jack was in a hurry to put his plan into action. His presence here put Annie in danger. He had another reason to act quickly, though.

He couldn't take much more of this.

Annie wasn't acting normal. She kept touching him. She seemed to look for excuses to touch him, and Jack was only human. And male. It was amazing how very male he could feel in his current condition. Every time Annie touched him he wanted to pull her down on the couch with him. Under him.

But if he did manage to get her where he wanted her, he wasn't sure he could *do* what he wanted. It would be a hell of a note if he collapsed on top of her before he was supposed to.

She obviously had no idea what her sweet touches were doing to him. Jack didn't mind—not the touches or the hovering, or even the way she tried to bully him into lying down all day long. Annie cared about him. She'd been up all night with him that first night. She wanted to coddle him, to protect him. It was a sweet and gallant notion, and it made him feel warm and happy inside.

It also meant that there was no way he could let her find out what he planned to do.

He sighed. The only way he could keep her in the dark was to lie to her, much as he hated it. She was going to be furious when she found out, but he'd rather have her mad at him than hurt. Or worse.

Jack was undoubtedly *not* lying down on the couch, Annie thought as she stared sleeplessly at the ceiling of her bedroom. It wouldn't hurt him much to be up for a while, but she'd have to go back downstairs soon so he didn't overdo it. He was a rotten patient.

Not that she'd expected otherwise. She had her brothers' example of the way active, athletic men behaved when illness or injury hit them hard enough to land them in bed. *Difficult* was one word for it. *Pigheaded* was another.

She sighed. It was a pity she was so blasted turned on by one particular difficult, pigheaded, impossibly sexy man. Between the humming in her body and the thoughts whirling in her mind, there was no way she was going to fall asleep now, no matter how tired she was.

Jack thought she was like him, that she dreamed of distant places. It had been a long time, though, since she'd thought of those dreams as hers. A very long time. Could she be happy following him all over the world the way her mother had followed her father?

When did compromise turn into unhealthy sacrifice?

Slowly Annie sat up and looked around at a room so familiar she usually didn't really see it. Just as she'd stopped seeing Jack clearly until their trip to Denver had forced a few truths on her.

Annie liked wood, and there was a lot of it in her room. The bed where she'd been trying to nap had solid oak posts; Ben had built it for her sixteenth birthday. Her dresser was cherry. It had been her mother's before her, and her grandmother's before that. There was a wooden rocker she'd bought in Denver, and a tall knobby-pine chest that she'd had forever. Wooden shelves held climbing gear, photograph albums, an old globe and a lot of books. Beneath the shelves were more books that she'd brought back from Denver and hadn't found room for yet.

It was an adult's room. Annie had a few things there from her teenaged years, but there was nothing that recalled the little girl she had once been...the girl who *had* dreamed of faraway places. Nothing except the globe.

Her mother had given her that globe for her sixth birthday. Every year after that, Mama had used the globe to show Annie where she and Annie's father would be.

Slowly Annie stood. It wasn't the globe that drew her, though, but the closet. On the top shelf, too high for her to reach without help, were all sorts of things she seldom needed—a file box, a zippered bag of old clothing, a couple of purses, and a faded shoe box.

It had been a long time since she'd taken that box down. Maybe it was time.

At the back of the closet was the little wooden stool a very small Annie had once used in order to reach the bathroom sink. She used it now to reach the shoe box, then crossed to the rocking chair. She settled there with the shoe box in her lap and took off the lid. Inside was a thick packet of letters tied with a frayed and faded ribbon that had once been blue. The ribbon was too old to unknot. She scooted it down a little at a time until she could pull it off without breaking it.

The letters on top were the oldest. They were short, written in block letters because Annie hadn't been able to read cursive yet when her mother wrote them. Annie hesitated, then set most of the letters aside. It was the last few she needed to see now. The ones her mother had written on the last trip she had taken with Annie's father.

"Dear Annie," one of them began. "We just got here, and already I'm missing you and the boys. Your father is, too, of course, but he's excited about this dig..." Annie skipped the details of that long-ago archeological expedition. She skimmed her mother's colorful description of the local bazaar and the funny story about the donkey. She knew all of that by heart.

She turned the sheet over. Near the bottom of the page was the last paragraph. "I'm so looking forward to you joining us once school is out—only a month to wait! I'm already planning the things we'll do once you get here...."

"Looking at your mom's letters?" Jack asked gently.

Annie looked up, startled, blinking the dampness from her eyes. Jack was leaning against the doorjamb. He looked pale and tired. "You climbed the stairs," she said accusingly.

"And didn't faint or fall down."

"But your head is hurting worse, isn't it?"

"My head is going to hurt for a while, no matter what I do." He shrugged impatiently away from the door and came into the room. "Those letters...that's what I was looking for that day."

"When?"

"In Denver. The *National Geographic* magazines made my point, but it was the letters I was thinking of when I started ripping open your packing boxes."

"Oh. They were here in my closet. I didn't take them to Denver with me." She looked down at the letter in her hand. "I was going to join my parents on a dig, you know. Before we heard about the accident. I had my bags all packed."

"I know. Your brothers each got to spend at least one summer with them, didn't they?"

"Yes." She touched the small pile of letters gently with her fingertips. "We had to be ten years old before we could go. That was the rule. Mom and Dad figured that ten was old enough to handle a long flight.'' She'd turned ten the year they were killed. Even after all these years she still got a lump in her throat when she thought about it. She'd wanted to go so badly. She had been waiting for years to be old enough to join them.

Annie looked up. ''You really ought to sit down. You're looking awfully pale.''

''Nag,'' he said, but he did sit—on her bed. He looked entirely too good there, she thought wistfully. ''How old were you the first time they left you?''

The question surprised her. ''I'm sure I've told you that.''

''Tell me again.''

She shrugged. ''Daddy had always been gone for several months of the year, but Mama didn't go with him until I started school. That was another rule. She stayed home with each of us until we were old enough to start school. Then she went with him again. Just for the summer, at first.'' Her father had expected it. That had made Annie furious when she was little—the way her father always expected her mother to go with him...and the way her mother had always gone.

Just like Jack had expected her to go. When he'd gotten that phone call about a job on their wedding night, he'd expected her to go away with him, just like that. And she...she had wanted him to care enough to stay.

''Summer lasts a long time when you're six,'' he said now. ''Did you think you were old enough for your mother to be gone all summer?''

''Of course not. A six-year-old doesn't understand that sort of thing.'' Annie traced the faded ink on one letter with one fingertip. Love, fairness, compromise, sacrifice...what had her mother considered a sacrifice? Staying home with her children when they were small? Or leaving them to be with the husband who couldn't stay in one place? What about her father? Had he thought of those few months he spent in the States each year as a sacrifice, or as a compromise between his needs and those of his family?

She began to tidy the letters again. "We did have Nana. It wasn't as if Mama left us with some stranger."

"No, she left you with a woman whose health wasn't good."

The sharpness in his voice surprised her. "Nana's heart didn't get bad until after Mama died. She never did recover from that." Annie didn't like to think of the year following her parents' deaths. She had lost her grandmother slowly rather than all at once—first to grief, then to a series of health problems that had led to her moving into a rest home. There she'd lingered another three years, but the vague, fragile woman who had finally died in her sleep hadn't been Nana. Not the Nana Annie had known. "But until then, her health wasn't bad. She'd slowed down, but I was pretty independent. It wasn't as if I needed a lot of looking after. And I had my brothers."

"Ben had moved out, though, hadn't he? He didn't move back home until your folks died."

"But he lived close by. We knew we could call on him if we needed him. Look, are we arguing about this for some reason?"

"I guess I'm angry on your behalf, even if you aren't. Not anymore, at least." A smile softened his face. "Though I seem to recall that you were pretty mad about it at one time."

It took Annie a second to realize what he was talking about. When she did, she chuckled. "That was the *first* time you got me in trouble. I had to pick up trash in the alleys for blocks and blocks."

"Hey, you weren't the only one who got in trouble. I was grounded for a month."

She felt a remembered pang of conscience. "I would never have done it if I'd known they were your aunt's dishes."

"That's why I didn't tell you where I got them."

From the boxes his aunt had planned to send to Goodwill. Oh, she did remember. Annie's fingers eased the ribbon back up over the packet of letters, but her mind wasn't paying attention to what her fingers did. It had drifted back to a distant fall day.

She'd been eleven when her thirteen-year-old brother had started hanging out with "that Merriman boy." It had been a difficult year. The first hard blow of grief had passed, followed by a gray period when she hadn't felt much of anything. But as the numbness wore off she'd discovered anger—a wretched, simmering anger that she hadn't known how to deal with. She'd been mad at everyone and everything.

One day Jack had come over to see Charlie. Instead he'd found her alone in the backyard, sobbing her heart out. She'd been mortified. When he'd asked her what was wrong, she'd sniffed and said, "I'm not crying."

"Then why is your face all wet?"

"Because I'm mad!"

"Okay, then. Why are you mad?"

"I don't know!" That had been the worst of it—to be so angry all the time and not know why.

"I bet you're mad at your mom for dying," he had said matter-of-factly. When she'd protested that she *couldn't* be angry with her dead mother, he'd said, "Why not? I was."

Jack had told her to come with him and he would show her what to do with her anger. She'd gotten on her bike and followed him to the alley behind the house where he lived with his aunt. He'd shown her his secret stash—a

collection of old pottery plates, cups and saucers. "You
only do this when you're really angry," he'd warned her.
"The knot-you-up-inside kind of angry, not just a regular
mad. You take a plate and think at it real hard, think about
whatever or whoever has you so mad you can't see straight.
Then you throw it as hard as you can." He held out a plate.

She'd been horrified. "I can't do that!"

"Sure you can. Like this." And he'd hurled the plate
against the seven-foot brick wall that surrounded his aunt's
property.

Annie still remembered the sound of that plate smashing
itself to smithereens. Jack hadn't had to work hard to get
her to try it after that. And he'd been right. Somehow
smashing those plates had cracked open the anger inside
her, breaking it into pieces small enough for her to deal
with.

"There's just something about the sound of a plate crash-
ing into a hundred pieces," she murmured now.

"Broken any lately?"

"Not on purpose." She frowned as she noticed the lines
that bracketed his mouth. "You're getting that two-days-
dead look again, Jack. You've pushed yourself too hard."

She stood up. "Lie down."

His eyebrows went up. "Propositioning me?"

"Not this time." She put her letters back in the shoe
box. "Come on. You can be a he-man and pole-vault down
the stairs or jog around the block later, after you've rested."
She came over to the bed and piled up the pillows so he
could lean back against them.

"I'm not lying down—"

"Jack," she said warningly, "weak as you are right now,
I can make you."

"Power mad, aren't you? What I started to say was that
I won't lie down unless you do, too. With me. There are
shadows under your eyes. You didn't nap, did you?"

She hesitated.

''That wary expression on your face is flattering, but I'm in no shape to do what you're afraid I might do. Unfortunately.''

Still she didn't move. There seemed no point in feeding his ego by telling him the reason she hadn't slept well was because she worried about him as much as she ached for him.

''Annie.'' He held out his hand. ''Let me hold you.''

She could no more turn away from his outstretched hand than she could stop breathing. She went to him.

He leaned back against the pillows she'd fixed for him, making room for her, drawing her gently down. She lay on her side, curled up against him in the bed she'd slept in since she was sixteen. His arm pillowed her head. And she felt as if she were drawing the first full breath of air she'd had since she'd heard about his accident. There was healing here, with the warmth of his body at her back, with his breath stirring her hair. Muscles she hadn't known were tense began to relax. How strange. He was the one who was supposed to need healing, not her.

''You were right,'' he said after a moment.

''About what?''

''I feel lousy.''

She smiled. ''Good thing for you I'm too tired to say 'I told you so.''' And she *was* tired, even drowsy. Desire hummed in her blood, yet her body was relaxed and comfortable. It was like waking up on a winter morning, she thought, when the cold air on her face made her feel deliciously alive, yet the rest of her body remained warm and limp, urging her to sleep a little longer. Of course, she'd always been one to respond to the life stirring in her blood rather than the quiet temptation of sleep…but just this once, she wasn't going to heed that stirring. It felt so good to just lie here with him….

* * *

Jack looked at the woman sleeping in the curve of his arm. He sighed. He was a selfish bastard. A stupid one, too, since he'd gotten himself into his present aroused condition on purpose. After he told Annie what he planned to tell her, it might be a while before he could touch her again. So he'd coaxed her into lying down and torturing him.

Selfish. Stupid. Also perverse. He must be perverse, because he was enjoying the torture.

The arm she lay on was the second part of his body to get stiff, but he didn't mind. She sure did look sweet, with her hair all loose and messy around her face. Her eyelashes made dusky shadows on the cream of her cheeks, and those kissable lips of hers were slightly parted.

He didn't have long to wait with his arm growing numb, his body aching and his thoughts uneasy, before she stirred. He wished she'd slept longer. She needed the rest, and he was dreading the coming argument.

She may not argue much, he reminded himself—and, true to his newly discovered perversity, he didn't like that idea, either. But Annie hadn't exactly been eager to move in with him until someone tried to crack his head open. Once she knew he was okay and thought he'd be safe, she would probably be ready to pull her head back into her shell, cautious little turtle that she was....

"Mmm," she said, blinking sleepily.

"Annie? You awake?"

"Hmm?"

"I need to tell you something. I should have told you earlier, but..." He let his voice drift off. "My conscience is bothering me."

She rolled over to face him. There were a few barely-there freckles on her nose, freckles so pale he had to be close like this to see them. "That sounds ominous."

He did his best to look embarrassed, but those freckles

distracted him. He wanted to lick them. "I've, uh, remembered about the attack. And there wasn't one."

"What do you mean?"

"I *did* try free-soloing that cliff."

She looked upset. Disappointed. "Why would you do something that stupid?"

He sighed. "I wasn't thinking straight. I was upset."

"I can't believe you were so dumb." She shook her head. "That was the first time you'd visited your aunt's grave, though, wasn't it?"

"Yeah." He wished it had been a little harder to convince Annie he'd been as much of a fool as he was claiming to have been. "Anyway, there's no reason for me to hang around here, keeping both Ben and you from your jobs. Tonight I'll go to go back to my..." He paused. It wasn't really his aunt's house anymore, was it? "To the house my aunt left me."

She sat up. "Jack, that doesn't make sense. Even if what happened two nights ago *was* your fault, there's still that warning you received, right after someone ran you off the road."

He gestured dismissively. "That was on the other side of the world, like you said. It must have been the black market people over there."

"But you're not steady on your feet yet. I'll go with you, of course, but—"

"You don't have to do that."

"Yes, I do."

He sat up, too—slowly, so the world wouldn't get light and whirly on him. "I don't want you to feel forced into anything. I know you wanted more time to think things over, and I can move around enough to take care of myself now—even if you think I should stay in bed for a week. And Ida will be there to handle meals and things like that."

She studied his face, frowning. "What's going on?"

"Nothing." Damn. She wasn't going to make this easy. "I'm trying to be considerate. I thought you'd be glad that I'm not pushing you."

"I'm ready to move in with you."

She wasn't just making this hard. She was making it downright miserable. He started to run his hand over the top of his head, stopping barely in time to keep from touching the knot on his skull. What was he supposed to do now? "I hadn't wanted to say this, but…well, I need some time, too. To think about things." That's what she'd said to him, so it must make sense to her.

Her eyes went big. "You—you've changed your mind."

"Oh, hell, Annie, don't look like that. I'm not—I—" He ran out of words and tried rubbing his face instead of his head. It didn't help. "I haven't changed my mind. I want you. Even in my current lousy condition, I want you. But I've been selfish, not stopping to think about what's best for you."

A spark of anger put a little color back in her cheeks. "Don't you think it's up to me to decide that?"

That's good, Annie, he encouraged her silently. *Get mad.* He'd much rather see her spitting mad than with that stricken look in her eyes. And he knew just which buttons to push to get her there. "I've been talking to Ben, and he and I have come to an agreement."

Her eyes narrowed dangerously. "You've come to an agreement. With my brother. About *us?*"

"He did make some good points." Jack made a mental note to make sure Ben knew what kind of advice he'd been giving. "He reminded me of how much you love Highpoint. I need to think about whether it's right for me to ask you to give up your home." He gave her his best smile and reached out to caress her shoulder, letting his hand drift down toward her breast.

She shoved his hand away.

''There, you see what I mean? I can't think straight around you. I'm too busy trying to get you in bed. And you're not thinking straight, either. Between your hormones and being worried about me, you're apt to do something you'll be sorry for later. I'm not going to let you do that.''

''You're not going to *let* me?''

The explosion was coming. ''That's right. I owe it to you to make sure you don't do anything you'll regret...the way you regretted marrying me.''

She went still. ''I—I didn't regret that, exactly.''

''No? You could have fooled me.'' He wasn't pretending when his voice turned hard. ''You called it the biggest mistake of your life. Then you took off your wedding ring.''

''And you said I was a sorry excuse for a woman. Did you mean that?''

''No. Stop trying to sidetrack me. If you would just calm down and be reasonable, you'd see that I'm right.''

''Reasonable? You want me to be *reasonable?*''

''Calm down, Annie.''

''Oh, I'm calm. I'm very calm. If I weren't, I might say something I didn't really mean. I might call you a stupid, insensitive moron with a death wish, since only a fool would try to free-solo that cliff in the dark! But I won't.'' She leaned forward, shoving her hair out of her face. ''And I didn't take off my ring until I woke up and found out you had left!''

When she mentioned taking off her ring, anger licked up from where it waited inside, always there these days, ready to flame. *Steady,* he told himself. Don't let this get out of hand. ''The point is,'' he said, trying to remember what the point was, ''that you are not coming to my aunt's house with me. You need time. You kept saying that, and now, by God, I'm giving you time. Whether you like it or not.''

''For my own good.'' Her eyes blazing, she pushed off

the bed. "That is the most stupid, high-handed, ridiculous thing you've ever said!"

"See? You're not thinking clearly." He considered asking her if it was "that time of the month," but decided he'd better not push her too far. "Trust me to do what's best for both of us."

"You do what you have to," she said, eyes shining, chin high and fists knotted at her sides. "And so will I. And that doesn't include listening to any more of your macho crap!" She spun around and marched out.

Jack watched her go glumly. He'd done a great job of making her mad, all right. He just hoped he could do as good a job of apologizing when the time came to do that. Especially since he suspected the truth would make her every bit as angry as the lie had.

He could handle that. He just wished he could be sure that the shine he'd seen in her eyes had come from anger, not tears.

Jack heaved himself off of her bed and waited to see if the dizziness would hit. When it didn't, he started for the stairs. He needed to call Fred, and then he'd better get out of here. He wanted to be gone by the time Annie got back.

He would stop by his aunt's house on his way. He needed to pick up some things, and he wanted to be sure Ida understood what to tell anyone who called and asked for him...anyone but Annie, that is. He didn't want Annie to know where he would be tonight, but anyone else who came looking for him needed to be given his room number at the motel. There wasn't much point in dangling himself like bait in front of his would-be killer if the man couldn't find him.

Chapter 11

Annie flew down the stairs, grabbed her jacket and her keys and made straight for the front door—nearly colliding with Ben in the hall.

"Hey!" His brows drew together. "What's got you all upset?"

"Nothing! Not one damned thing! I'm just going out for a while—with or without your permission. While I'm gone, feel free to *agree* with Jack about whatever you like, but don't expect me to go along with it!"

She slammed the front door behind her.

How dare he? she fumed as she jabbed her key in the ignition. Telling her what she would and wouldn't do—for her own good. She backed out of the drive, braked sharply, then paused. Where was she going, anyway?

Oh, it didn't matter. Binton's, she decided, for a game of pool and the company of people she wasn't related to. She headed west.

"Give a man an inch and he thinks he owns you," she

muttered. Jack had never tried pulling that sort of authority thing with her before, and she was not about to put up with it now. Just because she'd married him...

Something he needed to "think about" now. Away from her. Hurt tried to seep in beneath the anger, oily and unwanted. She scowled and closed a mental door on it. He had every right to think things over. Wasn't that what she'd insisted on herself?

He didn't have any right to make decisions for her, though. Or to come to an agreement with her brother about those decisions. She couldn't believe he'd done that. Jack *knew* how much she hated it when Ben pulled his big-brother-knows-best act.

Yes...he did, didn't he?

Annie frowned as she turned down Second Street. Jack also knew how furious it made her when some stupid macho male equated caring with taking over. And he knew that the worst thing to say to her when she was angry was "calm down" or "be reasonable." It was almost as if he had set out to enrage her.

By the time Annie reached Binton's, her mind was as crowded with thoughts as the parking lot was with trucks, vans and sports utility vehicles. The bar was something of a Highpoint institution, having been around longer than the town itself. It was a pleasant place to relax with friends, with pool tables in the back and a single arcade game that Ella Binton, the great-granddaughter of the original owner, had reluctantly added.

Annie found an open spot on the edge of the lot and turned off the ignition, then sat there a moment, brooding. Jack was up to something. But what?

Was he trying to drive her away?

Hurt nudged hard at the door she'd closed against it. She scowled and climbed out of her Bronco.

Inside, Binton's was just the way Annie remembered it—

warm, crowded and friendly, with the smell of fresh popcorn competing with tobacco smoke. The lights were never turned down seduction-low here, nor was the music too loud for conversation. Alan Jackson was singing about how everyone "might as well share, might as well smile," when Annie was called over to a crowded table that held some people she knew, some she didn't. She ordered a beer and tried to pay attention to the music and the company she'd thought she wanted.

Was Jack devious enough to try and drive her away by infuriating her?

Yes, she thought unhappily. He could be that devious...if he thought he had a good reason. The real question was why he would want to drive her away. All she could come up with was that either he wanted to get rid of her—period—or he wanted her gone temporarily for some unknown reason.

"Listen," she said brightly, pushing to her feet because she could not sit still another second. "Does anyone want to play some pool?"

Eric Smith's little sister, Meredith, did. The younger woman ought to make decent company, Annie thought, since she didn't feel like talking and Meredith did. She talked on and on about the problems she was having with a man she'd been seeing. Annie only needed to nod or murmur something sympathetic every so often. While they were waiting for a table to become available, Annie sipped her beer, greeted friends and acquaintances, listened to Meredith's troubles and thought about her own.

If Jack had decided he didn't want to be married after all, wouldn't he just tell her so?

Maybe not. He hated to hurt a woman's feelings. He would probably tie himself into knots to keep from hurting a good friend like her. Maybe he thought breaking up would hurt her less if she thought it was her idea.

Eventually Meredith's endless stream of complaints began to wear on Annie's nerves. "You know, if you're that unhappy with Steven, maybe you should tell him about it instead of me."

Meredith gave her a reproachful look. "I don't want to hurt him."

"Ah...right. Look, I think our table's ready," Annie said, relieved.

Was Jack really stupid enough to think that Annie would be hurt less if he drove her away instead of speaking to her honestly about his feelings—or lack of them?

She glanced at sweet, clueless Meredith and shook her head. Surely not.

Well, then, was he stupid enough to have climbed that cliff in the dark without any equipment? She frowned at her cue as she chalked it.

Annie won the break and actually sank one ball in spite of her distracted state. She was in position, her cue already in motion for a straight shot at the six ball, when another voice greeted her.

"Why, Annie! Fancy seeing you here!"

Her cue skipped off the top of the cue ball, which rolled gently up against the six ball and came to a stop. "Your shot, Meredith," she said grimly as she straightened.

Suzy Watkins, the woman Annie had told to get on with her life when she'd claimed that Jack couldn't be faithful, stood there smirking at her. She wore a Binton's T-shirt with her jeans and carried a tray with drinks on it.

Great. "So, how long have you been working here, Suzy?"

"Oh, nearly four months now. But then, you wouldn't know much about my life these days, would you?" The other woman's bright, malicious smile told Annie she was still smoldering over their encounter. "I'm glad you decided to stop by. I wanted to warn you."

"How ominous."

"You're wise not to take Jack's little friends seriously, but I did think you should know about this one. She seemed rather...intense."

Annie's eyebrows went up along with her blood pressure. "Jack's 'little friends'? If that's some cute way of hinting that Jack has girlfriends, you should know that I am *not* in a good mood."

"I'm just trying to warn you. She was in here earlier, talking about Jack and how *close* the two of them are."

Meredith had stopped playing pool and was unabashedly listening in. "Now, Suzy, just because some old friend of Jack's showed up—"

"Old friend? Honey, this woman was obviously more than a friend. Harry!" She called out to a man at the other pool table. "You were here when that little dark-haired cutie was in earlier, talking a mile a minute about her and Jack and asking how to find his house. Would you say they were 'just friends'?"

Annie frowned. The woman had been asking how to find Jack?

Annie didn't know the man who paused, grinned and said he wished he had a friend like that who would drop whatever she was doing to come when he called.

Suzy turned back to Annie triumphantly. "She said that he'd asked her to come here. That he sent for her. I'm not saying I believe her, mind, but that's what she said."

Jealousy fought a quick, cold battle with fear in Annie's heart. "What was her name?"

Suzy shrugged. "I didn't catch it."

"Suzy." Annie struggled to keep her voice level. "Stop with the games for a minute. Jack's in bed with a concussion because someone tried to smash his head in the night before last." At least, she was pretty sure that was what had happened—in spite of what he'd told her.

Meredith made a shocked exclamation. Annie ignored her, focused on finding out what she had to know. "This is important, Suzy. What did this woman look like?"

"Oh, come on. You don't think that little bitty thing could have hurt Jack, do you? As big as he is?"

"Just tell me what she looked like."

"Well—she was little, even smaller than you. More striking than pretty, but the kind of woman men watch, if you know what I mean. Then there was that hair of hers. God, what I wouldn't give for hair like that—about a mile long and dark as sin. She acted...I don't know." Suzy frowned. "Kind of odd. Excited, but tense."

Leah? Had Leah from Jack's office come to Highpoint? And bragged about the relationship Jack swore they didn't have—and asked where he lived?

Annie handed Suzy her cue stick. "Here." She started for the door.

"Where are you going?"

"To see a man about a bitch."

Jack was not comfortable. The canned laughter from the TV show that he wasn't watching made his head hurt. The motel's pillows were too soft, the bed was too hard, and he missed Annie.

Then there was the fact that he was here because he was waiting for someone to try to kill him. That was not a comfortable position to be in. Necessary, but not comfortable.

He had to do something to tempt the bastard out from under whatever rock he'd crawled beneath, though, and it made sense to try to provoke an attack on *his* terms, at the time and place of his choosing. That's why he was at a motel. The old house where Annie thought he was sleeping tonight would have been impossible to watch—too many rooms, doors, windows.

Jack had selected this motel room carefully. It was the only occupied unit on this end of the building, a situation he'd guaranteed by renting the two rooms closest to it as well. The door opened directly onto the parking lot so that Fred would be able to watch it from his vantage point there.

It wasn't a bad plan, he thought. Now all he had to do was wait.

Jack wasn't very good at waiting in the best of situations, and this was hardly the best. He was tense, his neck and shoulders tight, his head aching. Tense enough that he jumped when the phone rang.

Two rings. Then nothing. That was Fred's signal.

It was probably just room service, he told himself as he used the remote to turn the sound off on the TV. He'd ordered a hamburger, and Fred was supposed to let him know of any arrivals, even those of motel employees.

But maybe it wasn't room service.

Jack's heart beat faster as he reached into the duffel bag he'd set next to the bed and took out one of the ways Ben had chosen to help him—a nine millimeter automatic pistol. It felt heavy and cold in his hand.

A knock sounded at the door.

Jack didn't like guns. He knew how to use them, but he also knew what kind of damage they could do. If he had been in normal shape he would have relied on himself rather than a pistol, but right now he had the reflexes of a drunk and the strength of a tired kindergartner, while his unknown assailant might be armed and was sure to be in better shape. So he carried the gun with him when he went to look through the peephole in the door.

After a moment he shook his head in disgust, backed up to the bed and slipped the gun beneath one of the pillows. Then he went to open the door.

"What do you mean, Jack isn't here?"
Annie asked Jack's housekeeper.

Ida Hoffman was a short woman, but what she lacked in vertical inches she made up for horizontally. Her round face was no more made for worry than her gregarious nature was suited to keeping secrets, and her response to Annie came out sounding more hopeful than convincing. "He had to run some errands?"

"Ida, this is important. Really important. Where did he go?"

Her smile wavered. "Oh, well, I'm not...I'll tell him you came by to see him, all right?"

"Why don't I come inside and wait for him?"

A single worry wrinkle appeared in the older woman's forehead. "I don't think that would be a good idea."

Either Jack had told Ida not to let Annie in, or he wasn't planning to be back for hours. She sighed. "Ida, you and I have always gotten along pretty well, I thought."

The housekeeper nodded, her smile returning. "Oh, yes."

"Are you unhappy about Jack and me getting married?"

"No, no. I'm delighted. Just delighted. I cried when I heard. Elopements are so romantic, aren't they? Running off to Vegas to get married..." Her bosom heaved in a happy sigh. "I just wish he would bring you here and settle down for once and for—but of course he will. I'm sure he will. He just has to...there are things he has to do first."

Ida was obviously torn between loyalty to Jack and her own romantic inclinations. Annie chewed on her lip. "At least tell me this. Has a woman called for him? Or maybe come by? She's short, dark-haired—" She broke off. Ida's stricken expression told her what she hadn't wanted to learn. "You didn't tell her where Jack was, did you?"

"I don't—that is, I wouldn't—oh, I can't *do* this!" she wailed. "It isn't right. It just isn't right. He shouldn't have asked me. 'Tell anyone who asks where I am,' he said, 'except for Annie.' I argued, but he wouldn't...only he couldn't have been thinking of *her* when he said that. I just can't believe he would—that he—'' Her lip quivered. ''Jack may be a bit wild, but he's a good boy at heart.''

''He's not a boy anymore, Ida. And he's in trouble. I have to find him.'' When the housekeeper just stared at her, distressed but still loyal, she said, ''You can't tell me where he is if I ask, can you?''

She shook her head sadly.

''Well, could you tell me where you think that woman might be right now? The one with the long dark hair? You wouldn't be answering my question about where Jack is,'' she assured the housekeeper. ''You'd just be guessing about something and sharing your guess with me. Unless— you're not worried that I'll find Jack doing something he shouldn't be, are you?''

Ida blinked. Distress flowed off of her round face as smoothly as water flows off a windshield, leaving her bright with optimism again. ''Oh, I'm sure you won't! He wouldn't do anything really wrong. He couldn't have known that woman would come here looking for him.''

Like hell he couldn't, Annie thought grimly. But she kept that thought to herself.

''Now, Jack, I drove a long way to see you.'' Leah smiled. She'd slicked dark, reddish-brown lipstick over lips that Jack suspected had been plumped up with silicone. ''Aren't you going to ask me in?''

''No.'' Jack resisted the urge to look behind her and to the left, where Fred should be sitting in his blue Ford Escort, watching. ''What are you doing here?'' Surely Leah wasn't the one he was waiting for.

She leaned closer and put her hand on his chest. ''Ask me in and I'll tell you. Or maybe you'd rather I showed you.''

"Leah, I wasn't interested before I got married. What makes you think I'd be interested now?"

Those puffy lips turned down in a pout. "I quit ICA, so your stupid rule about co-workers doesn't apply anymore."

"I heard about that."

"Why, Jack! Did you try to call me at work? I'm flattered."

"I talked to Rebecca this morning, and she mentioned it." Jack didn't believe Leah had quit because of him. He had his share of male ego, but he couldn't believe this woman was so fixated on getting him in bed that she would quit a good job to pursue him. "It doesn't matter. There's another rule you may have heard of that applies. Fidelity."

"Oh, come on, honey." She walked her fingers down his chest. "You're not one of those uptight prigs who worries about that sort of thing."

He moved her hand away before it reached his belt. "What do you want, Leah?"

She leaned closer. "Let me come in and I'll tell you exactly what I want. In detail."

"If you don't tell me why you're here, I'm closing the door—with you on the outside."

"Oooh, threats. Is that nasty headache making you grouchy, Jack?"

"What makes you think I have a headache?" If she knew about his concussion, did that mean she was involved somehow? Or even responsible for it? Jack had a hard time taking the idea of Leah as his would-be killer seriously, but he couldn't ignore the possibility.

"I must have heard someone mention it." She put her hands on his shoulders and leaned her head back to meet his eyes.

Jack looked down at those sly, tilted eyes and the smiling mouth painted the color of dried blood. Was she here for the reason she kept implying—or was she here to kill him?

Neither seemed likely. Maybe she was connected to whoever had tried to kill him, and was supposed to—what? Distract him? Spend the night with him and then slip poison into his morning coffee?

Whatever her purpose, he wasn't going to learn much by keeping her standing outside his room. "You're right," he said. "I do have an ache that's bothering me."

"I can make it feel better, Jack." She wiggled up against him. "Much better."

His body knew when a female body was pressed up against it and responded accordingly. The rest of him didn't like it. "Maybe you could, at that." He took her shoulders and moved her back so he could look her over. She was wearing a stretchy little purple dress beneath an oversize leather jacket. Conceivably, she could have a weapon hidden under that jacket, or in one of the pockets. "Nice dress."

"You like it?"

"I suspect I'd like it even better without the jacket."

"Now you're getting the idea. I'd be glad to give you a better look, honey."

"Take off the jacket and I'll let you come in...to talk."

Her eyebrows lifted. "Kinky. Anything else you want me to take off before you'll let me in?"

He gave her a suggestive smile. "Whatever else I can talk you into. Or out of."

She chuckled and slipped the jacket off one shoulder at a time, turning the act into as much of a striptease as possible.

"Nice," he said, looking her up and down the way she expected him to. "Very nice." There couldn't be anything larger than a bobby pin hidden in that outfit, he decided, and held the door open wide. "So what are you doing out there in the cold? Come on in."

Should he leave the door open, he wondered as she

swayed past him, so that Fred could get inside quickly if
he needed to?

The idea made him feel foolish. He might not be up to
par physically, but surely he could handle this tiny slip of
a woman if she turned violent. And if all she had in mind
was seduction, he wouldn't need Fred's help.

He started to close the door.

Leah plastered herself up against his side, slipping her
arms around his waist. "Mmm, you feel nice and warm. I
don't think I'll need this jacket once you close out all that
chilly night air." She smiled wickedly. "Maybe not the
dress, either."

The phone rang. He tensed. "I'd better get that."

"You do that," she murmured, and let her jacket slip off
her shoulders and fall to the floor.

The phone rang again.

It had to be Fred. Was he letting Jack know that room
service was on the way? Or had he spotted Leah's accomplice? Jack needed to answer the phone quickly, before
Leah realized it wasn't going to ring a third time. His head
pounded. So did his heart as he sat on the bed, picked up
the receiver and said hello to a dial tone.

"Tell them you're busy," she said, sitting beside him on
the bed.

"No, no one's here," he said to no one while he slid his
hand beneath the pillow, his attention on the door he'd left
cracked open. Where was the damned gun?

Leah leaned into him and started pressing kisses to his
throat.

"Dammit—" There. His fingers closed around the pistol
butt.

"Relax, sugar," she said. "And get rid of whoever that
is." She put her hands on his shoulders—and pushed.

He fell back against the pillows, dropping the receiver.
But not the gun.

Leah followed him down, her hands and mouth avid.

The door crashed open. Jack yanked the gun out from under the pillow, swinging his arm to aim over Leah's shoulder, his finger on the trigger—and froze in horror.

"Get away from him," Annie said. She stood in the doorway, her eyes dark, her face pale.

His arm went limp. "My God, Annie, I nearly shot you!"

Leah looked over her shoulder. "Well, well. Look who's here. How awkward." She didn't sound the least bit discomposed.

Jack pushed her off of him and sat up, feeling sick. Annie was never going to believe him. God, how much more guilty could he possibly look? He'd argued with her, lied to her, left her house and refused to let her come with him—and then she found him here. In a motel room. With this female barracuda all over him. "Annie, this isn't—you have to let me explain."

Leah propped herself up on her elbow. Her dress was hiked up to her hips. She was smiling. "You do that, Jack. You can tell her we were having a business meeting. I'm sure she'll believe that."

Annie's lips thinned to a white line, holding anger in. "Jack and I have already talked to the Denver police about you. Keep going the way you have been and they'll be able to arrest you for stalking."

"Stalking? You've got to be kidding. You can't be so dumb you believe this was all my idea."

Annie bent, scooped the leather jacket off the floor and threw it at Leah. "Get out of here."

Leah tossed her head, sending some of her hair out of her face. "I don't think so. *You* weren't the one who invited me here."

"No one invited you, Leah," Jack said wearily. He stood, glanced at the gun still in his hand, and shook his head. "But for what it's worth, consider yourself invited to leave. Now."

She swung her legs off the bed. "You've got her wrapped around your little finger, don't you, honey? I think she actually believes you're my innocent victim."

Annie's eyes narrowed. She started for Leah. Jack stepped forward and grabbed her arm. Jack had never seen Annie get physically violent—but he'd never seen her quite this close to flame out, either. She was all but vibrating with anger.

She glared at him. "Let go of me!"

"Annie, she's needling you on purpose. She wants to start something."

"So? I know what she's trying to do, and I know what *you* were trying to do tonight, too, and don't think you're off the hook! But before I deal with you, I intend to get her bony butt out of here!"

"Bony?" That got Leah off the bed. "Listen, sister, just because you've got a few extra pounds yourself and can't keep your man satisfied—"

Annie tried to jerk out of Jack's grip.

The sound of footsteps outside had Jack's fingers tightening on the pistol he still held. His heart speeded up. He gave Annie a little shove, getting her out of the line of fire, lifted the gun—and Fred appeared in the doorway, dressed all in black. Jack had had to talk him out of blacking his face, too.

Jack sighed and lowered his arm.

Fred's square face managed to look worried and sheepish at the same time. "Thought you might need some help here."

"Sure. You can escort her—" Jack jerked his head in Leah's general direction "—back where she came from. Or anywhere else, as long as it's away from me." He set the gun down on the dresser.

"Uh—which 'her' do you want me to escort?"

"Which do you think? I—"

There was a loud, female shriek.

Jack turned. "Oh, hell."

Annie had a fistful of Leah's hair, right up near the scalp. "No more kicking," she said.

Leah spat at her.

Annie pulled on the hair she held. Hard. "Behave. Come on." She took a step toward the door, her grip on Leah's hair forcing the woman to follow. "You're leaving now."

Leah screeched and swung at Annie. Her hand wasn't closed in a fist, but spread to rake Annie's face with her nails. Annie ducked but had to let go of the woman's hair to get out of the way.

Leah struck out with her other hand.

Annie dodged, doubled her hand up in a fist and punched Leah in the face.

Leah shrieked again and threw herself at Annie.

Jack leaped into action. "Fred!" He went for Annie, wrapping both arms around her from behind, lifting her off her feet and turning to get her out of Leah's range.

Fortunately, Fred could move a lot faster than he could think. He was there in a second, pinning Leah's arms behind her back efficiently. His eyes met Jack's over the head of his squirming prisoner. "You didn't tell me you had a gun," he said reproachfully. "I hope you've got a license for it."

"What gun?" Jack said. His head was pounding. He felt dizzy and slightly sick to his stomach, and he wasn't sure his reaction had anything to do with his concussion.

"Room service!" called a cheerful voice from the doorway.

Everyone stopped moving—the two women being held captive and the two men holding them. Jack looked at the still-open door. A uniformed waiter stood behind a cart bearing covered dishes, his eyes growing wide as he took in the tableau in the room.

After a moment Annie said levelly, "You can let go of me now, Jack."

Chapter 12

"Maybe I should come back later," the waiter said, his face red.

"That might be a good idea," Jack agreed. The man fled, abandoning his cart. What did he think was happening in here—assault, kidnapping or something kinky involving all four of them? He glanced at Fred. "Do you suppose he's going to call some of your co-workers?"

Fred shook his head gloomily. "I hope not."

Annie tugged at her still-trapped arms. "Jack!"

He let go. "All right, but if you're going to take a swing at me this time, don't aim for my head, okay?"

Annie immediately stepped away from him. "Does your head hurt?"

"Like hell."

"Good."

Leah tried to wrench free of Fred's hold. "Let go of me, you moron! I'm going to kill her!"

Fred looked pained. "Now, I can't do that until you calm down."

Annie smiled. It wasn't a pleasant expression. "Not too smart of you to mention your plans in front of an officer of the law."

"What?" Leah went still, craning her head around to look at Fred incredulously. "You?"

"Yes, ma'am."

She relaxed suddenly, as if she were pleased by the news. "Maybe I should press charges against the bitch. She hit me."

"If you want to go down to the station, you can register a complaint," Fred agreed stolidly. "But so can Mrs. Merriman, if she wishes. Since I saw you strike the first blow, you might want to think about whether you want to do that or not."

Leah looked sulky and said something unflattering and almost certainly untrue about Fred's ancestry, adding that if he didn't let go of her she'd file a complaint against *him*. Fred did release her, but he stood close enough to grab her again if need be. "I'll walk you to your car, ma'am."

Leah gave Jack a cool smile. "I'll be in touch, honey. Let me know when you can slip away again."

Jack didn't dare speak. If he moved at all, he might throttle her.

Annie bent, grabbed the leather jacket from the floor and threw it at Leah. "Here. I think there's a vacant street corner down on Main, if you're looking for something to do tonight."

Leah opened her mouth to reply, but Fred took her elbow and propelled her out the door before she could say or do anything else. Jack closed it behind them, breathing a sigh of relief. One down. One to go...the one that mattered.

He turned and look at Annie. She was standing in the center of the room hugging herself, her expression tight and unreadable. "Annie? You okay? Where did she kick you?"

"My leg, but she barely got me." She held out her hand

and looked down at it. "My hand hurts, though. I didn't know it hurt that much to hit someone."

"It's better to aim for the stomach. No bones to bruise your knuckles on."

"I was aiming for her nose. I wanted to bloody it." She frowned as she opened and closed her hand a few times. "I've never hit anyone before. No one except my brothers, at least, and they don't count. I'm not a violent person."

"Could have fooled me for a few minutes there."

She slid him a quick, angry glance. "You look like hell. I hope your head is making you pay for your stupidity."

"It is." He came over to stand in front of her. "Annie, please. I have to explain about Leah and the motel room and everything."

"Damn right you have to explain." She moved away as if she couldn't stand to be near him, pausing by the TV, which was still muted. "When I figured out what you were up to I wanted to kill you myself."

"It isn't what it looked like." Desperate to make her understand, to make her *believe,* he followed her. "I didn't ask her here."

"You asked her in once she got here, though, didn't you? Dammit, Jack, how could you *do* that?" She spun around and started to pace.

"I know what it must have looked like." And what she must think. He grabbed her shoulders and turned her to face him. "But it wasn't like that. I wouldn't do that to you."

"I *know* that." She shrugged his hands off. "I'm not an idiot, Jack."

She knew that? And she looked…irritated. Exasperated. Not hurt or enraged or betrayed. "Annie? You believe me?"

"Of course I believe you. That doesn't mean I'm not furious."

He felt strange. Dizzy, and not from the concussion.

Something deep inside him loosened, something that had been wrapped up in a tight, small bundle for a very, very long time. "You believe me," he repeated uncertainly.

"I believe you about Leah. I *don't* believe that cocka-mamy story you fed me this afternoon about free-soloing that cliff." She scowled. "Quit grinning at me that way when I'm mad at you."

He couldn't help it. He felt too good not to grin. "You trust me."

"I don't trust you not to be an idiot! What were you thinking of, setting yourself up like bait?"

He blinked, surprised again. "How did you figure out that was what I was doing?"

"Well, what else would you be doing here? Once I calmed down, I knew you were up to something. You can be a real pain at times, but you're not quite as much of a jerk as you were pretending to be this afternoon."

"Thank you." He paused. "I think."

"Don't thank me. I haven't decided if I'm going to hit you or not. Of all the stupid, idiotic, harebrained ideas—you've got a concussion! You should be in bed, not chasing bad guys!"

"I wasn't going to chase anyone." Annie had been worried about him. That's why she was angry. Not because she believed what she had every reason to believe. Jack felt light and happy, and he just had to touch her. He started playing with a strand of her hair near her face. "The idea was to get him to come to me."

"Or her." Annie's voice was unsteady. "Don't do that."

"Or her," he agreed, looking at her mouth. "Don't do what?"

"That thing with my hair." His voice was firm. Her eyes were wistful. "This business of inviting your attacker to try again was not one of your brightest ideas, Jack."

Obediently he let go of her hair—and took her hand.

"Probably. I did get results, but I don't know what it means."

"You don't think that Leah...maybe you shouldn't do that, either."

He wasn't feeling *that* obedient. He continued to stroke the sensitive center of her palm with his thumb. "What were you saying about Leah?"

"Oh. Ah—you don't think she was Metz's partner? That she might have been the one who hit you on the head?"

"She's mean enough to do it, but she'd have to stand on a chair to reach that high." He shook his head at the image that evoked. "More important, I don't think she's bright enough to have been Metz's accomplice. She's in data entry, or was until she quit, so she might have been able to access shipping records, but altering them is another story." He liked the dazed look she got in her eyes when he circled the center of her palm with his thumb, so he did that some more. "I was expecting Herbie to show up, actually."

"Your boss?" She sounded surprised, then pleased. "I *said* it might be him, since he's such an expert on the system."

"So you did. Of course, he didn't show up. Leah did." He needed to taste her. Just a small taste. He lifted her hand, bringing it to his mouth so he could kiss the fleshy pad at the base of her thumb. "I still don't see how you knew what I was planning."

"I..." Her breath caught. "It seemed obvious. You stopped wanting me to move in with you right after the attack, and..." She frowned as if she'd lost track of what she was saying and pulled her hand away. "You need to stop distracting me if you want to talk about this."

"You know what?" He cupped her face with both hands. "I don't think I do want to talk right now. I like the distracting better."

Her eyes widened. "Jack, this isn't the right time. We have things we need to decide. I'm still mad at—"

He decided his mouth belonged on hers, and settled it there.

She went still. He stroked his tongue over her lips, pleasing himself with her taste. The quick punch of heat made him want to race, to take, but he managed to keep his mouth gentle and persuasive. His hands weren't so polite. His hands didn't want to ask, to court, to suggest.

He needed to touch her. Now. Everywhere. Her shoulders and the sweet dip of her waist...the soft, rounded shape of her hip, and the smooth vulnerability of her throat.

One at a time, her hands slid up to his neck. Her mouth opened to his. Their tongues touched, tested, began a slow duel. His hunger must have arced between them then, like the leap of electricity when a circuit is closed, because her hands turned greedy, too. She wrapped her arms around him and held on.

More. He needed more. "Annie," he said to the soft skin of her cheek, and kissed her there.

He was supposed to wait. He'd intended to wait, to give her time, because Annie needed to feel in control. She needed to feel that making love was her decision. But he whispered her name to the dusky scent trapped beneath her ear and licked her there, enjoying her shivery reaction as much as his own arousal, marveling at her.

How could one small woman be so brimful with life and passion? How could she fear the very life that filled her to overflowing?

"Annie," he said again, between kisses. "I don't want to wait. Don't make me wait for you any longer."

Annie's mind was mazed by the dizzy haste of desire. She pulled her head back, seeking air and clarity, and found his eyes on her—dark eyes, bitter-chocolate eyes. "Your head. You have a concussion. You shouldn't..."

"I won't pass out on you." He slid his hands up and down her body in a long, luxurious stroke, a smooth sculpting of flesh and need. "I need your skin against mine, Annie. I want to breathe you in and make you crazy." He cupped her face again and brushed his lips across hers, a gentle salute at odds with the way his hips pressed the hard length of him against her stomach. "You trust me. You proved that, and I... Don't keep yourself away from me this time. I need you."

And I love you, she thought. And all at once, that was enough—that she loved him. A bubble of feeling that had been trapped somewhere beneath her heart suddenly broke free, tickling on the way up like a sneeze about to happen. The bubble burst as soon as it reached the surface, there and gone in the same instant.

Bubbles, she thought, her head as light in that second as her heart was. Bubbles and instants and moments, rising one after another and bursting. That was all she had. All she ever could have. All the planning and thinking in the world wouldn't give her back one second of the past, or protect her from the future. She wanted to laugh and cry and kiss Jack.

There was no safety. Not in love. Not in life.

"Yes," she told him, smiling as she pulled his mouth back to hers. "Yes."

His mouth wasn't polite this time. It ate at hers, making her head swim so delightfully it seemed only natural when her feet left the ground. It wasn't until his mouth left hers that she opened her eyes and realized that he'd swept her off her feet and into his arms. Literally. And stood there grinning at her, pleased with himself.

"Your head," she protested, her arms circling his neck.

"I can make it to the bed. It's only three feet away." He proved that was true by carrying her there and easing her down on the rumpled covers, following her down, propping himself up on one elbow.

His eyes were as serious as she'd ever seen them when he looked down at her. "I want to take my time with you," he said. He reached for the first button of her shirt. Cloth brushed against her sensitized skin as he freed that button from its buttonhole. "But I want you awfully damned bad." Another button was eased out, and her shirt parted more. "If I lose it again, the way I did on the roof, tell me." One more button. "I'll slow down if you tell me I'm rushing you. I promise."

Funny how little air there was in the room, and how hot that air was. Lungs, heart, skin—all tingled with heat. "Should I also tell you if you're going too slow?"

His eyes lit with delight. "Too slow, huh?" And he grabbed the hem of her shirt and jerked it up, still partly buttoned, yanking it over her head. An eye blink later he had her bra unfastened and whisked away.

He gave her no chance to feel self-conscious. He brushed his fingertips back and forth across the peaked tip of one breast, sending ribbons of sensation from her nipple to her stomach, making the muscles there contract. Then he cupped the other breast, admiring what he saw with a pleased smile. And then with his lips.

When his tongue teased her nipple, those delicate ribbons of sensation became sharp twists of pleasure. She ran her hands over his hair, enjoying the softness there before moving on to the warmth of his skin, marveling at the way his textures changed from nape to throat to the hard line of his jaw. When he suckled her, she felt the action in the movement of his cheeks and in the quick throb between her legs.

She tugged on his sweatshirt. "I want you naked," she said, feeling free and daring and greedy. "I want you entirely naked."

He lifted his head. His mouth was wet from suckling her.

His eyes were hot. "Good idea." He grabbed the hem of his sweatshirt, yanked it off in one quick motion and tossed it to the floor.

Annie loved Jack's chest. She ran her hands over it, fascinated by the way his muscles worked beneath skin when he moved.

He grinned, wrapped his arms around her and rolled.

She ended up on top, her legs and his tangled together, his chest hard and hot and smooth against her breasts. When she leaned back, her nipples brushed his chest. "Hey," she said. "I like this."

"I thought you would," he murmured. "You like being in charge. But you're still overdressed." He slid his hands between them and unsnapped her jeans.

She froze, abruptly self-conscious. "I wanted you naked first."

He smiled. "In a minute." He cupped the back of her head, his long fingers splayed firmly at the base of her skull, and he kissed her—a deep, leisurely kiss, as if he felt no urgency, no rush, no reason to do anything but pleasure her mouth for the next hour or two.

But his hands weren't patient. They were in a hurry to unfasten her jeans, and they made hasty work of getting them out of his way, pushing jeans and panties down but not off, leaving her suddenly, shockingly bare. He cupped her bottom with one hand, the back of her head with the other, slid one leg between hers, and kissed her and kissed her.

His leg moved. Her breath caught. Rough denim rubbed against the inside of her thighs, against even more sensitive flesh. The sensation was delicious. Maddening. His tongue teased, his leg insisted, and abruptly she sat up and pushed her jeans and panties off. And reached for his zipper.

There was a very large bulge right beneath that zipper. She had to be careful—and she had to make him feel some fraction of what she felt. So she pulled the zipper down slowly, her knuckles pressing against that bulge, easing the zipper down a little at a time....

"Annie," he said, his voice hoarse, "you've got the right idea, but I might die before you finish." His hands pushed hers aside. In a few quick motions he'd shucked off his jeans.

That distracted her. She stared at him, at the whole naked glory of him sprawled across the bed—his chest and shoulders, thighs and hips, and the part of him that jutted out from a dark, curly patch of hair.

He was beautiful.

She reached out and touched him *there,* her fingers skimming skin as silky-soft as the muzzle of a horse. There was a drop of moisture at the tip, and she wondered suddenly what it would taste like. Annie had never kissed a man that way, but he made her want to do things she'd never done.

Curious, she wrapped her fingers around him and bent.

He groaned and grabbed her shoulders. "You will never know how much I *don't* want to stop you. But I'm hanging on by a thread here. And you're not ready."

She smiled, feeling vaguely shy and very pleased, and squeezed him. "Yes, I am."

He groaned again, his fingers digging into her shoulders. "No. You're not." He pushed her back then, rolling her onto her back and sat up to look down at her. "Let me show you what I mean." His fingers went to the place where she ached most for his touch, and teased her there— lightly, lightly, just stirring the hair.

"Jack—" She reached for him.

Gently he took her hands and held them out to either side of her. "You aren't ready, Annie. You won't be ready until you're as crazy with needing me as I am with needing you. Until you're ready to beg or scream."

Why would her heart pound suddenly with what felt like fear? "I—I'm not a screamer."

He just smiled and lowered his head. And showed her.

Had she thought she knew what desire was? She'd been wrong. Horribly wrong. Wrong, too, to think she knew this man. Jack was ruthless. He had no mercy in him, none at all. Despite the hunger that made his body tense and tremble, his breathing ragged, he was determined to take her to a place she'd never been, and had only dimly imagined.

She hit the first peak hard. He gave her no time to catch her breath. The sound of her cry still echoed in her mind when he sent her on a new climb, forcing her up where there was no safety, nothing to hold on to except him. His mouth took hers again and again; his fingers and the long, hard strength of his body drove her crazy. Time came loose, breaking up into ragged moments and fragments of sensation.

At last, at last, he sheathed himself and rose on top of her. She quivered, every part of her open for him. Desperate for him. He thrust inside.

And she screamed.

Jack held Annie close in the quiet moments after sanity shattered, before the world had finished re-forming itself around them. His chest heaved. He was sweaty and exhausted and his head hurt, but the rest of him felt better than he ever had in his life.

Except for being terrified.

She hadn't said it, he reminded himself. She hadn't said the words he didn't want to hear.

Yet he'd seen them in her eyes. Felt them in the way she touched him. Jack held Annie close while his heartbeat slowly steadied, but he wanted to run fast and far. He wanted to escape the trickery of those unspoken words, the broken promises. And the hope. The worst of it was the hope.

Her head was nestled on his shoulder. She stirred, tilting her head back to look at him with smug, sleepy eyes. "You don't look as relaxed as I feel. Maybe we should try it again and see if we can mellow you out properly."

She made him smile. In spite of everything, she made him smile. "Good idea. Unfortunately, my muscles have melted. I can't move." He ran his finger along the elegant line of her collarbone. He'd never seen her so beautiful, all drowsy and sated. And naked. The naked part was wonderful. "Have I mentioned how gorgeous you are without your clothes?"

Her cheeks turned pink. "I don't think you did."

"I've fantasized, of course. But the reality is much, much better." If he could keep her from saying those words, he thought—and keep himself from thinking about them—they would be okay. They would stay friends.

"About your melted muscles…do you think if we wait a few minutes they might begin to, ah, firm back up?"

He chuckled. "I love a greedy woman." The moment the words were out of his mouth he stiffened. Love? What was he thinking of? Annie would either think the word meant something—that he'd used it on purpose and begin expecting more than he could give her—or she'd realize he didn't mean it, and be hurt.

Quickly, he changed the subject. "I'm still wondering how you knew what I was up to." He ran his finger down her breastbone.

She was still smiling, but the glow was gone. He wanted to kick himself. "Well, there was the way you talked about needing time."

"You said the same thing."

"That's me. You aren't like that, wanting to mull things

over forever. But mostly what tipped me off was the fact that you'd lied about being attacked.''

"I could have sworn you bought that.''

She grimaced. "For a little while I did, when I was too spitting mad to think straight. Once I calmed down I knew better.''

"You did, huh?'' His thumb started making tiny, idle circles between her breasts.

"You wouldn't climb when you were upset. You might leave town or get into a fight or pull some other dumb stunt, but you wouldn't climb a cliff in that condition. So I figured that if you'd lied to me about that, it must mean you were doing something you didn't want me to know about. Something to draw the killer out. I wondered if maybe you'd remembered the attack.''

"I wish I had.''

She sighed. "Pity. Anyway, the more I thought about it, the more obvious it was that you'd decided to get me out of the way so you could play hero." She frowned. "While you had a concussion.''

"That's why I made sure I had backup.''

"Fred." She didn't look impressed.

"Among others.'' His didn't think this was a good time to mention that her brother had intended to help him with his plan. He hoped Fred had thought to call Ben and let him know he didn't need to stake out the parking lot at two this morning, after all. "My plan did work," he pointed out. "Even if I'm not sure what it means, I did get Leah to come after me.''

"Maybe. And maybe she was here for exactly the reason she wanted us to think.''

"She knew about my attack.''

Annie waved that away. "That doesn't prove anything. She could easily have heard about that when she was at Binton's earlier.''

"Just because we can't see the connection doesn't mean it doesn't exist. It's stretching coincidence too far for her to show up right after I put word out through Rebecca about the attack—and that my memory of it was coming back."

She sat up suddenly. "You did what?"

"I had to do something to make my enemy come after me," he said reasonably. "I wanted it to happen at the time and place of my choosing."

"You might as well have hung a sign around your neck reading Come Kill Me Before I Remember Who You Are!"

"I wasn't going to let anyone kill me. I've got a vested interest in winning this one."

"This isn't about winning or losing! God, of all the times for you to turn competitive, this has to be the worst, the dumbest, most ill-chosen—and I'd like to know just *why* you thought you had to lie to me. Why did you leave me out of your plans? I could have been your backup."

His eyebrows lifted in surprise. "That's obvious, isn't it? I didn't want you to get hurt."

She fell silent. After a moment she said quietly, "I don't think you can keep me from being hurt, Jack. I think it's probably inevitable."

He had a feeling she wasn't talking about physical pain. He swallowed. "I don't want to hurt you, Annie. Ever."

"I know." Her eyes lowered. After a moment she put her hand, palm flat and fingers spread, on his chest. "Have I mentioned that I'm crazy about your chest?"

"Not lately." To help her distract them both, he drifted his fingers slowly up the slope of her breast, stopping just short of the peak. "You know what? I think my muscles are starting to firm up again."

"Are they, now? Maybe you should show me what you mean."

He took her hand and put it where his meaning was most

obvious. Her eyes widened. Then her fingers tightened around him. The smile she slanted him brimmed over with mischief and something more, something he refused to think about. So he kissed her, and one thing led to the next with delightful inevitability.

It seemed that Annie wanted to be on top that time. She told him to just lie still and rest his poor head. He teased her about wanting to be in charge. She blushed and laughed, and she was smiling when he entered her several minutes later. He watched her eyes change, turning hazy with need.

This time they were both willing to go slowly, to savor. This time they hit the peak together and tumbled off in a sweaty, tangled mass of arms and legs and sated bodies.

This time, they didn't talk afterward.

Chapter 13

Annie liked sleeping with Jack. She liked waking up beside him even better, and as she blinked her way back to consciousness the next day, she decided that this was as much of a turning point in their relationship as making love had been. She might not be able to claim his love. But she would have his nights and his mornings, his warmth beside her when she went to sleep and when she woke up. That was a lot.

Jack had slept sprawled on his back, hogging the middle of the bed. She'd slept sprawled on top of him, with his arm around her waist and his heartbeat beneath her ear. When she felt him stir she smiled. "You awake?"

Silence for a moment. "Is it noon yet?"

"No."

"Dawn?"

"Probably."

He sighed. It made his chest rise and fall beneath her. She liked that, too. "I'd forgotten how you are in the mornings."

"Happy," she said, wiggling around so she could prop herself up on her elbows and look at him. "I'm happy this morning, Jack."

"I'm glad," he said softly. He reached out to toy with her hair, but his eyes were troubled. "But…"

Annie's heart gave a sudden, hurtful kick. "*But* is not a good word for you to use this morning."

"I'm happy, too. But I shouldn't have let you stay."

"I don't recall you doing any *letting*. Seducing, yes. Letting, no."

"I wasn't thinking last night. It's too dangerous for you to be around me right now." He looked away. "Once things are cleared up…I don't want anything to happen to you, Annie."

She sat up slowly, letting the sheet pool in her lap. He was trying to put distance between them, and it wasn't just because of the danger. She knew that, whether he did or not.

Damn the man. He wasn't going to make it easy for her to prove that he could depend on her, was he? "So what do you plan to do? Walk around with a T-shirt that reads Shoot Me for a few weeks? If no one does, will that make it safe for me to be with you?"

"I know what I *won't* do. I won't expose you to danger."

She shook her head in disgust. "And what do you think I'll be doing while you're taking care of things in your manly way?"

"What you've done all along. Stay with your brothers."

Anger was better than hurt, but neither were going to get her what she wanted. Annie swung her feet off the bed and grabbed her shirt and panties from the floor. "Wrong answer. You're stuck with me now."

"Annie, I can't let you move in with me until everything is cleared up. Until it's safe."

But there was no such thing as safety—not in life, not in love. She'd finally figured that out. Annie stood and gave him a long, cool look. "What makes you think you can stop me?" And turned and stalked into the bathroom.

He couldn't stop her.

Jack thought of leaving while Annie was in the shower, slinking away like the coward he was. His feet itched to go, but he couldn't do it. He couldn't leave Annie here alone when his would-be killer might still show up at the motel looking for him.

She emerged from the bathroom damp and sexy and not speaking to him. He grimaced and went to take his own shower. When he came out, he found coffee waiting, along with a silently steaming woman. "Thanks for ordering the coffee," he said, giving her a hopeful smile. Maybe she was ready to be apologized to.

She looked him over coolly. Her expression said plenty about her opinion of what she saw, but she didn't say a word.

That worried him. A lot. Annie had a temper. He knew that, and usually it didn't bother him. But usually her temper led her to tell him in detail why she was mad and exactly what a jerk he was. He poured a cup of coffee and drank half of it, trying to wait her out, but he couldn't stand it. "Dammit, why don't you go ahead and tell me what you think of me?"

Her eyebrows went up. "I don't use that kind of language."

When he walked out of the motel room, he didn't really think she'd follow. She wasn't too happy with him right now. But she was right there with him when he got to his car. "You don't want to leave your car here, do you?" he said reasonably.

"I'm going with you."

That was all she said, and her expression was still stony. But for some reason, his heart lifted. "All right," he said, sliding in and unlocking the passenger door. "But you're getting out at your house."

"Only if you push me out on my butt." She pulled the seat belt across and clicked it shut. "And then you won't have to worry about who's trying to kill you, because Ben will do it."

Once Annie had broken her silence, she went on to make a few things clear. By the time they pulled up in front of the big old house he hated, she'd told him that barring his door to her wouldn't work. She was his wife now. His home was her home. She'd call a locksmith to let her in if she had to. Or she might just camp out in the front yard. She didn't think Ida would be able to keep her locked out for long, even if Jack could. He couldn't.

"I could go back to Denver," he growled as he got out of his car. "That's what I probably should do, anyway. So I can get to the bottom of things."

She got out, too. "I can go to Denver, too," she said sweetly—and slammed the car door. Hard. "I couldn't camp out in front of your apartment, but I could stay close enough often enough that someone with a ridiculously overdeveloped sense of protectiveness might think I was in danger."

Jack started to run a hand over his hair, winced when his fingers touched the knot on his skull, and gave up.

He felt too much. Dammit, why did she keep doing this to him? He didn't want to feel all these emotions swirling around inside him—anger, fear, disappointment, relief, worry. At least the fear and the worry made sense. He couldn't stand it if anything happened to Annie. The relief wasn't as logical. It had hit the moment he realized she'd followed him out of the motel, that she was determined to stick with him no matter how angry she was.

He didn't have the foggiest idea where his anger and disappointment were coming from.

Annie followed him up to the porch in stiff silence. When they reached the door he took her elbow. "Annie..."

She slid him a glance every bit as haughty as any her orange cat might have given him, had he been rude enough to touch the beast without permission.

"Would you really camp out in the front yard?"

"I said I would."

His lip curled in scorn. "Right. You said you'd stay with me in sickness and in health, too. That promise got old pretty quick, didn't it?"

"I'm here now. And I'm staying."

Well, he thought, his lips tight as he fit his key in the door, at least now he knew where the anger was coming from—the same place where it had lurked, sullen and immune to reason, for the last two months. "I guess I'm supposed to take you at your word."

"Maybe not yet," she said, stepping past him into the entry hall. "But you will. Sooner or later, you'll see that I mean it."

He was frowning as he went inside after her. Deep down, he *was* taking her at her word. In spite of the anger, in spite of the way she'd let him down before, he believed her this time. Annie would do whatever she had to do in order to be with him—whether he liked it or not.

What was different? Was he fooling himself, or had something really changed?

Dumb question. Of course something had changed. They'd made love. Everything had worked out the way he'd planned; once Annie had gone to bed with him, she'd felt committed to him.

And that was where the disappointment was coming from.

He shook his head, disgusted at himself. This was what

he'd wanted to happen, even if he hadn't been thinking about his plan last night. Why in the world would her reaction disappoint him now?

She was watching him warily, her own unsteady mix of emotions showing in her eyes. He was being a real ass about this, wasn't he? He sighed. "You want some coffee?"

"I guess so." She didn't sound enthusiastic. "Have you thought about what you're going to do with this place?"

Mostly he tried to think about this house as little as possible. "I can't do anything with it. Ida loves it here. She doesn't want to retire."

"Oh, Jack." She shook her head, her eyes softening. "Just when I'm ready to swear you're the most insensitive man on earth, you say or do something impossibly sweet like that."

He frowned. "Kids and puppies are sweet. Valentine's Day is sweet. I am *not* sweet."

"Not many people would keep a huge white elephant like this just because their housekeeper needs a job. It must cost a fortune in taxes, maintenance and insurance. Then there's Ida's salary."

"I can afford it." The subject of his inheritance made him edgy, and he started toward the kitchen. "I'm not planning to spend any of the money my aunt left me on myself. It might as well go toward keeping the house so Ida can stay here."

She followed him. Her voice sounded troubled. "You don't want anything to do with your aunt, do you? Even now that she's dead. You're still really angry with her."

"I'm not angry. It's just too late for the money to help." He thought of all the times when his mother had needed the money she should have inherited from her father. Times when he'd hardly seen her because she was working two jobs, trying to get enough money together to pay whatever utility someone was threatening to cut off. Times when she'd been sick and had gone to work anyway, unable to afford time off or a visit to the doctor.

Not that she'd let Jack go without medical care when he'd needed it. She'd always found a way, even if it meant begging her sister for money. "My aunt didn't think it was right to go against her father's wishes," he said bitterly. "She helped my mom occasionally, but only if it involved me."

"Your grandfather disinherited your mother, didn't he?"

"Yeah." Jack sometimes wished he could have met his grandfather so he could have spat in the old man's eye. "I don't want his money."

"Why don't you give it away, then? The house and the money both. There are bound to be several charities that could use a place like this, and you could make retaining Ida as housekeeper part of the deal."

Jack stopped in the middle of the hall and turned to stare at her. With one simple, sensible suggestion she'd exploded all the illusions he'd been hiding behind, illusions that he'd taken for reality. He didn't want to give up the house. He hated it. He didn't want to be here. But he didn't want to give it up. What kind of sense did that make?

He was still dealing with the echoes from that explosion when Ida came hurrying up the hall, wiping her hands on a kitchen towel.

"I thought I heard you, Jack! And Annie, too! Mrs. Merriman, I mean," she corrected herself, beaming. "I'll have some breakfast on the table in two shakes. I am so glad— that is—you *are* staying, aren't you?"

Annie shot Jack a look. "Oh, yes, I'm staying. And please—I've been Annie to you forever. Let's not change that."

"Well..." Ida flushed with pleasure. "If that's what you want. But, oh my, I don't have the place ready for you.

The sheets...I don't even know which bedroom you'll be using...?'' The last statement drifted up at the end into a question she directed at Jack.

Damn. Chances were, Annie wouldn't be interested in sharing the couch in the parlor with him. ''We'll figure it out and let you know,'' he muttered.

''Of course,'' Ida said, and started to turn away. ''Oh, I almost forgot.'' She dug into the pocket of her apron. ''I was so excited about Annie being here—but this must be important, because he was calling from some teensie little country. One of those places with a name I can't say to save me. I told him where you were, just like you wanted me to.'' She paused to give him a reproachful look. Ida hadn't approved of his plan to keep Annie in the dark about where he was. ''He said he would try calling you there, but now you're here, so he may have missed you.''

''*Who* called, Ida?''

''Oh, didn't I say? That nice Mr. Deerbaum from ICA.'' She held out the scrap of paper. ''I made a note of it,'' she said proudly.

''When did he call?'' Probably last night, he thought. Ida was a fantastic cook and a meticulous housekeeper, but she either garbled messages or forgot them altogether.

''About an hour ago. I—'' The phone rang. ''Maybe that's him again. I'll get it.''

But Jack was already halfway down the hall.

''Hello?''

''Jack, you son of a bitch, I've been looking for you!'' There was an unusual amount of static on the line, but that hearty voice had no trouble making itself heard over the buzzing. ''Why are you hanging out in motels instead of staying home in bed with your new wife?''

''I was hoping to coax Metz's killer out of hiding.''

''The police said Metz killed himself.''

''I think they're wrong. I think he became a liability to

whoever was in it with him. Did you try calling me at the motel?''

"Called you at home from the airport, called you at the motel from the plane, then had to call you again from the plane because you wouldn't stay put. I'm over the Atlantic right now, and it costs a fortune to call from one of these damned commercial jets." He gave a quick bark of laughter. "Good thing I've got a fortune! Now, I don't want you playing Hercule Poirot anymore, Jack. Too risky."

Jack's voice hardened. "I can't let it go. Not when there's still someone on the ICA payroll who helped Metz steal from the organization—and from the people we're supposed to help."

"Damnation, you think I'm dropping the ball? Amos Deerbaum drop the ball? No way in hell, boy, no way in hell! I read your report—makes it clear Metz had someone else helping him. No other way it could have gone down, eh? But I can take it from here. Should have done it before, but I didn't realize you were damn fool enough to put yourself at risk! Wanted to finish up my little trip first, but this is more important."

With genial obscenity Deerbaum went on to exhort Jack to quit getting his brains bashed in, then offered him lewd advice on how to spend the next several days while he healed and the police caught the culprit.

He also offered Jack the keys to his own mountain cabin.

"You deserve it after all you've been through! And don't worry about the investigation. I've got the money and the balls to kick some official butt," Deerbaum boomed. "I'll get the damned police to do their job. You be sure to pick up those keys—get you and your little bride tucked out of the way where no one can find you. That's an order, Jack— ICA needs your brains inside your skull!" He gave his distinctive bark of a laugh and disconnected.

Jack was frowning when he hung up and met Annie's eyes.

"What did he say?" she asked. "Is he going to investigate?"

"He says he's going to make sure the police get moving on the investigation. I'm supposed to stay out of it now."

"Why do you look so worried, then? The police are better equipped to investigate a crime than you are."

"True." The muscles along his shoulders and neck had tightened, and his head was aching again. He made an effort to relax. "I guess I'm having trouble letting go. For a long time I've been the only one who cared enough to keep digging. Now I'm supposed to step back and let someone else handle everything." His frowned deepened. "It would have been nice if Deerbaum had decided to 'kick some official butt' a couple months ago."

Now she was frowning, too. "What kind of man is Deerbaum? Will he do what he says? If he does, you'll be out of danger. The investigation wouldn't stop even if…if something did happen to you."

"He's tough, but fair, and he's never gone back on his word that I know of. The only thing we butt heads over is his trophy hunting. He does like to get his way. If Deerbaum puts pressure on the police, they'll feel it." He rubbed the back of his neck, trying to ease the tension and rid himself of an uneasy feeling he didn't understand. "This is kind of anticlimactic, isn't it? One phone call, and suddenly everything is over but the shouting."

Her forehead pleated. "Not quite. Until the killer knows that you aren't involved anymore, you're still in danger."

"Actually, Deerbaum had a suggestion about that, too. He offered me the use of his cabin to get me out of sight…and for a belated honeymoon." Suddenly he felt a little better at being shut out of his own investigation. A week in the mountains alone with Annie sounded like a slice of heaven.

"Oh." She chewed on her lip.

"Apparently his land butts up against the Rocky Mountain National Park." He put his hands on her shoulders and eased her closer. "You know how gorgeous it is around there at this time of year, Annie. Deerbaum's place ought to be pretty special. The man likes to have everything first-class. And it will be private, a great deal more private than—"

Ida called down the hall. "Breakfast is almost ready. I do hope you're both hungry!"

Jack grinned. "See what I mean?" He slid his hands up and down her arms and thought about the other places he wanted to touch her, places he'd barely begun to explore last night. He didn't think he would ever get enough of touching Annie. "Deerbaum said he would call his care-taker and tell him to leave us the spare set of keys. What do you say? Want to take off on a honeymoon after breakfast?"

She didn't look swept away by the idea. "Getting you out of sight is a good idea, but I've got responsibilities here. I'm supposed to teach on Tuesdays and Thursdays, and I've got some jobs lined up."

"Come on, Annie. Surely you can find someone who will substitute for you if you tell them you're going on your honeymoon."

"Well…Karen might be able to take my classes for a week. I could ask her. I do have a detailed lesson plan to give her. But I have a job today I can't put off."

"I can help with that. I don't just stand around with my clipboard and tell people what to do on a site, you know. I've laid pipes and dug ditches, and I can tell one end of a hammer from the other pretty well."

"Of course. But those jobs next week—"

"Annie— Isn't it time to think about giving up your handyman work?" If she was going to go away with him, she would have to. "It was supposed to be temporary, anyway, wasn't it?"

She opened her mouth, then closed it again without saying anything. Her eyes held a hint of panic.

"I'm not trying to pressure you." Like hell he wasn't. The anger licked up, trying to make him say things he knew he'd regret. He turned away. "We'll talk about it later."

"Jack." She put her hand on his arm. "I'm not good at sudden changes. It hit me that I'd be leaving Highpoint soon, and not just for a honeymoon. It's scary."

Annie did intend to go with him. That was what counted. He put his hand over hers. "It'll be okay, Annie. You'll see."

"Of course it will. I'll adjust." She nodded firmly, as if she were trying to convince herself. "If you're going to work with me today, wear old clothes. We'll be painting Mrs. Northrop's garage. But you've forgotten something."

"What's that?" He stroked his fingers along hers.

"You haven't apologized for trying to ditch me earlier."

"I got the idea you'd already decided to quit being mad at me."

"I wasn't mad. I was furious."

He grinned. "See? You used the past tense. You aren't mad anymore."

She considered that for a second. "You're very annoying, you know that?"

"Yeah." He bent and gave her a kiss that he intended to be quick, but the taste of her made him forget haste, breakfast, Ida and everything other than the magic of Annie. After a few deliciously forgetful moments, he straightened. "Let's go pick out a bedroom."

"Why? If we're leaving this afternoon—"

"I wasn't planning to sleep in it."

She was trying not to smile, but the corners of her mouth twitched. "I don't think—"

"I just took the biscuits out of the oven," Ida called.

Jack groaned and grabbed Annie's hand. "Come on. If we hurry we can get upstairs before she catches us. She won't come in without knocking. And if you make the same delightful noises you did last night, she won't knock."

"Jack!" Her cheeks were three shades beyond pink and her eyes were shining. "We can't just—just—besides, it would hurt Ida's feelings if we didn't eat the breakfast she's fixed."

"Yeah." He sighed. "I suppose it would." Reluctantly he let her tug him in the direction of the kitchen.

Ida had pulled out all the stops. She steered them into the dining room, where she'd covered the massive claw-footed table with a lace tablecloth that was older than Jack was. Two places were set with the good china and the ornate silverware Jack had sometimes had to polish as penance for his teenaged sins. He hated the stuff.

"I know you don't like a fuss, Jack," Ida said happily as she poured coffee from a silver coffeepot, "but I thought just this once we should make things special."

"I'm glad you fussed. It will be at least a week before you can drag us into the dining room again. Annie and I are planning to take a little trip together. We'll be leaving this afternoon."

"A honeymoon?"

He grinned and nodded.

"That's wonderful. Just wonderful." Ida heaved a huge, happy sigh. She was humming the wedding march under her breath when she left.

Annie wanted to talk over breakfast. Normally Jack would have obliged her, but he was distracted. Was it ego that made him want to keep investigating on his own? A need to stay in control? Or was it instinct?

"I get the feeling you're only about half with me," Annie said after polishing off the last of her eggs. "Where's the rest of you?"

"Sorry. I can't seem to shake this feeling..." He shook his head, unable to put it into words. "It just feels wrong to step back from the investigation."

"Do you think Deerbaum intends to sweep things under the rug, the way Herbie wants to? Or...is there any chance *he's* involved?"

He shook his head. He'd considered that. "There's just not enough money involved. For a man like Deerbaum, 'financial trouble' would come with a lot of zeros tacked onto the end—he'd be after millions of dollars, not the thousands that the sale of those drugs would have netted on the black market."

She reached for another biscuit, frowning thoughtfully. "So are you worried he isn't going to push the investigation the way he said he would?"

"He didn't get worked up about the thefts until I got hit on the head, and I have to wonder if he'll lose interest."

"Tell me something. Did you inherit a lot of money from your aunt?"

"What does that have to do with anything?"

"Humor me." She split open the biscuit neatly.

"All right. Yes, I inherited a pretty good chunk of money. No, I'm not going to touch it—not for anything except keeping the house up and paying Ida." Had any woman except Annie asked him that question, he would have thought she was seeing dollar signs in her future. But not Annie. There was no one like Annie, no one in the whole, wide world. He ought to know. He'd seen a pretty big slice of it, and he'd never met a woman who came close.

Nevertheless, fear pricked him. Annie said she was going with him when he left on his next job, but she wasn't happy about it. He was probably a selfish bastard to make her leave Highpoint—but he couldn't lose her. He *wouldn't* lose her.

Even if it meant giving up his job?

"I was thinking that if you're not convinced that Deerbaum and the police will do everything they should, you could hire a P.I. That can be pretty expensive, though. If you don't want to touch your inheritance, we probably couldn't afford it." She chuckled. "For sure I couldn't, anyway."

We. The sound of that simple pronoun hit Jack like a clapper striking a bell. The echoes rolled around in his mind while he considered her suggestion. Surely, he decided, his dislike for his grandfather's money wasn't as important as knowing that he—and therefore Annie—was out of danger. And the only way to be absolutely sure of that was to see that the killer was identified and locked up. "We'll have to pass through Denver to get to Deerbaum's cabin. I guess I could talk to someone."

"It wouldn't hurt." She slathered strawberry jam on her biscuit. "It's a good thing we're getting away from Ida's cooking. Very much of this and I wouldn't fit in my clothes anymore."

"Annie."

She glanced at him.

"I want you to be happy." He needed to say more. All sorts of feelings were pressing up inside him, urging him to say more, but he didn't have the words. "Remember what I told you the day before I left for college?" Annie had still been in high school when Jack and Charlie had gone off to college, and she'd been upset at losing her brother and her friend.

She looked at him for a long moment, her eyes clouded

and unreadable. Then she touched his hand lightly. "You said we'd be friends forever. I remember."

"Think you can finish up without me?"

Annie glanced over at Jack and grinned. She'd let him use the paint sprayer while she tackled the trim on the detached garage, and his face was speckled with white paint. So were his hair, his shirt and his jeans. She must be pretty far gone, she thought, because she thought he looked awfully sexy covered in paint spatters. "You aren't cutting out early on me, are you?"

"I need to see the lawyer before we leave. I don't have any checks for the estate account—I've left all that in his hands. If I'm going to talk to some high-powered detective agency, I'd better have access to more funds than I've got in my own checking account right now."

"I suppose that's a decent excuse, as excuses go."

He came over and gave her a kiss. "You're a good boss, even if you do taste like paint. I'll be back to pick you up in an hour or so."

"I'll need to go home—I mean, to my old house—to pack before we leave."

"Tell you what. I'll see if Ben can swing by and pick you up."

She sighed. "You're trying to get him to baby-sit me, aren't you? Jack, I'm not in any danger."

"Probably not," he agreed. "Ben won't mind picking you up, though."

As soon as he left, Annie got back to work, humming because she was pleased with herself. She'd gotten Jack to dip into his inheritance. It was a start, she told herself as she stroked green paint along the last stretch of trim.

She didn't care what he did with the money. He could keep it, spend it, give it away—whatever suited him. She just wanted him to come to terms with his feelings for his aunt. He was frozen in place, she thought as she swished her brush in the can of paint solvent. Ever since his aunt's unexpected death, Jack had been unable to move forward because he wouldn't admit to the feelings that were holding him back.

Pretty much what he'd accused her of, she thought as she began putting up her painting gear. And he'd been right.

Annie didn't consider herself an expert on many things, but she understood a lot about grief. *Funny,* she thought. Jack was the one who had shown her that anger was a natural part of grieving. Why couldn't he admit he was angry at his aunt for dying?

Maybe because he hadn't admitted that he'd cared for her.

Annie sighed. Jack had a problem with the whole idea of love. But she thought she knew out how to deal with that. He wanted a friend. He needed someone he could count on. She would get him used to the idea of being loved, a little at a time. As long as she didn't use the words, didn't tell him what she really felt for him, he wouldn't panic and push her away.

That thought depressed her so much she had to turn the radio on extra loud and sing along to drown out her regrets.

Chapter 14

Jack pulled up in front of the McClains' home a little after one. He wished they were already on the road. Annie wasn't safe here. Deerbaum might be ready to rattle official cages, but he wouldn't be landing in New York for several hours, and it would be tomorrow before he could reach Denver. Who knew how long it would take the killer to realize that Jack's death wouldn't halt the investigation?

He knocked on the door. A moment later it swung open to reveal Annie's glowing face. "Jack, you'll never guess who's here! C'mon." She grabbed his arm. "Come see."

For one second, he had thought that glow was for him. "Mel Gibson?" he asked, keeping his voice light. "That other guy, Brad Somebody."

"Even better." She tugged him inside. "See?"

Standing in the arched entry to the living room was a lean, dark-haired man with watchful gray eyes—Duncan McClain, the middle brother. Duncan wasn't as husky as Ben or as lively as Charlie, but there was a silent power to the man that spoke of tests endured.

"Duncan," Jack said. "Good to see you again."

Duncan nodded. He seldom used two words when one would do—or one word when a nod or a glance was enough. "Annie's been telling me about your situation. I understand you're planning to hire a P.I. You have someone in mind?"

"Not yet."

"If you don't need to leave immediately, I can get you a name. Someone good."

Not for the first time, Jack wondered exactly what Duncan did in the Special Forces. He had some odd connections for an enlisted man. "I'd appreciate that."

Duncan nodded and headed for the phone in the kitchen. Annie started to follow, but Jack put a hand on her arm. "Annie, do you want to stay here for another day so you can visit with Duncan?"

She shook her head. "No, I want you where your attacker can't find you. Where you'll be safe."

It was typical of Annie that she didn't consider her own safety. Jack returned some comment, but his mind wasn't on the conversation. He was thinking about family. He was planning to take Annie away from her family and her home, and what was he offering her in their place? Friendship. Sex. A chance to face her fears and maybe rediscover a dream she'd once had. And all of that was important, he thought as the two of them entered the slightly shabby charm of the McClains' kitchen. But so was what she already had—the solidity of family, the kind of ties Jack had never possessed and couldn't give her.

Keeping Annie with him was right for him. He had no doubts about that. Somehow he had to make sure it was the right thing for her, too.

The investigator Duncan sent them to sure didn't resemble Magnum, PI, Annie thought wryly as they were escorted into the man's office. With his shiny bald head and shiny round glasses, Harold Straight looked more like an accountant. His office would have suited an accountant, too, with its rows of file cabinets and computer equipment. A very successful accountant, however. The chairs they sat in were leather. The file cabinets, like the desk, were hand-rubbed cherry, and the computer equipment looked state-of-the-art.

Jack outlined the situation. After asking a few questions, the investigator leaned back in his chair, tenting his fingers in front of him. "I'm inclined to agree that the motive for these crimes must be monetary. I have a suspect I intend to focus on, but I would prefer to get complete financial backgrounds on everyone in the ICA main office who might have the knowledge and the access to have created the fake shipment records. Obtaining such reports will be costly, however. Not all the information is available through public venues."

Jack shrugged. "I've got money from an inheritance. I can't think of anything better to spend it on."

That brought a twinkle to the eyes behind those round glasses. "Then you are a most unusual man."

"Who is it you suspect?" Jack asked.

"Leah Pasternak. She is almost certainly involved in some way."

Annie nodded. "I'll bet she wrote the anonymous letter I got."

"Possibly. In considering such a question, it often helps to look at the results of an action and see who benefited. In this case, the result of the letter was to bring Mr. Merriman back to the U.S. Presumably the person who wrote the letter thought that once Mr. Merriman was home again he would stop investigating. My next question is, would Ms. Pasternak have had access to the shipping records?"

"Yes," Jack said, "but Leah isn't bright enough to alter them undetectably. Whoever did that was good."

"But would the man who died—Metz—have had the necessary knowledge to instruct her?"

Jack frowned. "I'm not sure. I don't know enough about his background. I could accept Leah as Metz's accomplice based on her morals—or lack of them—but I have trouble thinking of her as some sort of criminal mastermind."

"But there is no evidence that we are dealing with an expert criminal, save the expertise involved in falsifying the shipping records. If Metz was able to teach an accomplice how to do that, his accomplice needn't be particularly clever. One of the things I find reassuring about this case, actually, is the clumsiness of the recent attack on you, Mr. Merriman. Had a professional killer been hired, you would not be alive now. I suspect Ms. Pasternak hired a thug with some experience of violence but no great skill. Her visit to you at the hotel supports that theory. No doubt she wanted to learn if you had remembered anything about the attack."

Annie felt a profound sense of relief. "You really think Leah might be behind everything?" Leah was vicious enough to be dangerous, but if she *was* the one trying to kill Jack, Annie had no doubt that this prissy, competent little man would catch her. "But what about the attack on Jack overseas?"

"That may have been what Mr. Merriman originally surmised, an attempt by local black market agents to frighten him away. I don't want you to relax your guard, however. Remember that we don't have all the facts yet."

Yet everything he'd said made so much sense. It was only as the fear slid out of her that Annie realized how frightened she had been. She barely listened to the rest of the discussion as the two men agreed on a retainer and Jack made out a check. She was thinking giddily about being at a mountain cabin with Jack. Alone. Just the two of them, tucked away where no one could find them. It took a moment for the investigator's final words of advice to register.

"You think Jack should have a bodyguard? At the cabin with us?"

"I recommend it, yes," Mr. Straight said. "Although I don't anticipate any problems, it's best to be prepared. Unfortunately, the man I use for such jobs won't be free until tomorrow afternoon."

Annie met Jack's eyes. She didn't want someone else around at all, but if they had to have someone there—and she supposed they did—she was more than willing to put it off. "I, uh…as far as I'm concerned, tomorrow will be fine."

Between stopping in Denver to talk to the private investigator and driving through a late-afternoon thunderstorm, it was dusk by the time they left the public highway for a narrow gravel road. Thirty minutes of bouncing through ruts and up a series of switchbacks took them into an increasingly isolated section of mountainside.

"I'll bet no one can get in or out of here in the winter without a snowmobile," Annie said. "This road is terrible."

"No kidding." Jack was in the driver's seat. He'd claimed that he needed to drive because he was the one who knew how to get there. Annie suspected that was just an excuse to get behind the wheel, but she didn't mind indulging him. "The people who live along here must be more interested in privacy than convenience. This road would certainly discourage casual visitors."

"Deerbaum must be crazy about privacy, then. I haven't seen another house for at least ten minutes."

"That's not surprising. We've only gone ten yards in the last ten minutes."

It was an exaggeration, but she knew what he meant. "Are you sure we haven't passed the cabin?"

"He said we couldn't miss it. Of course, people always say…hey, guess what?" he said as they rounded a tight turn. "He was right. That would be hard to miss."

"Wow." The road dead-ended at the base of a cliff. Tucked up against that cliff was Deerbaum's "cabin"—a modernistic, split-level structure with lots of glass. This wasn't a house designed to blend with its setting, she thought. It was an arrogant building—beautiful, but intended to dominate. "When he said his place was at the end of the road, he meant it, didn't he? But I sure wouldn't call it a cabin."

"Only in the sense that the Kennedys' summer place is a beach cottage." He pulled up in the circular drive. The yellow glow of the porch light left on by the caretaker spilled over the terra-cotta tiles of the terrace, where wrought-iron chairs were set out invitingly. The house itself, however, looked exotic and unwelcoming to Annie. "At least we can be sure no one will find us here."

"Not likely," he agreed, going to the rear of the vehicle to unload the suitcases.

She climbed out and stretched, looking around. The house might not be to her taste, but its setting should be magnificent by daylight. Maybe they could have breakfast on the terrace. She inhaled deeply, tasting pine and ozone from the recent rain. Mountain air, she thought happily. It had a flavor all its own. "You want to go hiking tomorrow?"

Jack raised both eyebrows. "You must have a different idea of what happens on a honeymoon than I do."

Annie blushed. She could feel herself doing it, and it annoyed her. "We can't do that *all* the time."

"Want to bet?" He set down the suitcases and felt in

the planter next to the door, where the caretaker was supposed to have left the key.

"I don't think so," she murmured as she bent to get the groceries from the back seat. The caretaker was supposed to have stocked the place for them, but they'd picked up a few things in a tiny town nearby, just to be sure. "Think how disappointed I would be if I won."

"What? I didn't quite catch that." Jack set the suitcases down beside the open front door. His smug expression told her he'd heard her just fine.

"I said I won the coin toss, so you're fixing supper."

"Funny. I don't remember tossing a coin." He stepped forward and took the sacks of groceries from her, bending to set them down—and pick her up. "I thought I should carry my bride over the threshold."

"I think that's supposed to happen when you get back from the honeymoon." She wrapped her arms around his neck. "But I guess we can practice."

"A threshold's a threshold." He carried her across that one, stopping just inside. His smiling eyes told her what he was going to do next.

Annie's arms tightened around his neck. She met his mouth gladly with her own. Held high against his chest, she could feel the quick, hard beat of his heart pounding out a hasty measure to match the one her own heart was drumming, and she knew that Jack wanted her. She gave herself up to the moment, the feeling, and the man.

He broke the kiss slowly, easing her down. Her feet touched the ground and she clutched his shoulders, dizzy with him.

I love you. The words pushed at her, begging to be spoken, jamming at the back of her throat and dimming the feelings she'd exulted in a second ago. She pasted a smile on her face as she eased out of his arms, glancing around. "Look, there's a fireplace."

"Fireplaces aren't uncommon in mountain cabins," he said dryly. "Even 'cabins' like this one. Is something wrong, Annie?"

"Of course not. I was just glad to see it. I, um, have this fantasy about a fireplace."

He smiled slowly. "There's no bearskin rug."

"Thank God. After what you told me about Deerbaum's trophy hunting, I was afraid we'd find the place decorated in early embalming."

"I'm kind of relieved about that myself. Having a moose staring at me from the wall might be inhibiting."

Everything was going to be okay, she thought. She just had to keep things light and friendly. "I tell you what. While you're putting away the groceries and fixing supper—"

"You want to remind me just when we tossed that coin?"

"I did it for you," she assured him. "You lost. I thought I'd take a hot bath and, ah, change into something more comfortable while you're busy."

"You look pretty comfortable to me right now. A little overdressed, maybe." He reached for her.

She put her hands on his chest. "Jack, I'd like to pretend this is our real wedding night and do things…traditionally."

"You mean with the bride spending hours in the bathroom doing who knows what while the poor groom paces anxiously outside? Then you come out wearing one of those billowy things that covers up way too much?"

She grinned. "Something like that, except that I don't have a fancy negligee. There wasn't time to go shopping for one."

"That's okay. Come to supper naked." She choked on a laugh, and he gave her a quick kiss. "I'll put together some sandwiches if you promise not to linger too long in the bath. We can eat them in front of the fire on the rug that didn't come from a bear, and you can tell me about your fantasy.''

She irritated herself by blushing again. ''We'll see. Um…would you mind giving Ben a call? He wanted to know we arrived safely. Normally I wouldn't indulge him this way, but with everything that's happened lately, I guess he's entitled to do a little worrying.''

Something was bothering Annie. Jack knew that much, even if he couldn't figure out what it was. Probably the same thing as always, he thought glumly as he put away what remained of the ham he'd sliced for sandwiches. She didn't want to leave Highpoint.

But he was making progress. She wasn't happy about leaving her home, but she was going to do it. In return, he would do everything in his power to make sure she didn't regret that. And she was with him tonight. Upstairs, he thought, glancing up as if he could see through several walls to the sybaritic bathroom where she was soaking right now—naked and wet, her skin probably flushed from the heat…

He grinned. Annie had been right to insist on tradition. There was something decidedly erotic about waiting for his bride to go through the feminine ritual of preparing herself for him.

He put their plates on a black lacquer tray he'd found, added wineglasses and a corkscrew, tucked a bottle of cabernet sauvignon under one arm and a small paper sack beneath the other one.

He also tucked his borrowed gun into the waistband of his jeans.

The living room was not a cheery place at night. The outside walls contained vast expanses of undraped glass that made Jack feel as if he were on display, though the house was so isolated he knew there was no one to peer in. The view would undoubtedly be spectacular in the daytime, he thought as he set the tray down near the fireplace. But the only view he was interested in seeing tomorrow was the one from the king-size bed in the bedroom where he'd left their suitcases.

Jack found wood in a canvas carrier and kindling in a small brass chest nearby. He knelt and laid the fire, adding bark and wood chips around the base, then closed the tempered glass doors and looked around. He wanted to get everything right. To fulfill Annie's fantasy. No lights, he decided, and moved to turn them off. The glow from the fire would be enough.

He grabbed some pillows from two big couches and arranged them invitingly on the thick rug in front of the fireplace, then opened the small sack he'd brought in along with the supper tray. It took him a moment to find a discreet place to put the box of condoms that he took out of the sack, but finally he settled for tucking it behind one of the biggest cushions. A fantasy called for a little subtlety. He slid the gun just underneath the couch, regretting the need to keep it near, then looked at the scene he'd set and nodded. The logs were already catching. His glance fell on an elegant, silver-toned phone sitting on the nearest end table and he grimaced. Oh, yeah. Might as well call Ben so Ben didn't call them at a particularly annoying moment. He picked up the receiver.

The line was dead.

The bathroom was warm and steamy. Annie had pulled her hair up on top of her head to keep it dry while she soaped, shaved and soaked herself. A few tendrils had escaped, and the hot, moist air had made them frisky. They curled around her face, tickling her cheeks when she bent and smoothed lotion on her legs.

She straightened and put a hand on her stomach. Nervous

jitters were jumping around like crazy in there. It was ridiculous. Everything she did felt portentous, as if she were about to turn some corner, make some unalterable commitment that would change her life forever. Never mind that the commitment had been made over two months ago, and consummated twice last night.

Tonight she felt very much like a new bride.

She pulled her nightgown on over her head. It was a soft, brushed-cotton knit in a vivid turquoise. The neck was wide and elastic, the sleeves little puffs that tended to slip off her shoulders. It was a summer gown, but sexier than the football jersey and thermal leggings she usually slept in at this time of year.

The mirror was still hazy. She took a towel and wiped it off, frowning at what she saw. The nightgown looked so…ordinary. Pretty enough, but hardly special.

Well, she thought as she tugged the covered band out of her hair, she was ordinary, too. Pretty enough, but ordinary. But Jack knew what he was getting. He wasn't waiting for some sultry centerfold to join him downstairs.

A tingle of excitement went through her, and she brushed her hair quickly. Jack was waiting for *her*.

She left her robe hanging on the bathroom door. She wouldn't need it tonight.

Jack had just hung up the phone when he heard her.

Or maybe he felt her—a quiet tingling under his skin, a chemical change in the air he breathed. However it came about, he knew Annie was near. He turned.

She stood in the arched entry that led to the bedroom level. Her gown was a long drift of color as bright as the sunny seas of the Mediterranean. The light from the hall was behind her, creating a slim silhouette beneath that clinging ocean color.

She took his breath away. His voice came out husky. "Annie."

Her smile was sweet and a little shy—a bride's smile. She came forward, leaving the brightness of the hall's artificial lighting for the dim, firelit room where he waited.

Jack found himself on his feet, though he didn't remember standing. She seemed more fantasy than reality in that moment, a slim wraith made from mystery and longing, less substantial than a dream.

He held out his hand.

She reached him and put her hand in his, and became real. Flesh to his flesh. His fingers tightened around hers. "Is this anything like your fantasy?"

"Better." Firelight painted her skin in primitive shades, dancing shadows across her face when she tilted it up to him. "Much better. This is real."

Very real. His heart was pounding as if they'd already touched, kissed, placed the heat of their bodies together. But all he held was her hand. "I want it to be right, Annie." He touched the play of fire and shadow along her cheek. "I want everything to be perfect for you."

Mischief brightened her eyes. "Well, if we don't get it perfect the first time, we can always try again."

He smiled. "And again." He bent and brushed his lips across hers once, twice. "And again." *For the next forty or fifty years.* The thought startled him into straightening.

"You're not supposed to frown like that after you kiss me."

"Sorry." He didn't know how to describe the peculiar feeling that had come over him when he thought about spending the rest of his life with her, so he spoke of the other thing that was bothering him. "I tried to call your brother a minute ago. The line is dead."

She shrugged, and the gown slipped off one shoulder.

"There was a storm here shortly before we arrived. I imagine the lines are down somewhere."

Lines did go down, especially in remote areas. "I'm probably worrying over nothing, but I don't like being cut off."

"My worrywart of a brother talked me into bringing my cellular phone with me."

His mouth twitched up. "Does that mean we can expect a call from Ben if we don't check in with him right away?"

The mischief was back in her eyes. She put her hands on his shoulders. "Only if I turn it on."

"You'd better do that then." He brushed a kiss across her lips. "Later." He touched her lips with his again, intending to play around the edges of the flames for a while before passion grabbed them both and flung them wherever it would. But Annie put her arms around him, brought her body up against his, and hunger bit hard. *Slow,* he reminded himself, and cupped her head in his hands, savoring the feel of her hair. When he probed gently with his tongue, her lips parted. Heat rolled through him in a wave. He deepened the kiss.

There was nothing playful about the fist that seized him and shook him and made his hands tremble when he suddenly swept his hands over her shoulders, pulling her nightgown off her shoulders, down her arms, until it fell in a turquoise puddle at her feet.

"Jack!" She sounded flustered.

He was anything but flustered. He was hard as a rock and his breath was trapped in his chest, making his head light and dizzy—but he was not flustered. He managed a grin. "I told you to come to supper naked."

Her eyebrows went up. The haughty look went well with the blush on her cheeks. "You're thinking of eating supper *now?*"

"Well...maybe not supper." He cupped her breasts, run-

ning his thumbs over the tips. She shivered. "You are so
beautiful, Annie."

She paused a moment. "Thank you."

So polite. And so sure he didn't mean it. He shook his
head. "I get the idea you don't believe me, but if you could
see what I see…" He ran his hands down to her waist.
"Your hair is all messy from my hands, your eyes are dark
and mysterious, and your skin is so smooth. The fire makes
you glow."

The color in her cheeks deepened. "It's not the fire making me glow," she said softly, and reached for his shirt.
"Why do I have to keep pointing out that you have too
many clothes on?"

A shiver of pure hunger hit him when her fingers began
undoing the buttons. *Go slowly,* he reminded himself. "I'm
a greedy man. I like to get you naked first." He bent and
took her mouth with his.

So good. So right. He eased her down, down onto the
rug with him. The pile was thick, warmed by the fire—but
not as warm as Annie's flesh. She ran her hands over his
body while he tugged off his shirt, getting in his way and
making him go a little crazy.

It was plain that Annie wanted him, and she wanted him
now—no easing into passion this time, but a quick, hard
plunge. His cautious Annie didn't make love like a careful
woman. No, she burned for him, throwing herself into the
fire with reckless haste, all the life crammed into her small
body spilling out in passion. Her hands and his, her lips,
his tongue—all found places to test, to tease, to devour.

Jack lost everything, and he lost it fast—his shirt, his
sense, his pants and his good intentions. He knew only the
feel of her hands, the silk of her thighs, the musky, private
scent of her where he pressed his mouth. He drove her up
quick and hard, using his mouth and his hands. When her
cry struck the air and her body jerked and quivered, when

he was so full of her he couldn't wait a second longer to fill her with himself, he moved up her body. With one quick, sure stroke he sheathed himself inside her.

"Annie."

"Jack," she gasped. "Oh, Jack, I love you so much."

He froze. Panic wrapped dark wings around him, smothering him. He couldn't move, couldn't speak, couldn't think.

Her eyes glistened. She blinked fiercely and grabbed his shoulders. "Damn you," she whispered, and thrust up with her hips.

He groaned, and his body took over.

The fire snapped and popped. A log shifted, sending sparks flying. Annie stared at the flames in the fireplace, her eyes dry and her heart aching. Jack lay beside her, his arm over her waist, his front cupping her back. He hadn't spoken since calling out her name…just before she told him she loved him.

God knew she hadn't intended to say it. No, she'd been holding those words inside, afraid of his reaction. If she'd had any doubts about whether that was the right thing to do, Jack had certainly settled the question. She kept seeing the look in his eyes and trying to decide what, exactly, he'd felt. Fear? Panic? Or sheer horror?

At least it hadn't been pity. Pity would have been worse.

Silence coiled between them, winding tighter and tighter as the fire hissed and popped and the sweat dried on her skin. She shivered.

"Are you too chilly?" Jack asked.

She shook her head.

"You're awfully quiet."

"I've already said too much, haven't I?" Abruptly she was angry. She rolled onto her back so she could look at him. "I'm not going to take the words back, or pretend I didn't say them."

"I didn't ask you to."

"No, but you've been asking me not to say them, haven't you?" She sat up, pushing her hair out of her face. "Not out loud. But with everything you've said about love, everything you've told me you wanted—and didn't want—from our marriage, you've been telling me to keep quiet about my feelings."

He sat up, too. His face was tight. "I wanted to avoid exactly what's happening now. I didn't want you hurt."

She tilted her chin up and held on to her pride with both hands. "You knew I loved you, then. You just didn't want me to say it."

He looked away. "I don't…think in those terms."

"You mean that you avoid using the *L*-word even in your thoughts."

"If you want the flat-out truth, I was sure as hell hoping you hadn't fallen into that trap. Romantic love is a fairy tale. It keeps people reaching for something that isn't there, keeps them from appreciating what they *do* have. Of course I didn't want that for you. I care about you."

"You care about me." Annie's lip curled. "But you don't think I know the difference between reality and fantasy?" She couldn't stand to lie there beside him another second. She grabbed her nightgown, tugged it over her head and scrambled to her feet. "Well, guess what? You're wrong. I love you, and it doesn't have anything to do with fantasy, because if I were chasing after a dream I could sure come up with a better one!"

His eyes hardened. He stood more slowly than she had and didn't bother to reach for his clothes. "Are we going to replay what happened on our wedding night, when you told me how much you regretted marrying me?"

"No! No, that's not what I mean. Jack, if you don't think

romantic love exists, why do the words bother you so much? Are you that frightened of something that isn't real?''

"Because of what's happening right now! Dammit, Annie, can't you see? You're hurt and angry, and why? Because you think we're supposed to have something more than what we've got, when what we've got is *perfect.*"

"I'm angry because you don't want me to love you! Not because you don't love me. That would be n-nice, but—" She blinked quickly to keep the tears inside. "I'm not going to edit my feelings to suit you."

That cold look was back in his eyes. "Okay, Annie. Let's say this love you feel is real. How long have you been in love with me?"

"I..." She swallowed. "For years, I guess."

"Then you loved me when you dumped me on our wedding night. And you want me to respect that feeling?" He shook his head. "No, thanks. I don't want anything to do with an emotion that unreliable."

Annie stared at him. Realization belled through her, striking chords of memories, echoing back into the past and rearranging everything. "You want to be safe," she whispered. "I thought I was the one who was afraid of risk, but you are, too. You're scared to death of love. You want it, but anytime you start to reach out for it you get scared and run the other way."

His face went blank. "You don't know what you're talking about."

"All this time I thought you'd rejected everything about your aunt. But you're just like her in one way—you don't trust any deep feelings."

"You've said enough, Annie."

"You won't even admit that you cared about her, that you're grieving her death. Just like she never admitted to caring about you."

He grabbed his jeans and pulled them on, then jammed his arms into the sleeves of his shirt. He reached for his shoes and socks. "If I stay here we're just going to fight. I'll be back when we've both cooled off." As soon as he was fully dressed he headed for the door.

This was just what he'd done on their wedding night. He'd walked out when their argument got too intense. "You didn't use a condom when we made love just now. What will you do if I'm pregnant? Will you run away from that, too? Give me some money, maybe, and stay gone the way my father did?"

He froze, his hand on the doorknob. Then he pushed the door open. Cold air poured in, washing over Annie. And then he was gone.

For a long time Annie stood there staring numbly at the closed door. She didn't hear the Bronco start, which meant he must be walking. Or running, running off into the night rather than face her feelings—or his own.

Finally she sank down on the rug where they'd made love such a short time ago, drawing her knees up close to her chest and resting her head on them. She watched the fire and thought about compromise and sacrifice. The key to understanding them, she thought, lay in the difference between "want" and "need."

Leaving Highpoint was a compromise. She loved her hometown and wanted to stay there, but she didn't *need* to stay the way Jack needed the diversity and the challenge of his job. It wouldn't be a sacrifice for her to wander the world with Jack. She might even like it once she got used to it, especially if she were able to teach.

But sacrifice…yes, she understood what that was now. At least for her. Sacrifice meant squeezing herself into shapes that didn't fit. She would still be Annie whether she was in Timbuktu or Denver or a tiny village in the Andes.

But she wouldn't be herself if she pretended that she didn't love Jack Merriman.

She couldn't do that. Not for his sake, or her own.

Tears welled up in her eyes. Even if loving him was the one thing she could do that would drive him away.

He was a fool.

Only a fool took off down an unfamiliar path through a mountain forest at night without a flashlight. Jack had jogged down the road blindly for the first few minutes, but when he'd glimpsed this path leading away from the road his feet had taken it. As if they knew better than he did what he was doing. As if he had somewhere to go.

Only a fool rushed outside at this time of year without a jacket, but that's what he had done. Though it was mild for a fall night in the mountains, "mild" meant a damp, chilly forty degrees. He was cold and his shoes were wet from some puddle he'd splashed through, and while it made sense to keep walking to stay warm, it would have made more sense to walk back the way he'd come—back to the warmth of the borrowed house. Back to Annie.

He didn't turn around.

The path he followed might have been made by deer originally, but it was probably used mostly by motorcycles and mountain bikes now. On either side of him trees loomed, walls of pine and spruce unseen in the moonless night except as a blacker darkness. Their needles made the path spongy beneath his feet. Their branches, wet from the recent rain, dripped and dampened his shirt when he brushed against one.

He couldn't see where he was going by looking down at the path. Instead he followed the echo it cast in the faint lightness above it—a strip of sky mostly bare of branches, where a sprinkling of stars offered the only light.

Only a fool would hurt Annie.

His feet faltered and stopped.

He'd been so sure he'd known what was best for both of them. So sure, and so blindly selfish. Annie needed to be loved. It was that simple and that impossible. Jack stared at the blackness around him and felt the yawning of a similar darkness inside. She'd said she only wanted to be free to love him, to speak the words. Maybe that was true. But she deserved more. She deserved to be loved back.

If he couldn't give her that, he didn't deserve to keep her.

But how could he give her something he knew didn't exist? Or if it did...if it did, it was as far beyond his reach as those sparks of light overhead. Farther. All he knew about love came from the impossible dreams his mother had spent her life chasing. How could he give Annie something he knew only as the ghostly fragments of someone else's dream?

Annie thought love was real. Jack thought that if she was right—if love truly existed as something more than a dream—then it existed in Annie.

"You're scared to death of love. You want it, but anytime you reach out for it you get scared and run the other way."

He'd certainly run this time, hadn't he?

Jack stood motionless in the dripping forest and listened to the wind shiver through the trees. He shivered, too. He needed to keep moving to stay warm. His feet wanted to move, to carry him on and on. But he had nowhere to go, nowhere he wanted to be, except back where he'd already been. With Annie.

He looked up.

The stars were cold and bright and tiny, sources of power so distant that much of the light he saw now was older than the mountain he stood on. He couldn't touch the stars. He would never be able to reach them, to claim them. But their light touched him.

God's freckles, Annie called them. The opposite of people's freckles, she'd said, because it takes darkness for us to see them.

His eyes squeezed closed. How could he give her up? She was in every part of him—bone, breath, mind and memory. Everything he saw, everything he was, had pieces of Annie attached.

Could a man who didn't believe in love learn how to love?

No. No, he was still hiding from the truth. The real question—the one that made his stomach constrict and his mind shy away—was whether love was possible for a man who was scared to death of it.

Maybe...maybe if he just stood *still* long enough for Annie's love to reach him, he could learn how to reflect that feeling back. Maybe, if Annie would be patient with him, would give him time...

The first faint hope flickered to life inside him.

Jack turned around. He'd taken the first step back when he heard a sound that didn't belong to the night and the forest. A voice? It was faint, but yes, that was a human voice coming this way, he thought. A woman's voice. Annie? No, the voice was coming from the wrong direction, from farther down the path.

A light blinked through the trees—a flashlight, he realized. Then he heard a man's voice, still some distance away but loud enough to carry. A deep, impatient voice. A voice Jack knew. "Quit your bitching. It isn't far."

"Don't see why...couldn't get...car a little closer."

"Because we don't want the damned car seen, and the only way to get it closer would be to park on the damned road that leads to my cabin."

Deerbaum. That was Amos Deerbaum coming up a dark path that led to his house when he was supposed to be in New York City. Deerbaum—who hadn't wanted his car seen, so had parked it elsewhere and was tramping through the woods to reach his cabin.

And the woman with him—

"...why you had to send...godforsaken wilderness," she said, her voice shrill enough to carry clearly.

The woman with him was Leah.

Quickly, and as quietly as he could, Jack started to run. Back to the house. Back to Annie.

Chapter 15

Annie huddled into the corner of the couch with her robe on. The fire was dying down and she was cold, so cold. Where was Jack now?

Some noise from outside penetrated her misery. She frowned, uneasy. Had Jack locked it behind him when he left?

Her question was answered in a crash when the door slammed open. Jack raced in. He bent, reached for something under the couch with one hand then grabbed her hand with the other. "Come on. They're not far behind me."

She stared. "They..?"

"Deerbaum and Leah. I heard them, but when I tripped over a root they heard me, too. We've got to get to the car before they get here." He pulled her with him toward the door—and he had Ben's gun in his right hand.

Annie didn't know what was going on, but fear kicked her from a stumble to a run. Her bare feet slapped the hall, then landed on the tile terrace in one running stride, an-

other—then there was a loud *crack!* followed by a dull
thunk. Jack stopped so suddenly she ran into him. He
shoved her back inside the house, slammed the door shut
and locked it.

Belatedly her brain processed the sounds: the *crack* of a
rifle. The *thunk* of a bullet hitting something terrifyingly
close. Amos Deerbaum was shooting at them.

"That won't slow him for long. Come on. We've got to
get away from these windows." They ran back to the hall
that led to the stairs—the only spot on the ground floor
without exterior walls. He turned to her, his face intent. "I
haven't checked the house out, Annie. I don't know where
the exits are. Have you seen a back door? A side door?"

"I—I don't think there is a back door. There are sliding
doors in the dining room, but they open onto the front of
the house, too. If h-he's out there, he'll see us." And shoot
at them. Her skin was clammy, her stomach tight, and her
heart was doing a crazy fear-dance in her chest. "There's
a balcony. On the upper story, off our bedroom. But I don't
know where we could go from there."

"It's a way out. Let's go."

They'd reached the hall on the second floor when she
heard the front door crash open a second time. "You stay
outside," a man's voice boomed. "Keep 'em penned up in
here. For God's sake, look before you pull the trigger.
Don't screw up and shoot me."

Annie didn't listen for the reply. She was too busy running.

The bedroom with the balcony lay at the far corner of
the house. None of the lights were on up here, and she
stumbled into something right inside the bedroom door—a
massive armoire.

"Perfect," Jack said, closing the door quickly and moving to the far side of armoire. "Help me tip it over. We
have to block the door."

She sprang to lend her strength to his, but the armoire was impossibly heavy. Feet pounded up the uncarpeted stairs. Oh, God. They couldn't tip it over, not in time. Deerbaum was nearly here. No, wait—their end was off the floor an inch. Two inches.

She shoved with everything in her, felt Jack straining beside her, and the armoire fell over with a huge crash. Its upper end blocked the door.

They raced for the sliding glass doors on the far wall. Annie reached for the lock, but her fingers were stupid with haste and fear. The crack of a gun sounded again—loud, extraordinarily loud inside the house. Wood splintered in the door they'd just barricaded.

Jack leveled the gun at the door and snapped off a shot. Wood splintered—and on the other side of the door, Deerbaum laughed.

She whimpered and bit her lip—and got the door open.

The balcony was small and it went nowhere. The house was built on a slope, putting them at least thirty feet above ground, though it was hard to be sure in the darkness.

"If we can't go down," Jack said, "we'll go up."

He handed her the gun and vaulted onto the railing, balancing himself with one hand against the house as he straightened, tilting his head back to study the roof. The edge was within grabbing distance, but there was nothing to grab onto—just a smooth, shingled slope that ended over his head.

A loud thud on the bedroom door announced Deerbaum's attempt to shove it and the armoire out of his way. There was another ear-blasting shot. He couldn't get through the door, but his bullets could.

Jack jumped down. "Get on my shoulders, Annie," he said, his voice pitched too low for Deerbaum to hear. "It's not the usual climbing technique, but it will work."

She saw what he intended, and shook her head. "Right

idea, wrong shoulders. I could make it to the roof from your shoulders, but I couldn't get you up. I'm not strong enough. You go first, then pull me up.''

He hesitated.

"Dammit, Jack, I can take your weight for a few seconds. Just don't pause to admire the view.''

He nodded and jumped back onto the railing.

Annie set the pistol down and stood at a right angle to the railing so she could brace herself by leaning against the house with her palms flat, her arms locked and her feet shoulder-width apart for stability. She prayed that the adrenaline that had her heart doing triple-jumps in her chest would let her draw on reserves of strength she couldn't normally tap. She could do this, she told herself. She had to.

"Ready?'' he whispered.

She drew a breath and nodded.

A crushing weight pressed down on one shoulder, then he stood on both shoulders—then his weight was gone. She glanced up, heard him grunt and saw his legs rapidly disappearing as he levered himself up.

The railing felt a lot more narrow when she climbed up on it than it had looked when Jack kept jumping on and off. Annie stood shakily, her shoulders aching, her hand on the side of the house for balance. Jack's arms were already there, stretched down for her. She passed him the gun. His hands locked tight on her arms. He pulled.

For one dizzy second his body slid sickeningly, her weight dragging them both down. She kicked out with her legs, getting her feet against the building to push up as hard as she could. Her shoulder muscles shrieked and her body rose. The edge of the roof scraped her breasts and belly through the thin nightgown—then she had one knee up—then her whole leg. Her foot knocked against something—something cold and metallic that started to slide. The gun

But neither she nor Jack could free a hand to grab it as it fell from the roof.

Oh, God, she'd lost their only weapon. She heard it hit the ground far below, and then Jack gave another heave, and she was on the roof with him. He rolled to his hands and knees, glancing at her with his finger held to his lips. She nodded, got onto her hands and knees and followed.

It wasn't an elegant ascent, but silence was more important than style. If Deerbaum didn't hear them he might not realize where they'd gone. Maybe, she thought with a small surge of hope, he would assume they'd risked the jump to the ground. Maybe he would look there for them. People with even a mild fear of heights tended to forget to look up for a route.

They paused near the crest of this section of the roof. "Any chance Deerbaum's afraid of heights?" she whispered.

"I doubt it," he whispered back. "He flies his own plane."

She grimaced. The adrenaline rush had faded enough for her to notice things—like how cold the wind was, and how it blew right through her nightgown and robe. And the way the scrapes on her body stung.

"I'm sorry about the gun," she whispered, miserable with guilt.

He touched her cheek lightly. "Not your fault. I shouldn't have put it there. A handgun wasn't going to be much defense against a high-powered hunting rifle with a night-scope, anyway."

It had been better than nothing, though. Which was what they were left with. "What's going on, Jack?"

"I wish I knew. I...had wandered down a trail a ways when I heard Deerbaum and Leah talking. They intended to sneak up on us, and I knew there was no good reason for that."

"But Amos Deerbaum...how could he be involved? The man's rich!"

"I don't know. I do know I was a fool to bring you here. He set me up."

"But even the investigator we talked to thought it was okay." The wind was picking up. She shivered, and he put an arm around her. She stiffened for a moment—but no longer. They both needed the body heat, and if his body had another effect on hers, this was one time she wouldn't be tempted to act on it.

Jack put his mouth close to her ear. His breath was warm. "We can sort out motives later. We know the important part—Deerbaum's here, he's got a rifle and he plans to use it. We'd better concentrate on getting away from here."

She glanced around. Where?

Jack whispered in her ear. "This way."

Still on hands and knees to avoid the chance of an audible footfall, they crept to the side of the house nearest the cliff. But it wasn't until Jack stood, craning his head back as if he could actually see hand and footholds in the darkness, that Annie realized what he had in mind.

Abruptly he leaned forward.

Annie couldn't stifle a gasp, but he bridged the three-foot gap between the roof and cliff easily, his feet remaining on the roof, his hands moving over the granite face of the cliff, hunting for a hold. And if he found a good hold or two, she wondered, what then? Would she be able to use them? She didn't have his inches, his reach or his upper body strength. She'd never free-soloed. She was used to bolts, fixed climbs, ropes.

Annie bit her lip. No time like the present to learn.

Jack stretched an arm up and up—and his legs swung over to join the rest of him. He hung by his hands while his feet hunted, hunted—then one toe found a niche. He pushed up with that leg, his right arm reaching for the next hold.

Annie moved to the edge of the roof. She would follow if she could. She tilted her head back. Jack's clothes made his body hard to spot in the darkness, but his hands and face were light enough for her to follow his progress. He climbed a few yards, then angled sideways.

Suddenly light blazed on the other side of the crest of the roof. Floodlights, she realized, at the front of the house. The light didn't reach the back of the house, thank God, or the cliff Jack was inching up.

Deerbaum shouted from the front, "Leah! Dammit, woman, have you been watching the house? They've gotten out!" Leah's voice wasn't loud enough for Annie to make out her reply, but it, too, came from the front of the house. Annie relaxed slightly.

Jack started back down. When he was almost back where he'd started, he shoved off from the rock wall, arching backward to land softly—but not completely silently. Deerbaum was busy berating Leah for having supposedly allowed Annie and Jack to get away, though. He couldn't have heard Jack's landing over his own harangue.

She leaned closer. "Did you find a route, or the start of one?"

"There's a good crack farther up, but you wouldn't be able to use the holds I used to get there. They're too far apart. I tried to find another route up, but couldn't. I'm sorry."

She swallowed. "You go, then." Jack could do it if anyone could. She'd seen him "crack climbing" before—no bolts, no rope, nothing to hold on to but a fissure in the rock on one side and a few vague dents on the other.

Even in the darkness she could sense his incredulity. "And leave you? You think I would do that?"

"There are houses farther down. I saw lights when we

were driving up here, and where there are lights there are
people. You can get help.''

Jack shook his head. "Forget it. Once I made it up the
cliff I'd have to hunt for a way back down that didn't drop
me back in Deerbaum's lap. Then I'd have to hunt for a
house in the dark, in unfamiliar territory—hell, without a
map or a compass I might end up going the wrong way.''

Relief loosed her shoulder muscles even while fear dried
her mouth. She didn't want to stay here alone. She also
didn't want Jack here, where people were trying to kill him.
"Deerbaum hasn't even thought about the roof. I'll be
okay," she assured him in a whisper.

"Yes, you will." Though he spoke in a whisper, she
heard something odd in his tone, something impossibly
tender. She thought he was smiling. "You'll be fine, Annie.
I won't let anything happen to you.''

For some reason that made her heart jump in alarm. "I
don't want anything to happen to you, either.''

"I'll be okay, too." He bent and pressed a kiss to her
mouth, a soft kiss that asked for nothing and made her long
to give him anything. "There's no one like you, Annie. No
one.''

She swallowed. "Don't say that as if—" As if he were
saying goodbye.

"Do you remember where you left your cell phone?''

The sudden change of subject jolted her. "In the bedroom." Remorse hit. "I could have grabbed it—God, I'm
so stupid! We were just in there!''

"I didn't think of it, either." He paused. "I don't hear
them.''

Neither did she. Deerbaum and his rifle, Leah and her
gun, might be anywhere.

Jack put his hands on her shoulders and his mouth next
to her ear. "Here's what we're going to do. First I have to

find out where they are. Then I'll distract them while you—"

She grabbed his wrists with both hands and whispered fiercely, "No!"

"Just listen. You'll have to get back into the bedroom on your own. It won't be easy, but if I can get them away from that part of the house you won't have to worry about being quiet. That should help. Get the phone and call 911. Then hide right there in the bedroom. He'll have already searched it, so he won't look for you there."

Her fingers tightened desperately on his wrists. "And what will you be doing?"

"I'll let myself down off the roof at the front, where it's only one-story high. An easy drop. I'll make sure they hear me, but aren't too close. Deerbaum likes to hunt. He likes the chase. He'll come after me. Leah may stay behind, but as long as she stays outside on guard like he's had her doing, you'll be okay until help gets here."

"I'm going with you."

"No. You'd slow me down."

He was right. He was right, dammit, and she couldn't stand it. Annie had never hated her short legs as much as she did in that instant. "I won't do it," she whispered. "I won't let you risk yourself that way. He's got a rifle. He doesn't have to get close!"

"It's not that much of a risk. The trees are only ten yards or so from the house. Once I'm in the forest, he won't have a clear shot. Ten yards—that's nothing."

"Not with Leah out there watching, lights flooding the area—"

He made a scornful noise. "She's got a revolver. How many people can hit a moving target at any distance with a handgun?"

"No. Go up the cliff. Get help that way."

"I'm going to do this, Annie. You can either do what

I've asked and call for help, or you can stay up here on the roof.''

Her eyes squeezed closed. He made his plan sound so reasonable—but it wasn't. He meant to offer himself as a target. The thought of Jack dodging bullets made her want to scream, but he'd given her no choice. She couldn't stop him. Annie gave a single, tiny nod.

He squeezed her shoulder. ''I'll locate Deerbaum and Leah,'' he whispered. ''You go back to where we climbed onto the roof, be ready to swing down onto the balcony once you know Deerbaum is coming after me. I'll make sure you hear. Don't move too soon.''

''Jack, be careful. Please. I—'' She had to say it. ''I love you.''

He went still. ''Yes,'' he said in a soft, strange voice. ''I believe you do.'' She could see the whites of his eyes shining in the dark when he cupped her face in his hands. His fingers moved gently over her cheeks. ''If I'd had more time…if only I'd had more time.''

He gave her one last quick, hard kiss, then turned and moved swiftly away.

God, Jack thought, trying to catch his breath without audibly gasping. Who would have thought a man Deerbaum's age could move so fast?

He leaned against the trunk of a tree, his chest heaving. One arm hung useless at his side, and blood dripped into his curled hand. He didn't think he'd lost enough blood to slow him down, though. Not yet.

Good thing Leah really did have only a handgun, and even better that she wasn't much of a shot with it. At least she only got his arm. Jack had known Leah had been too damned close when he let himself off the roof. He really hadn't known what kind of gun she had when he told Annie it was a handgun, of course. He'd just wanted to keep Annie from worrying about him when she needed to focus on her own safety.

Where was Annie now?

Jack felt as if he'd been running and dodging for an hour, but it probably hadn't been more than fifteen minutes. But that was enough time for Annie to have gotten down from the roof, called 911, and maybe be tucked away in a closet or under the bed. If he could keep Deerbaum busy for another thirty minutes, maybe help could get here.

Thirty minutes, he thought. If he could stay alive that long, Annie would be safe...as long as Leah didn't take her little pistol and go looking for her in the house.

He told himself not to think about that. Deerbaum was by far the greater threat. Leah had fired wildly at Jack when he'd raced for the forest, emptying her gun and hitting him more by accident, he thought, than by aim. Deerbaum had come charging around the corner of the house, bellowing at her to reload and make sure ''the woman'' didn't get away. So Leah should be on guard outside the house still.

He hoped.

Keeping Deerbaum on his trail was easier said than done. He couldn't risk getting too far ahead, because Deerbaum might go back to the house for Annie then. He had to stay close to the man hunting him. Deerbaum was big, loud and arrogant—but he was a hunter, and he knew how to move silently when he had to, making it hard for Jack to keep track of him. In fact, Jack hadn't heard anything of the man for the last couple of minutes. He'd better double-back and see if he could spot him.

Jack started back one soft, careful footstep at a time. Brush rustled some distance ahead of him. He froze. The sounds continued—a twig cracking, a branch shoved aside. Careless, heavy footsteps moving quickly, without any effort at silence.

Moving quickly *away* from Jack. Back toward the house.

Jack followed, making so much noise that he couldn't believe the man didn't hear him. But Deerbaum was well ahead of him and apparently no longer paying attention.

At the edge of the trees Jack stopped, crouching to watch. What did he do now?

"Leah!" Deerbaum boomed. "Get off your butt and go in the house. I want you to find me Jack's pretty bride and bring her out here."

Annie crouched in the darkness and tried not to sneeze. She was sitting on the floor of the tiny coat closet near the front door, her knees huddled up to her chin, the handle of an umbrella digging into her hip, and her bare feet freezing. The rest of her was warmer, since Jack's denim jacket had been hanging here. She hugged it around her and tried not to fall apart.

Jack. Oh, God, Jack.

She had heard the shots. One after another after another. She'd been on the balcony and she'd nearly gone crazy, but she'd held on to enough control to run into the bedroom and grab her cell phone. She'd punched out the numbers and told the operator in a frantic whisper where she was, that someone was trying to kill them and to please hurry— while she was racing downstairs. She couldn't have stayed up in the bedroom, not knowing what had happened to Jack. She just couldn't.

She'd run to the front door, where she'd pressed her ear up to the wood. Silence. She'd stayed there for several minutes, shaking with reaction, unable to hear a thing. Finally she'd decided that must be good. If Jack had been shot, wouldn't Deerbaum have said so in his loud voice? Wouldn't he and Leah have come back into the house to look for Annie? So she'd ducked into the nearest hiding place—the coat closet.

It was probably a dumb place to hide. She knew that,

but couldn't make herself move. She simply had be as close as possible to the front door, as if that made her closer to Jack.

What was that? She lifted her head, straining to hear. Voices? Yes, that was unmistakably Deerbaum outside, though she couldn't catch the words. Then she heard something scrape against the tile of the front terrace. And then the front door opened.

"Check upstairs first," Deerbaum ordered.

"I'm getting sick of the way you yell out orders and then yell out curses at me," Leah said from much too close to Annie's closet. "This was supposed to be easy. All I had to do was come up here with you, wait while you did them, then tell my sad tale to the cops. I didn't agree to all this other stuff."

"Don't worry," Deerbaum said soothingly. "You'll get extra for this night's work."

"I'd better."

"Leave the door open so I can call you if I need you."

Annie opened her mouth so her panicky breaths wouldn' sound quite so loud in the dark closet.

Jack didn't know what to do. Deerbaum was sitting in a chair on the terrace, his rifle at the ready, looking as calm as if he were unwinding after a rough day at the office.

Maybe if Jack could draw the man away he could ambush him. Then he'd figure out how to get Leah out of the house. He moved away from the tree he'd been crouched behind, letting himself be seen, then ducked behind another tree.

Deerbaum chuckled. "Not this time, Jack," he called out. "You had me going for a while, I'll admit that. But I'm no fool. I saw what you were up to—trying to lure me away from the house and that little wife of yours, weren't you? I decided to sit down and let you come to me instead.''

What did the man think? That he was going to step out and get shot? Jack clenched his jaw. He might. He would, if it would buy Annie more time, enough time for help to get here.

"You know, Jack, I'm going to win this one because you're so goddamned noble. You must be, or you wouldn't have kept making trouble about those piddling few drugs Metz sold." He shook his head. "That stupid bastard caused me no end of trouble. So have you, but I like you. I tried to warn you off, but you were too damned noble to listen, just like you're too damned noble to let your little wife get hurt."

He leaned back in his chair. "Right now you're thinking, 'That SOB is going to kill her, anyway.' But I don't have to. It would be simpler, I admit that, but I don't have to. Let me tell you what will happen if you cooperate. I'll shoot you—that part won't change, Jack, sorry to say—then I call the police. Seems I loaned you my place so you could get away with your wife. But you were a bad boy. You brought your girlfriend instead of your wife. That's Leah's role—your piece of ass.''

Jack went cold all over. The letter Annie had received— from Leah? And the scene with Leah in the motel room— that had been staged. Leah was supposed to make it look like they were having an affair. No wonder she'd seemed pleased to learn that Fred was a cop. He would make a great witness to the argument between Annie and Leah.

"Your wife followed you here," Deerbaum continued. "Poor little thing was all upset. It got ugly. In a jealous rage, she shot you—bang!" He held his finger and thumb out like a kid and mimed the shot. "By the way, what the hell did you do with that damned gun you had? I know you don't have it anymore, or you'd have tried to shoot me while we were playing hide-and-seek in the woods. Pity. Would have made things simpler.''

The gun Annie had knocked off the roof. Jack smiled grimly. Deerbaum wouldn't be able to find it in time to use it on them.

''Where was I? Oh, yes. Your wife shoots you. That's where I show up, here on ICA business. Now, originally I had planned to make it a murder-suicide. Poor little wife sees what she's done and shoots herself. But like I said, I don't have to, because I've got Leah. She'll swear it all happened like I said. Your wife—what the hell is her name, anyway—Lainie? Amy? Whatever—she'll tell her story, Leah and I will tell ours. Who will they believe?''

Annie. They'd believe Annie. Because there were things Deerbaum didn't know about—like the call Annie had already made, and the detective Jack had hired.

''But if you make me drag your poor little wife out, I'm going to tell a different story. Same setup, but in this one you tried to get the gun away from her and accidentally shot her. Then, crazy with remorse, you went off into the woods and shot yourself. So I can play this with her alive, or with both of you dead. It's up to you. Stay where you are, and as soon as Leah finds her, I kill her and hunt you down. Come out, and she can stay in whatever little hidey-hole she's found until the cops get here.''

Jack didn't believe him. Deerbaum had no intention of letting either of them live. But if he came out before the man got his hands on Annie, she'd have a little more time. ''All right,'' he called. ''I'll come out if you get Leah to stop looking.''

''Leah!'' Deerbaum bellowed. ''Get your pretty ass out here, chop-chop!'' He looked in Jack's direction. ''Your play.''

Jack stepped out from behind the tree. ''You don't really

want to shoot me with that rifle. It would screw up your story."

"That's right," Deerbaum said agreeably as he stood, pointing the rifle at Jack. "I'd rather shoot you in the house with that cheap little Saturday night special Leah clipped you with. It can't be traced. But I'll shoot you with this if I have to, and work out the details later."

"Your plan isn't going to work, you know," Jack said as easily as he could as he walked toward the staring black eye of the rifle's muzzle.

Deerbaum looked amused. "If it makes you feel better to believe that virtue will triumph in the end, you go right ahead."

"Virtue will have some help from a detective I hired—Harold Straight."

"You haven't hired Straight. You can't afford him. Think I don't know how much you make, how much you've got in the bank right now? I'm a businessman, boy. I know your balance to the penny."

"I paid him with funds from my aunt's estate. I've got the receipt in the pocket of my jacket. I can show you."

Deerbaum chuckled and stood. "Nice try. Whatever the hell you've got in your jacket—a knife, maybe?—can stay there."

He was almost there. If he could get close enough, maybe he could rush the man. Deerbaum was sixty years old. Jack was younger, faster, stronger—even if he only had one arm working. "Several people saw Annie and me together today. Her brothers saw us leave, the detective saw us in Denver, and the girl who checked us out at the grocery store saw us just before we got here. Leah's story about coming here with me won't hold up."

That made Deerbaum frown, but only briefly. "The brothers would lie for her, and you're lying about the rest. You're just trying to bluff me, Jack. You didn't see a damned detective, and you didn't stop for groceries. Why did you think I had my caretaker stock the place for you?'' He stepped back. ''I know how to plan, Jack. Right now I'm planning on having you go in first.''

Fear was a sour taste in Jack's mouth. Deerbaum's arrogance made him dismiss anything that didn't fit his plan. *Just twenty more minutes,* he thought. If he could delay the man for even twenty minutes, maybe the cavalry would arrive before Deerbaum found Annie.

''Move it,'' Deerbaum said, motioning with the rifle.

Reluctantly, he did. Deerbaum followed, stopping just inside the door, next to the coat closet. ''That's far enough.''

Jack turned to face him. *What now?*

Leah came from the hall that led to the stairs. ''What do you want this time?'' She wandered in a few steps into the living room, stopped and stared at Jack. ''God, what a bloody mess! I don't know why you wanted me down here. I'm not killing him. I don't like blood.''

''Squeamish, Leah?'' Jack asked.

''You don't have to do a damned thing but what I'm paying you for. Here, give me the damned gun.'' Deerbaum shifted the rifle to his left hand, keeping it trained on Jack, and held out his right hand for the gun.

She moved forward, making a wide circle around Jack, and held the little .22 pistol just out of Deerbaum's reach. ''Say please.''

''What the hell...?''

''Just once you're going to say please instead of barking orders at me.''

Deerbaum smiled, showing his teeth. ''Please give me the damned gun, Leah.''

''There, see?'' She put it in his hand. ''That wasn't so bad, was it?''

''Not too bad.'' He pointed the gun at Jack. ''There's

one part of the story I didn't mention, Jack. Your little wife also shot your lover.'' He moved his arm a few inches and shot Leah between the eyes. Those eyes opened wide as her knees folded gently.

The explosion from the gun was still echoing in Jack's ears as the gun swung back toward him—and the closet door swung open, hitting Deerbaum's arm.

The gun went off, but the shot went wild.

Annie flew out of the closet and grabbed Deerbaum's arm. Deerbaum backhanded her, pointing the pistol at her as she stumbled back.

''No-o-o!'' Jack yelled, halfway to them and running flat-out.

The pistol moved again.

Jack heard the shot. He felt a blow to his chest—no pain, just a hard jolt. Some part of him knew he'd been hit, but it didn't slow him yet. He collided with Deerbaum an instant later, his good hand grabbing for the rifle. Deerbaum cursed loudly. The two of them staggered back, struggling for control of both guns.

Jack still didn't feel any pain, but strength was pouring out of him. He seemed to weaken with every pulse, and he only had one good arm.

He wasn't going to be able to stop Deerbaum.

Annie—I'm sorry, Annie, so sorry....

Suddenly Deerbaum let go of the rifle. Jack had it—but he staggered, slipping in what he dimly realized was his own blood, and fell to the floor. All at once the pain hit—crushing, searing pain, pain that blotted out thought and every feeling except the horrible knowledge that he'd failed Annie. He couldn't move, could barely see through the film descending over his vision—but he saw Deerbaum's grin, saw the pistol pointed right at him.

And he saw the wooden handle of an umbrella crash into the back of the man's head.

Deerbaum's eyes flew open wide, just as Leah's had, but he didn't fall.

Jack blinked back the darkness and saw Annie, his wonderful Annie, holding the umbrella as if it were a baseball bat. She had it hauled back over her shoulder—then she swung it again, hard, as if she were going for a home run.

Jack heard the crack when it connected that time.

The impact made Deerbaum's head bounce forward, then back in a whiplash effect. His eyes rolled back in his head. His knees bent. And he fell, toppling over backward, out of Jack's line of vision.

"Annie," Jack whispered before the elephant sitting on his chest crushed out the last of his breath. She'd done it. Annie had done it. She'd be safe now. Peace settled in him, sweet and restful. Just before the darkness swallowed him completely, he thought he heard the faint and distant howl of a siren.

Chapter 16

Afterward, Jack remembered nothing of his admission to the hospital and little of the twenty-four hours immediately following his surgery. He did remember flashes from the ambulance ride into Denver—noise and lights that blurred and melded with the pain. A man's voice. A needle in his arm. Annie's hand wrapped around his. Words that he spoke...or maybe he had just thought he said them aloud.

Two days after the surgery, he was moved from CCU to the surgical floor. It was another day before he was able to persuade Annie to leave him so she could get a full night's sleep, and she only agreed then because Ben hustled her out. She must have needed the sleep badly. It was eleven the next morning when she came to see him.

"Good morning," she said softly from the doorway.

He turned his head. She looked beautiful—and rested, too, he noted with satisfaction. Sleep had erased the dark smudges beneath her eyes. She held a shopping bag in one hand. "New sweatshirt. I like it."

"It's kind of bright."

It was a blazing yellow, in fact, with a daisy appliquéd on the front. "I like bright. Did you smuggle me in some real food?"

"Of course not." She came over to stand beside his bed and took his hand. "The doctor wants you on a liquid diet for at least one more day."

He grimaced. "Traitor."

"I did bring you some pajama bottoms."

Jack hadn't liked the hospital gown the nurse had tried to put on him when they moved him to this room yesterday. He'd disliked it so much that at the moment he wasn't wearing anything under the sheet except bandages.

"I brought you a newspaper, too," Annie said. "Deerbaum's talking, and the story has hit the front page." She handed it to him, folded so he could hold it in his good hand.

He took it, but didn't look at it right away. "Every time I woke up last night I saw Ben sitting in that chair, scowling at me."

She grinned. "That sounds like Ben."

"I guess staying here with me was the only way he could get you to go back to my apartment and get some sleep."

"I needed the sleep," she admitted. "But Ben stayed here because he wanted to. He was watching over you. You know how he is with family—we're all his little ducklings, in need of his sheltering wings."

Jack was beginning to understand how Annie felt about her big brother's overprotectiveness—why it chaffed her, and why she put up with it anyway. "I guess I can't complain. Not after the way things worked out."

"I know. I never thought I'd be so glad for my Ben's habit of checking up on me."

The sheriff had pulled up in front of Deerbaum's cabin only moments after the shooting—much faster than they'd had any reason to expect help. Later he'd told Annie why he'd gotten there so quickly. When Annie didn't call to let Ben know she'd arrived safely and Ben couldn't reach her on her cellular phone, he'd called the sheriff's department. He'd made such a nuisance of himself the sheriff had reluctantly agreed to drive out there, fully expecting to annoy two people who were interested in a little privacy from their overprotective relatives. He had been halfway to the cabin when Annie's 911 call had come in. He'd turned on his siren and radioed for backup—and an ambulance.

If he hadn't, Jack probably wouldn't be alive now.

Jack glanced down at the paper and started scanning the article. He scowled. "Has Deerbaum cut some kind of deal? The bastard's spilling his guts. His former business partners aren't going to like that."

"The D.A. has promised me he's not making any deals on the murder charge, and that he intends to put Deerbaum away for life for Leah's death. I don't know about the other charges, though."

Deerbaum's motive had been just what Jack's detective had suspected: money. Not the few thousands Metz had gotten from selling the drugs intended for the clinic, however. Deerbaum had been after millions.

He had arranged with a foreign criminal syndicate to use ICA as the "mule" for getting drugs in and out of a number of countries. For the past year, twice as many shipments had been passing through regional ICA offices as were supposed to. As ICA Director, Deerbaum had known exactly how to use the system to hide the records of the extra shipments; his frequent visits to regional offices had given him the opportunity. Leah's job had been to alter records as needed at the main office. Deerbaum knew the system almost as well as Herbie, and he knew the passwords. He'd just needed a good data entry person who would do as she was told—someone more interested in money than morality. Metz had been Deerbaum's flunky in the field. He'd arranged the delivery of some of the bogus shipments.

The operation might have gone undetected for years if Metz hadn't gotten greedy and decided to run his own small-scale scam and sell off some of the regular drugs for the clinics. Deerbaum had undoubtedly arranged Metz's death, though the D.A. didn't expect to find proof of that, in an effort to stop the investigation. But Jack had refused to quit digging.

Jack finished the article and tossed the newspaper on the floor, disgusted. "This stupid reporter makes me sound like some kind of hero. There's even a quote in here from Herbie about my 'dedication to everything ICA stands for.'"

She smiled, amused. "Well, you *are* a hero. Even Herbie can see that."

"Poor Herbie. He's busy trying to put a positive spin on things. This is going to be bad for ICA." He sobered. "Actually, I had a call from one of the board members this morning."

"Already?"

"The board had an emergency meeting. They, ah, want me to serve as acting director." He shifted slightly. Damned chest. It hurt. "It's that 'positive spin' business. I'm the one who uncovered the fraud; putting me in charge would give everyone from customs officials to potential contributors the right message."

She was silent a moment. "I know you don't want an office job, Jack, but you're going to be recuperating for quite a while, so you won't be able to go into the field anyway. I take it this would be temporary?"

"Herbie hinted that it might become permanent, if things work out...if I want it to."

She frowned. "You sound like you're considering it."

"I'd be here in Denver most of the time. I know you

don't like the city, but you'd be close to Highpoint and
your family. And I'd still travel sometimes.''

"Jack." She reached for his hand. "No."

He frowned. "What do you mean, 'no'?"

"You love what you do. I don't want you to give it up
for me."

"You love Highpoint."

"Not as much as I love you."

She said it so easily, so naturally. This time, her words
didn't make him want to run. They made him feel warm
and happy—and they made his throat tight. "I don't deserve you, or your love. After the way I ran out on you
that night, you might not be sure you want to stay with me.
But—"

"I'm staying, Jack."

He felt those words deep inside him, a promise he knew
he could depend on. "I'd do anything for you, Annie.
Changing my job wouldn't be such a big deal. I, uh…"
The words wouldn't come. His throat—hell, his whole
body—seemed to have locked up around them, and his
heart was pounding as rapidly as it had when he'd fought
Deerbaum. "Hell. There's something I want to say to you.
Something important. I thought—did I say anything in the
ambulance on the way here?"

She shook her head. "You were pretty much out of it."

"Hell." This would be easier if he knew he'd already
done it once.

She laid her fingers over his. "You don't have to say it,
not right away, at least. I know you love me."

He blinked. "You do?"

She smiled tenderly. "I was slow figuring that out. Not
as slow as you have been, but it took me a while. I wasn't
paying attention. I was so hung up on the words that I
wasn't listening to everything you told me without words.
You married me. You came back to me when you were

still so hurt and angry you didn't know whether to kiss me or yell at me, so you did both. You put my safety over your own, over and over. And you made love to me…" Her smile turned wicked. "I should have known it then, but I didn't. Not until I watched you throw yourself at Deerbaum. You were going to give your life, not even to save mine, but—oh, Jack." Tears stood in her eyes. "You did that just on the *chance* it might save me. I don't know what else that could be except love."

"It is. I mean, I do." His chest was hurting, but the pain there wasn't what made him stumble through his sentences like an idiot. It was another, much older pain that held him back. He took a slow, shallow breath. "Annie, you were right. The words do matter." It was partly because of the words he hadn't said to his aunt, and the ones she'd never said to him, that this was so hard now. Jack didn't have any experience of loving without losing. Deep down he felt as if saying the words meant he would lose Annie.

But she had told him she would stay. He believed her. "I think…whether you need to hear the words or not, I need to say them."

"Okay." She waited.

His heart pounded. His skin felt clammy, and he held her hand so tightly he was afraid he was hurting her. "I love you."

Her eyes squeezed closed—then opened again, shining with love and tears and the promise of a future together. "Oh, Jack. I love you, too. So much. I think I always have. And if I don't kiss you in the next two seconds, I just might explode."

Her lips were warm and careful. She tasted like coffee and morning and all the sweet beginnings that lay ahead of them. Jack had one good arm and he used it, threading his fingers through her hair to hold her close and deepen the kiss. Now when his heart pounded, there was no fear. Only pleasure.

When she pulled back, he urged her silently to lay her head on his shoulder. He was able to get his good arm around her, to smell the subtle perfume of her skin and stroke his fingers along her throat, where her pulse pounded for him just like his did for her. "I didn't understand," he said haltingly. "I've always felt good around you, and the feeling got deeper as time went on, but I didn't know what that meant. Everything is more real when I'm with you. The colors are brighter and things *mean* more. I feel more like myself. Does that make sense?"

"Perfect sense." She lifted her head and stroked his cheek. "I'm more 'me' when I'm with you, too."

That called for another kiss. He was tiring already, though, and hurting, so he didn't linger over her lips as much as he wanted to. "Are you sure you don't mind traveling with me?"

"I'm sure. Because you were right, too. I want to see some of those exotic places myself, not just in photographs."

"I've been thinking…you remember what you said that night? About how I forgot to use a condom?"

She bit her lip and nodded.

"Do you think you might be pregnant?"

"It's possible." She ran her fingers over his arm. "Not very likely, maybe, but it is possible."

"If you are, I'll either arrange a transfer to the main office, or I'll quit."

"Jack—"

"No, hear me out. I'd like to have a few more years to travel with my job. I want to take you all over the world with me. I think you'd love it, too. You can teach, and I can build. But when we do have children, I'm not leaving them to be raised by someone else half the time.'' The way her parents had done.

She nodded, her heart in her eyes. ''And if I'm not pregnant yet? Do you want children, Jack?''

''Of course I do.'' He hadn't thought about being a father, but now that he did—yes, he wanted children. With Annie. Jack smiled and started playing with her hair. ''But if we can wait a couple of years to start our family, that would be good. I could use the time to practice saying it.''

''Saying what?'' She didn't really have to ask, though. He could tell by the smile on her face that she knew.

Jack had never felt this happy or this free in his life. This time he said it easily, without fear. ''I love you, Annie.''

* * * * *

If you enjoyed what you just read,
then we've got an offer you can't resist!

Take 2 bestselling love stories FREE!

Plus get a FREE surprise gift!

MONTANA MAVERICKS
Big Sky Brides

Legendary love comes to Whitehorn, Montana,
once more as beloved authors

Christine Rimmer, Jennifer Greene and Cheryl St.John

present three brand-new stories in this exciting anthology!

Meet the Brennan women:
SUZANNA, DIANA and ISABELLE

Strong-willed beauties who find unexpected
love in these irresistible marriage of
covnenience stories.

Don't miss
MONTANA MAVERICKS: BIG SKY BRIDES
On sale in February 2000,
only from Silhouette Books!

Available at your favorite retail outlet.

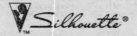

SILHOUETTE'S 20ᵀᴴ ANNIVERSARY CONTEST
OFFICIAL RULES
NO PURCHASE NECESSARY TO ENTER

1. To enter, follow directions published in the offer to which you are responding. Contest begins 1/1/00 and ends on 8/24/00 (the "Promotion Period"). Method of entry may vary. Mailed entries must be postmarked by 8/24/00, and received by 8/31/00.

2. During the Promotion Period, the Contest may be presented via the Internet. Entry via the Internet may be restricted to residents of certain geographic areas that are disclosed on the Web site. To enter via the Internet, if you are a resident of a geographic area in which Internet entry is permissible, follow the directions displayed on-line, including typing your essay of 100 words or fewer telling us "Where In The World Your Love Will Come Alive." On-line entries must be received by 11:59 p.m. Eastern Standard time on 8/24/00. Limit one e-mail entry per person, household and e-mail address per day, per presentation. If you are a resident of a geographic area in which entry via the Internet is permissible, you may, in lieu of submitting an entry on-line, enter by mail, by hand-printing your name, address, telephone number and contest number/name on an 8"x 11" plain piece of paper and telling us in 100 words or fewer "Where In The World Your Love Will Come Alive," and mailing via first-class mail to: Silhouette 20ᵗʰ Anniversary Contest, (in the U.S.) P.O. Box 9069, Buffalo, NY 14269-9069; (In Canada) P.O. Box 637, Fort Erie, Ontario, Canada L2A 5X3. Limit one 8"x 11" mailed entry per person, household and e-mail address per day. On-line and/or 8"x 11" mailed entries received from persons residing in geographic areas in which Internet entry is not permissible will be disqualified. No liability is assumed for lost, late, incomplete, inaccurate, nondelivered or misdirected mail, or misdirected e-mail, for technical, hardware or software failures of any kind, lost or unavailable network connection, or failed, incomplete, garbled or delayed computer transmission or any human error which may occur in the receipt or processing of the entries in the contest.

3. Essays will be judged by a panel of members of the Silhouette editorial and marketing staff based on the following criteria:

   Sincerity (believability, credibility)—50%

   Originality (freshness, creativity)—30%

   Aptness (appropriateness to contest ideas)—20%

   Purchase or acceptance of a product offer does not improve your chances of winning. In the event of a tie, duplicate prizes will be awarded.

4. All entries become the property of Harlequin Enterprises Ltd., and will not be returned. Winner will be determined no later than 10/31/00 and will be notified by mail. Grand Prize winner will be required to sign and return Affidavit of Eligibility within 15 days of receipt of notification. Noncompliance within the time period may result in disqualification and an alternative winner may be selected. All municipal, provincial, federal, state and local laws and regulations apply. Contest open only to residents of the U.S. and Canada who are 18 years of age or older, and is void wherever prohibited by law. Internet entry is restricted solely to residents of those geographical areas in which Internet entry is permissible. Employees of Torstar Corp., their affiliates, agents and members of their immediate families are not eligible. Taxes on the prizes are the sole responsibility of winners. Entry and acceptance of any prize offered constitutes permission to use winner's name, photograph or other likeness for the purposes of advertising, trade and promotion on behalf of Torstar Corp. without further compensation to the winner, unless prohibited by law. Torstar Corp and D.L. Blair, Inc., their parents, affiliates and subsidiaries, are not responsible for errors in printing or electronic presentation of contest or entries. In the event of printing or other errors which may result in unintended prize values or duplication of prizes, all affected contest materials or entries shall be null and void. If for any reason the Internet portion of the contest is not capable of running as planned, including infection by computer virus, bugs, tampering, unauthorized intervention, fraud, technical failures, or any other causes beyond the control of Torstar Corp. which corrupt or affect the administration, secrecy, fairness, integrity or proper conduct of the contest, Torstar Corp. reserves the right, at its sole discretion, to disqualify any individual who tampers with the entry process and to cancel, terminate, modify or suspend the contest or the Internet portion thereof. In the event of a dispute regarding an on-line entry, the entry will be deemed submitted by the authorized holder of the e-mail account submitted at the time of entry. Authorized account holder is defined as the natural person who is assigned to an e-mail address by an Internet access provider, on-line service provider or other organization that is responsible for arranging e-mail address for the domain associated with the submitted e-mail address.

5. Prizes: Grand Prize—a $10,000 vacation to anywhere in the world. Travelers (at least one must be 18 years of age or older) or parent or guardian if one traveler is a minor, must sign and return a Release of Liability prior to departure. Travel must be completed by December 31, 2001, and is subject to space and accommodations availability. Two hundred (200) Second Prizes—a two-book limited edition autographed collector set from one of the Silhouette Anniversary authors: Nora Roberts, Diana Palmer, Linda Howard or Annette Broadrick (value $10.00 each set). All prizes are valued in U.S. dollars.

6. For a list of winners (available after 10/31/00), send a self-addressed, stamped envelope to: Harlequin Silhouette 20ᵗʰ Anniversary Winners, P.O. Box 4200, Blair, NE 68009-4200.

Contest sponsored by Torstar Corp., P.O. Box 9042, Buffalo, NY 14269-9042.

ENTER FOR
A CHANCE TO WIN*
Silhouette's 20th Anniversary Contest

Tell Us Where in the World
You Would Like *Your* Love To Come Alive...
And We'll Send the Lucky Winner There!

Silhouette wants to take you wherever
your happy ending can come true.

Here's how to enter: Tell us, in 100 words or less,
where you want to go to make your love come alive!

In addition to the grand prize, there will be 200
runner-up prizes, collector's-edition book sets
autographed by one of the Silhouette anniversary
authors: **Nora Roberts, Diana Palmer,
Linda Howard** or **Annette Broadrick.**

DON'T MISS YOUR CHANCE TO WIN!
ENTER NOW! No Purchase Necessary

Silhouette®

Where love comes alive™

Name:

Address:

City: _____ State/Province:

Zip/Postal Code:

Mail to Harlequin Books: **In the U.S.:** P.O. Box 9069, Buffalo, NY
14269-9069; **In Canada:** P.O. Box 637, Fort Erie, Ontario, L4A 5X3

PS20CON_R